NICHOLAS OF HAITI

Bert—

Nicholas is perfect
reading. It's one
of year.

11-18-19

NICHOLAS OF HAITI

JOSEPH COURTEMANCHE

Published by Commotion In The Pews Publishing, Saint Paul, Minnesota, www.commotioninthepews.com
Cover design by Joseph Courtemanche

DEDICATION

This work is dedicated to my wife Kip.
She has been my other half for most of my life.
I couldn't ask for a better friend, wife, editor,
and soulmate.

ALSO BY JOSEPH COURTEMANCHE

ASSAULT ON SAINT AGNES

ACKNOWLEDGEMENTS

First kudos go to my dear friend, Pastor Timothy Moynihan. He took the gibberish I'd scrawled and turned it into excellent back-cover copy. Look him up if you want to read a great book: Prodigal Avenger. (Available late 2018) Second kudos go to Michael Brooks, who graciously modelled as Andre in some of the artwork we considered for the cover. Thank you, Michael, for stepping out on faith.

Now, to Brenda, who is a great cheerleader. Kathie Chambers Underwood, whose name I spelled wrong in the dedication to Assault on Saint Agnes, was also a great encourager in my early writing days. Carol Addison who puts up with my nonsense also contributed to the book. Renee, who talked me off the ledge and motivated me to finish this book. My friend Larry, who is such a big deal that he got a primary character named after him. My co-worker Karen, who graciously annotated all the errors she found in a beta version of this book. She also holds the record for the most copies purchased of *Assault on Saint Agnes*.

Noel, Joe, and Hannah all deserve what they get in the book. All of you should enjoy how the story unfolds. It is sufficiently brutal.

My family, who all know that "Crazy Uncle Joe" is an author and smile politely when I begin to babble about books.

Nancy B., who provided the final beta read on the book and validated some ideas I'd not yet put in the text. She helped me up to the next level and made it a much better book.

My wife Kip, who waited patiently for me to give her the manuscript to edit. She did a magnificent job of finding my flaws as a writer and pointing them out gently.

The wonderful folks at Athanatos Publishing Group, especially my mentor Tony Horvath. I promise, Tony, that the sequel to Assault on Saint Agnes will be finished before you die. Debbie and Dillon Thompson get special kudos for taking an earlier edition of the manuscript and pointing out some story issues that I have hopefully resolved in a satisfactory manner. Gary Thompson gets props for honouring me with a voice-over project and some fine raspberry moonshine that had nothing to do with writing, but were both fun.

My friends at KTIS radio, especially Rich, Jason, Julene, Jennifer, Mark, and Dan who took us to our first mission experiences and opened the door to a pair of very reluctant missionaries.

My friends in the Haitian mission field are amazing. Jeff, Mike, Elisa, Don, Carolyn, Keith, Meredith, Katie, Russ, Dave, Grace, Max, Jean… the list is virtually endless. You have all inspired me beyond your wildest beliefs and created the foundation of this book with your kindness and ideas. You are all a gift from God and give me much to aspire to in this life. You just may see yourselves somewhere in this work.

CHAPTER ONE
Salt Lake City, Utah
January 05

Jean Silver shifted her slender frame seeking some padding. As she did, she caught a glimpse of herself reflected in one of the multiple monitor screens that surrounded her. With a jerk of revulsion, she produced a makeup set and a brush from a purse that probably should have been equipped with wheels. It was large enough to have hidden a polar bear, but today it contained a copious quantity of makeup and a laptop computer.

Simultaneous with the last dab of lip moisturizer, the door to the room opened a crack and that federal agent stuck his head in for a peek. Her now glamorous face turned into a hard mask. She motioned for him to get out and shut the door. It clicked closed an instant later.

"Who's that?"

Snapping her head to the left, Jean saw her brother's eyes for the first time since she arrived. "You sound awful, Nick. But even a croak is an improvement. How long have you been with us big brother?"

Nicholas descended into a coughing jag. Jean poured him a sip of water in a disposable cup. After a few pulls at the straw, he was able to whisper again. "What happened to me?"

Jean stared at the mess in the bed. All his dark black hair, including eyebrows and eyelashes were burned off. This left him with a bright red char on every exposed area from the neck up. His hands were burned a second degree as well. God spared him third degree burns, but not by much. The bomb that destroyed the aircraft directed its force to the rear of where he had been standing, but the fireball set him ablaze before he was sucked out of the first-class cabin. Instead of being a chubby 43-year-old engineer, he looked like a sunburned sixty-five-year-old derelict. The gray stubble on his chin wasn't doing much for his appearance, but he couldn't shave for at least two weeks.

"What happened, Nick? Your plane exploded. I was in Florida, but I got here that night. Nobody really knows why it happened. It seems there was a bomb in the passenger cabin. Don't you remember anything?"

1

Nick shook his head. "I don't even know where I am. Well, I know it's a hospital, but that's it."

"You're in Salt Lake City, Utah. The explosion happened just after take-off. You landed, without a parachute, in a snowdrift at a ski resort. Your survival is a total miracle. But some aren't buying it as a miracle, including the horde of cops waiting to interrogate you. They're camped out in the lobby, the cafeteria, and the hallway outside this room. You're quite popular with the boys in blue."

"You might as well get the cops in here. I'd rather tell the story one time, and it will be short as I don't remember a thing."

"As your attorney, I recommend you tell me first."

"I was sitting in first class and I woke up here."

Jean stood up and started pacing a five-foot long track in the floor. "Nick, you're the sole survivor of that plane crash. You're also the primary suspect in the bombing for the same reason. In addition, you're the most famous man in the Western world this week. It's twenty-four/seven about the crash on the cable news networks. That guy who just stuck his head in here is one of an army of federal agents who want to talk to you about the flight. Right behind the feds are a couple of hundred news people and media types. Everybody wants to buy the rights to your story since it's not every day that somebody falls 10,000 feet without a parachute and survives. I'm sure that your landing 40 feet away from those poor ski patrol people is going to scar them for life.

"I get a voice mail from another publisher every half hour. I took the liberty of issuing a press release on behalf of my bachelor brother that I was representing him legally. Unfortunately, given my business as a show-biz manager, they all assumed that meant I controlled the rights to the story. I told the feds to bug off until I could talk to you in private. Your coma put a crimp in things, but now that you're awake, I need the full story."

Nick started to respond but took another mouthful of ice chips instead, and chewed them thoroughly before responding.

"Jean, I got up go to the bathroom. Too much coffee in the terminal. Last thing I can swear to, the flight attendant gave me a dirty look about being out of my seat with the seatbelt sign on. I kind of remember flying through a blizzard and that's it."

Jean smiled. "I didn't think you were a mad bomber. However, they're going to ask you the same questions about twenty different ways until they're satisfied. Nick, your clothes were full of explosive residue when they got to you in the hospital, and it's pretty strange that you're the single guy to survive. Especially after your wingless descent into an avalanche zone. Nobody understands how you survived that experience. They searched for a parachute until the ski patrollers convinced them you just plummeted from the sky. Jeez, I'm even freaked out just thinking about that happening."

"Nobody else survived?"

A spiderweb formed across Nick's burned face: white lines of emotional anguish gave witness to a personal Hell. The plane was full of young families who no doubt knew what was happening for a few seconds before they died. Nick welled up with tears and sobbed in a fog of pain, opiates, and guilt.

Jean grabbed a tissue from the box next to his bed and dabbed at the tears rolling down his face with the lightest touch she could muster. Her main concern was not to rub off any of the burned tissue. "Hey, you're a miracle, Nick. It's okay. Well not yet, but it will be when you get better. Go ahead and cry. It's got to be a shock to find out you're the lone person to make it out alive.

"What's wrong with me?"

Jean's breath hitched for a moment: "Sweetie, you've been out for three days. The doctors were worried about Traumatic Brain Injury syndrome. You were unconscious when you got to the hospital, and they put you into a coma to keep your brain cool until they could get all the tests run. You've got a clean bill of health except for the burns and a busted-up ankle. The brain injury was more like a bad concussion. You hit the back of your head at some point during the explosion and landing. It may be a few days before the stuff they used to put you into the coma wears off."

"My eyes hurt. Not working right."

Jean watched as Nick's eyes spun back in his head and he convulsed, setting off the alarms on the pole. She was ushered out as the medical team rushed in to help.

3

CHAPTER TWO
Port-au-Prince, Haiti
January 08

Violene pulled the piece of old blanket tighter around her bony shoulders. Huddled in a ball, she fought to keep some of her body heat before the night air whisked it away. Losing warmth meant burning body fat: she didn't have any to spare.

Her mind raced between her empty stomach, her burning thighs, and her bloody left hand. She ate a bowl of rice for breakfast twelve hours ago and worked hard all day. Her hand snagged on the edge of the washboard while she did her owner's laundry. That earned her a beating for getting blood on the clothing and ruining a pair of socks.

She twitched at the memory of the rigwaz biting into the back of her thighs: fresh heat burned deep into her skin with the thought. This wasn't the first beating in the last three years, but it was the most savage. Just twelve years old and she had the scars of an ancient butcher's block across her backside. Loneliness may be the worst of the wounds: she hadn't seen her birth family since they were forced to sell her into bondage at age nine.

Her owners were from a wealthy clan of powerful business moguls, all of whom had nice things. Violene had three dresses and two hair ribbons. Nothing else was hers. At night, she was locked in a utility room at the back of the home. They kept her there until an older girl let her out to help the woman known as "Cook" begin breakfast and prepare the coffee. The older girl had been with the family for seven years and was due to be released in one more year. That suited the owners; she was far harder to handle than Violene and no longer "fresh" according to the master.

Violene wasn't forced to sleep with her owner yet. She knew it was coming: she'd seen the looks he gave her when she cleaned in the kitchen. He was touching her shoulders and face more often.

Violene knew she couldn't leave. Who would take in a Restevek if she escaped? Her owner might demand the money back from her family, and they'd spent it already just to remain alive. There was no place she could run. She had no hope. She had nothing but God. Violene fell asleep hungry, bloody, cold, and lonely. Her lips moved a bit in that last moment before slumber: she was praying. Perchance God could help her to be free; that nobody on this Earth seemed to care about her plight was her last thought of the day.

"Special Agent Himmler, how nice of you to drop in on us again. Where is your associate, Special Agent Goebbels?"

No smile crossed the man's face, nor was there any sign of one in the past week. Jean Silver suspected the last time he smiled, there was a tortured kitten involved.

"Special Agent Gabler is busy elsewhere. You're stuck with me. My name is pronounced Schimmler, not Himmler. You know, we can save a lot of time if you just grow up a bit counselor. I'm not expecting much, but the juvenile name-calling is a waste of our time. You want me to be gone; I want to go. How about we try it as though you were an officer of the court, instead of some princess with an axe to grind?"

Schimmler had just tap-danced into the one minefield that no human wants to explore with Jean Silver: her faith.

With the same jocular smile she used a moment before to taunt him, Silver asked, "Special Agent Schimmler, whatever do you mean by that?"

Schimmler caught himself before a syllable was uttered. Taking a moment to allow some moisture back in to his mouth, he said, "I think my meaning was clear. You're not royalty, and I won't be treated like a peasant."

"Oh? I was pretty sure you were making a reference to my religious choice. And it was a choice! I married a Jewish guy and converted to do so. But you didn't figure that out because you're lazy, and stupid. Basic research would have shown you that Nicholas and I were not born Jews. That would have been funny: a couple of Jews named Bacon.

"You wouldn't be the first Nazi bigot to call me a JAP (Jewish American Princess.) But I can promise you this, Himmler: if you ever drift down that road, or think about it, you will be on your way out of your precious agency before you can say "Sieg Heil." You may have suspicions that "my people" control everything behind the scenes. Well, you're right. Jews rule the world, and I'll be making sure that every member of the tribe has their moron detector set on high when you walk into the room. Don't cook your goose, Himmler. Be very careful from here on."

Schimmler slapped down a folder on the bedside table in Nick's hospital room and opened it for him to see. "No problem, counselor. Now, Mr. Bacon, we have some questions about your travel over the past few years. The explosion on the aircraft and your surprising survival have left us baffled. Are the dates on this list accurate?"

Cobras lack the striking speed Jean Silver displayed when she snatched the folder and pulled it away from Nick. Nick continued to eye the television hanging over his bed where the aircraft explosion was still taking up a good five minutes out of every half-hour cycle. His picture was displayed in the corner of every report on every channel. The single barrier keeping the reporters from knocking down the door for interviews was the ongoing investigation and the two Salt Lake City cops posted outside the door twenty-four hours a day to protect him. Or was it to deny him access to the public?

After looking over the document, Jean flipped the folder shut and slid it back toward Schimmler. "Special Agent, you know that this is nothing but a fishing expedition. My client will not be participating in filling out any travel surveys for your agency. Unless he gets a free week in Vegas for rating hotels around the world."

Nick held a hand up so that both combatants could see him. "Hello, don't I get a say in this? I'm not hiding anything. I just had the craptacularly bad luck to be flying on that plane when it blew up. What harm could there be in looking at the form?"

"You'll have to pardon my brother Nicholas: he's an engineer. He has this perverse view of the world that tells him that things are digital: one way or the other. Shades of grey don't play into his conceptual process. Ask him to design a water filtration plant on the coast of some Third-World hell-hole, and he'll use his graphing calculator to build it for you with chewing gum and toothpicks. Ask him to talk to a girl in a bar and get a date, and he'll fail every time because he thinks honesty works. Kind of a shame, if you ask me, because before he was so grievously injured in the plane incident, he was a good-looking guy. The brush haircut was a bit dorky, I'll admit that, but his cherubic features and gentle eyes attracted girls all his life. Once he opened his mouth, however, they either played him for a sucker or dumped on him."

7

Nicholas stared at his sister in obvious dismay.

"You're like an undercover cop in a bar, Himmler. You're trying to seduce my brother into talking himself into a jail cell. You don't have his best interests at heart. You don't want to catch the jerk that blew up that plane. You view him like any predator would. Your victim is trapped in a hospital bed, and you find it easier to pin this on him than do all that nasty investigating that is required to find the real bombers. So, the answer is "NO," and it will remain so for eternity. We answered the questions germane to your investigation without reservation. But now you're to the next phase. He's not going to be the next Olympic Park Bomber if I can help it. And I can. So now you take your little folder and get out. My client needs his rest."

Schimmler picked up the folder and tapped it on the table. "You'll be getting a subpoena for a grand jury if that's the case. That, Mr. Bacon, is a big room with lots of people in it. Not a single one of them will be your attorney. You will have to answer truthfully in front of a grand jury. Why not do it the easy way and get this over with?"

Nick reached for the folder and almost got his knuckles broken when Jean knocked it out of Schimmler's hand. "Special Agent, do you really want me to contact the Office of Professional Responsibility and tell them that you're trying to break the attorney client relationship here? That you're lying to my client about a grand jury?"

Schimmler picked up the folder from the floor and headed to the door.

Jean's words stopped him in his tracks. "Hold on a minute, sonny. You might want to hear this next little bit: Nick, don't talk to him unless I'm in the room with you. Ever. There won't be a grand jury. They have no reason to empanel one, no reason to drag you in front of one, no evidence that in any way connects you to any activity that has a bearing on this case. He's playing outside the rules, and if he persists, I will have his badge. Now, Special Agent Schimmler, get out of our faces and don't come back unless you have a warrant. It's that simple."

Schimmler smiled as he left the room. He was gone for a count of five, and then whipped the door open. Strutting to the table, he reached into his left inside pocket and pulled out a document.

Spreading it flat on the table, he said, "It's a court order for Mr. Bacon. He's not allowed to leave here because he's officially in our custody as a material witness in the terrorist bombing of Flight 1642 on January second. As his counsel, you need to advise him of his rights and responsibilities regarding this order. Failure to remain in our custody will result in criminal penalty. Because he is in our custody, and we do not wish to impact his recovery, he remains here, in this hospital, until his doctors release him to a rehabilitation clinic of our choice. Do you have any questions, Ms. Silver?"

"That means you get the bill, Schimmler."

"Not for his stay to this point. My understanding is that he no longer needs hospital level care. For his burns and ankle to recover, a couple of weeks in a recovery and rehabilitation center will be adequate. It's very convenient that Salt Lake City has several excellent facilities to choose from. We hadn't planned on picking up his tab; consider it a form of house arrest. If you like, counselor, we could arrange for him to stay at Uintas. Sadly, in Utah, we don't have a federal facility that could handle his medical needs, so we rely on our state friends for short-term stays. There's also the issue of safety and security. That's where we'd put him until we get our issues sorted out, Uintas. If you like, Counsellor, we could execute the transfer later this afternoon. Why, I dare say it's even convenient for you; it's just down the road in Draper."

Jean looked up from her smart phone. She checked on Uintas while he was talking and now turned brilliant red. "Bite me, Himmler. He's not going to Utah's supermax unit so you can keep him away from me. There isn't a judge in the circuit that would stand for this nonsense. I know that fancy lawyer talk boggles you, but even night-school lawyers like you understand the concept of habeas corpus. Mr. Bacon's insurance plan more than adequately covers a stay in a rehab facility, so we'll undertake that on our own. But he's going there to get better, and once he is sufficiently recovered from his injuries, he leaves. I suggest you stand ready to be in court tomorrow morning and fight that little chunk of recycled napkins that you got some idiot to scribble on with a crayon."

Schimmler smiled like the cat that ate the canary, "I think that Judge Addison would be mortally offended that you characterized him that way. He, by the way, is not just the senior member of the bench for this circuit, but he happens to be a fellow alumnus of Marquette Law, seven classes ahead of me."

Jean pointed at the door.

"I expect you to notify me of where you transfer your client before he moves any farther than the lobby. You have my number. Call me 24/7. The two gentlemen from Salt Lake's finest will be giving him an escort when he moves. Have a pleasant day."

Schimmler walked out and let the door click behind him. Jean and Nick waited for him to come back with some other surprise. The door stayed closed this time.

"That guy is an utter scum bucket. Nick, don't say anything to him, don't look at any papers, or cooperate in any way at all. He's one of those rotten lawyers that can twist your actions and words into meaning what he wants, not what you intended."

"So, you mean he's just like you?"

"Exactly. This will turn into open warfare if we don't make sure he's always on the defensive. I have to keep it subtle enough to be nasty and yet not provoke him into taking action. I'll have to be on my best behavior until this is over.

"On the brighter side of things, I did locate a really nice place for you to stay. It's designed for addicts who have life-threatening injuries. I never realized Utah had such an issue with drugs and alcohol. That squeaky-clean LDS (Latter Day Saints) image they present to the world has a pretty dark underside. The place is kind of pricy, but Larry has offered to pay the difference between your insurance plan and what the fees are at Pinedale Services. That's some boss you have."

Nick smiled. "Larry is a great boss. I think I'll stick with him until retirement. Tell me more about this place, and are they going to have someone who can clear up the eye thing?"

"Pinedale has a nice name, and it's a nice place. I took a tour this morning. You'll have your own bedroom, bathroom, and even kind of a living room. It's more of a hotel suite than a hospital room. No cooking available, but they run a dining facility that's a three-star restaurant for all practical purposes. You won't go hungry. As to the eyes, your doctors want to do a couple of brain scans before you leave here and see if they can figure out your "shadows." You've got them stumped."

Nick patted his stomach and smiled. "Mmmmm, room service?"

"Good to see the eyes don't bother you that much if you're worrying about room service. No, room service is not part of your coverage level. But Pinedale has its plusses; it's a doggone spa. You'll get the deluxe treatment with massages, music therapy, movie nights, probably even a dance where you can find a date. On second thought, never mind. Dating in a rehab facility isn't that great an idea."

Jean sat down in the recliner next to his bed and waved him to the other chair. "You may not realize it, but you're still more than a little goofy. You've been crying out in your sleep and shouting about someone whipping you. You've even got an imaginary friend you talk to when you get tired. Docs say it will clear up in time, but that's one of the reasons I put it right in Himmler's face the other day: you currently are not competent to answer questions. If you try to do so, I'll get a court order as your guardian to have you civilly committed. That will keep him at bay. You want me to do that?"

Nick was sitting on the edge of the chair with his mouth gaping open. His feelings were worn on his sleeve.

"I thought not. Sorry, Nick, but that's the truth. Listen, you know I love you with all my heart. Part of love, Nicholas, is telling you the truth when it hurts. Right now, it's not safe for you to be on your own. Your balance stinks with that bum ankle, and that will be weak for a long time unless you get daily therapy. I've got to consider your mental state as well. You have a brain injury, and for some reason you're not clearing the drugs out of your system like you should. One of the doctors was pretty blunt. It can take up to six weeks for the intoxicating effects to finish drawing down in people with your kind of wounds. The stuff holds out in fatty and damaged tissues. You've got plenty of both."

Nick had a tear coming from the corner of his eye and looked like the dam was about to burst. "I don't know if that makes me happy or sad. Fact is, my head hurts most of the time, and I do have trouble differentiating between dreams and when I'm awake. I keep seeing this little girl with terrible scars. It's upsetting. I catch her out of the corner of my eye, but she's gone when I look directly at her. Jean, am I going nuts? Is this really going to pass?"

Jean reached out to put her hands on the sides of his head, cupping his face like he was a small, frightened puppy with something in its eye. Pulling his head toward her, she kissed the top of his skull where the burned skin was starting to flake off in sheets. Shifting in her chair as close as she could manage, she moved her hands to his shoulders,

11

embracing her older brother and holding him like the sad, lost little boy he was at that moment.

"Nick, I'll do everything I can to help you. That's one of the reasons I picked Pinedale: they can help you get the drugs out of your system. Best of all, they'll work with you on some pain techniques that hospitals don't deal with very often. Let's face it, this place just gives you more dope when you tell them you hurt. Pinedale Services will help you cope, not use dope. Hey, that rhymes! I wonder if I can sell them the slogan…

"I'll stay as long as you want. I can do everything I need to do from a hotel room, and Jeff is traveling in China this month. Don't fret. And if that little girl you keep seeing in the corner gives you any crap, tell her she's got to deal with me."

Nicholas sniffled for a moment and then snorted out a laugh between the tears, making a mess of his hospital robe. "Great. Mean Jean is making a comeback beating up on little black girls, and I'm shooting snot like a cannon."

"I'll kick anyone's butt for you, Nicholas Bacon. You're my big brother and you're the last family I've got left. Count on me in the clinch. Now, let's put you in a fresh robe, get a wheelchair, and go down to the restaurant in the lobby. I need a steak, and you need to get out of this room. If it's haunted with tortured children, we'll give them the night off."

"Jeannie, I don't think this girl is dead, but someone's whipping her and…"

"Nick, let's drop it. Nobody here but us chickens. And that rat Himmler. Let's go before he comes back with another gift from his friend the idiot judge. I'll wait in the hallway while you change out of that disgusting robe."

Stepping out of the room, Jean let the police officers on the door know they were going downstairs and needed a wheelchair. The older cop headed off to the nurse's station while Jean entered the visitor's lounge.

Accessing her contacts list she dialled "Celebrity Cleaners" in Saint Paul, Minnesota. The phone rang three times before a man's voice answered, "Yes."

Jean smiled. "Lopez, I have a job for you. It's a fed named Schimmler. The usual plus a deep look. He's the main agent here in Salt Lake. Any problems?"

"Nice to chat with you. Usual fee plus 50 percent: feds are tougher than the average bear. You know how to get it to me. Three or four days for the first level. The rest depends on how bent he is. I'll call when I have something."

The line went dead as the first cop wheeled by with Nick's chair. Jean followed him to the room, a definite spring in her step for the first time in days.

CHAPTER FOUR
Salt Lake City, Utah
January 30

"Six more steps Mr. Bacon. You can do that easily."

Nick's eyes stung from the tsunami of sweat that roared down his charred forehead. Reflex caused him to swipe the sweat out of his eyes, his hand jarring to a stop just short of where his hairline used to be. Too tender to risk it. He needed a sweat catcher, but his scalp still exploded with pain every time the shower hit it. A hat couldn't be tolerated.

Nick's face screwed up in pain as he glanced about the room. The physical therapy gear was bad enough, but they built the place with ballroom fixtures, so they could hold social events here when needed. He was uncomfortable at a dance, and this place looked more like a dance studio than a physical therapy room. Various tasks were simulated at work stations around the room, with doors that led nowhere, stairs to climb that would have done Sisyphus proud, a host of textured rugs and floors to test crutches and canes on, and a kitchen cabinet layout where they practiced with grabbing devices so that wheelchairbound patients could survive in their own kitchens once they got home. Worst of all, in his salty view, there were more than a few ceiling-length mirrors for practicing, and watching from the reverse angle, as the patients did their tasks — reminiscent of a ballet studio now that he pondered it in depth.

Turning his concentration to the three steps up and the three steps down, he let go of the railing and tried it without support. The room swirled around him as he caught a glimpse of the little girl looking at him from a corner. She cringed in terror when he bounced off the parquet flooring. No matter what he told the shrinks, she was always just at the edge of his world.

"Well, I guess you're not ready for that, but the effort was nice. Did you hurt yourself, Mr. Bacon?"

Nick looked up at the ceiling, avoiding eye contact. He hadn't even made it to the first step when he had plunged out of the therapist's reach and slammed to the floor.

"Just my dignity. I thought I could at least stand on that leg and lift the other one."

"Good thing you missed the mats, they get bloodstained and that's harder to remove than from the wooden floor. Try to hit them the next time though, that floor will jack you up if you do that too often. You're too big to do that, sir. Please, in the future, when I tell you to hold onto the railings, hold onto them."

A voice erupted from the doorway: "I saw that, you pushed my client down. He didn't fall. Nobody would be stupid enough to try and walk up those stairs without holding the railing. My brother is many things, but he's not stupid."

Nicholas turned an even darker shade of red. "Well, I am stupid. I'm exhausted. But, my therapist said six more steps. Six more it is."

With great effort, Nick pulled himself up the steps. Little used muscles twitched beneath the skin as he kept a death grip on the railings. Pausing on the top step to get his balance, he waited a moment to let his heart settle. Way too much like work. Turning around in ten-degree slices, he led with the good foot and went back down the simulated staircase again. Determination and agony fought for his facial real estate as he traversed what was, at this moment, his life's greatest challenge.

His therapist met him at the bottom and helped him to a chair.

Grabbing his water bottle from the table, Nicholas emptied it in gulps. He never worked this hard in his life. With the weak ankle, the uncomfortable brace, and the lack of balance since the accident, he was a mess. The main thing that kept him moving along was the morale-boosting visits from his sister.

"Jean the Queen. What great news do you have today? Another deposition on video? A blood sample taken directly from my left eyeball? Perhaps a visit in person from Special Agent Himmler?"

"None of the above. I think Himmler got the point when I served him a restraining order today. I haven't laughed so hard in years. My, but the look on his sour puss was priceless. He had to apologize in the judge's chambers for being such a sleaze ball. He'll be good for a while. If he shows up here without me, the judge will break him into little pieces."

Nick grinned at the image of Schimmler eating crow in front of his pal the judge. Not much brought him that kind of joy since the bombing. Even sleeping was causing him dread. Before, he'd escaped the omnipresent little girl when he closed his eyes, gaining a few hours' break every day. Now the dreams had changed for the worse, and the little girl was talking to him in his dreams every night, sometimes several times. The dreams were vivid, always taking place on a mountaintop that looked out over a desert and an ocean. It was the most barren landscape he'd ever seen, and he'd visited some doozies.

"Alright, Nick, I'm here to pilot your wheelchair back to your room. You are to take a shower and then put on some decent clothes. I brought a few nice things from your house and left them in your closet. Your house isn't nearly as messy as I figured it would be. Nick, is it possible you're growing up?"

Nick was tired of looking at himself in hospital scrubs and Utah Jazz sweat gear. The thought of clothes from home brought forth a glow in his eyes. As did his sister's presence: it had been a long week without her while she took care of clients in other cities. The crushing loneliness was about to win.

"You look pretty good, other than lying flat on your back on the floor. Looks like you're putting on extra weight with the cuisine around here. On the other hand, that noggin of yours is as scaly as a lizard's butt. That's got to itch something fierce."

"Thanks. I managed to forget for almost two minutes."

"You're welcome. Tonight, we're going out to a German place I found last week. The best schnitzel you'll ever eat. But not until you hose off and make yourself presentable. You gonna shave?"

"I'm letting it grow. It keeps me from obsessing about the scars. Now that it's a decent length, it doesn't itch so bad. The stuff on top of my head doesn't help with the itch, but the beard is an improvement."

"That's great. Hey, are you cleared to walk with a cane yet?"

Nick's therapist chimed in, "Not yet. Crutches if he wants them, but I prefer he uses a walker. Canes are a balance issue. Another week or so, but we'll have to see how it goes."

"What about a walking staff? You know, like hikers use."

"If it is comfortable and he tolerates it, it should be okay in a few days. But please, don't risk a fall. Use the walker, or crutches, until I clear him for a staff."

"No problem. Nick, things just keep getting better. You've gone from flat on your back in bed to crutches in just three weeks. Another week and you'll be zipping around with a cane. Take time to heal; you're not in a rush to go anywhere.

"I'm ready to leave now. I really want to go home."

Jean motioned for the therapist to give them some privacy.

"We can't be having this discussion every time I see you, Nick. I talked to the doctors. You're still having vision issues and your balance isn't even worth the name. Until those clear up you're not safe on your own. This isn't home; I get it. But you must do stairs to get to your bedroom and bathroom. Unless you have a secret rambler where you live part-time, I'm afraid you can't go home for safety reasons."

Nick scowled. "By safety you mean that I'm nuttier than a Snickers bar and you can't trust me not to talk to Schimmler and his goons. Or, do you mean that anyone who sees tortured little girls in the corner of the room, and auras around people, has a screw loose and shouldn't be around sharp things?"

Jean pulled back for a moment as the wave of frustration and rage coming across the table slammed into her. She reached out and placed her fingertips on his forearm, stroking his skin. "Nicholas Bacon, if you think I'm trying to keep you locked away, I can leave. I can find another attorney to represent you, and I'll just keep you in my prayers. But if you think I'm right and just hate being cooped up and mistrusted, tell me now. We can't go forward with this friction.

"I can't help you unless you're honest with me about your health. Unlike the staff here, I'm not good at detecting the lies and half-truths that come from addictions and drugs. My Hollywood clients and writers are all drug-addled zombies, so I don't trust a single word they say. I love you, Nick, and I want you to be well and trustworthy. Do you understand the hurt I'm feeling?"

Nick used his towel to blot a last dribble of sweat from his forehead. Dropping the cloth to the floor, he slumped in his chair as the anger boiled off like smoke from dry ice. Leaning his head back, he closed his eyes and took a deep breath. After a ten count, he sat up straight in the chair and scrubbed at his eyes with his palms. "I'm sorry. I don't like feeling out of control. Not that I'm wild, or that I want to hurt myself, but events are racing on all around me and I can't stop them. I can't even choose much beyond what I have to eat and what I watch on television. Thank God for streaming video is all I can say."

17

Looking off toward the set of steps he'd just climbed, he went on, "I do see that little girl. I saw her as I was falling. She's — upsetting. It unnerves me every single time. I'm a lot less cloudy in the last week, but I'll admit my head isn't always clear. I have some pretty vivid hallucinations with this aura thing. Seriously, some people just about vanish in the shadows they cast.

"I hate it. I hate everything. All my life I've prided myself on thinking like a calculator and now it's gone in a morning. I laugh when people tell me there's a reason for everything. What's the purpose of my seeing ghosts? Tell me that, Jean, because I can't fathom why I need to be tormented with ghosts. Tortured ghosts. Jeez. Maybe I need to be here forever? Can a guy who hallucinates be trusted to drive a car? Design water plants? Even cook a meal without poisoning himself or someone else? What are the limits?"

"I don't know, Nick. Is it possible that girl was on your flight and you have survivor's guilt? The doctors said that you might experience that as the sole survivor."

"No. She wasn't on the plane. Never saw her before the crash. She's a little black kid, Jean. Maybe ten years old. Dressed in a plain dress with her hair done up in a ribbon. But she's got scars all over her back, and I see them through the dress like an x-ray when she walks away. She's pleading with me to help her. I don't understand the words she speaks; I don't even know what language they are sometimes. She uses something that sounds like French, but I haven't taken a French class in 20 years. Other times it's pidgin English. But I get her meaning. It's right out of an episode of the *Twilight Zone*. And it's making my life miserable."

The two of them sat in silence for a few minutes. Neither knew how to comfort the other. But love seemed to settle over the wounds like an airborne mist that just needed a little more time to hit therapeutic levels.

"I'm due to end my shift, is there anything else I can do for you?"

Nick looked at his poor therapist across the room. The man was trying so hard not to intrude. "We're good. We'll let the desk know when we're done and have them lock the room. Guess I'll see you tomorrow?"

"No, tomorrow's Saturday. But I'll be back Monday for your session. Just check your schedule for the time."

"Thanks. See you Monday."

18

Turning to Jean, Nicholas looked more devastated than before. "See, I don't even know what day of the week it is. I was sure it was Wednesday. Jean, am I ever going to be me again?"

There was no answer for that question on this dismal Friday afternoon. At least not one that Nicholas Bacon could hear.

CHAPTER FIVE
Port-au-Prince, Haiti
February 16

Violene contorted her body in anticipation of hitting the ground. Falling from that height would break her like a dish dropped onto the kitchen tile, shards ricocheting against everything in sight and leaving a mess. Instead, she landed in what must have been a pile of feathers.

The man was back again tonight. He was holding her hand as the two of them tried to move toward the dim light above them. Violene was cold, so the man wrapped her in his arms to warm her.

Popping above the surface, she realized it wasn't feathers but snow on a mountain. She saw it on a television in the driver's apartment when she had to clean for him. There was no snow in this part of Haiti. She wasn't sure if it ever snowed anywhere in Haiti.

On top of the snow pile, the man held her close, but he fell asleep. Violene traced the places on his forehead where his eyebrows should have been. Instead, she smeared ash — his face was burned in a horrible manner. He sighed at her gentle touch.

Violene never saw a man like this before. His skin was red from the burns, a patchy quilt of damaged skin and freckles. All the people she knew had skin as black as hers. This man was not cruel like other adults. Nor was he interested in her like "that." No, this man was protecting her from something. He comforted her. That was it. He let her know he was a voice of truth. He spoke little but had said that he would save her and heal her wounds. Was he Jezi (Jesus)? She didn't think he was: Jezi lived a long ago. But this one, who walked in her dreams with her, and who flew with her, he came to her in her sleep, and let her know she would be taken care of one day.

Violene awakened as the door to her bedroom/closet jerked open. The work day had begun. Could the man with no eyebrows come in time to save her from what she knew was coming?

CHAPTER SIX
Salt Lake City, Utah
February 20

"Special Agent Schimmler, my client has been answering your questions. The fact that you choose not to listen, and then endlessly repeat your inane points, is what's slowing us down. How many times does he have to tell you that he doesn't remember anything about the incident except plummeting toward the ground below?"

Nick looked around the room and sighed. Designed to be used as a conference room for the facility's doctors, it was turned into a branch office of the federal government. Arrayed around the table were ten special agents from every alphabet agency concerned with the explosion on the aircraft. Even the airline sent a lawyer to sit in as an observer. Two video cameras recorded the depositions, and every cop in the room had a recorder running on the table in front of him. They stopped every two hours so that Nick could take a break and hobble around a bit while they changed memory chips, but it still was sucking all of the energy out of him.

Grabbing his walking staff, Nick levered himself out of the chair. "Hopefully, you can all continue bickering without me. I'm going to have lunch and take a nap. If you're still hanging around after that, give me a shout. For now, I'm off to eat and snooze."

Turning toward the door, the bells on the top of his walking staff jingled as he moved away from the glares behind him. His ankle was doing well, but he still needed some kind of support if it started to hurt or swell up. His sister got him this hand-carved monstrosity and presented it to him the day before. Over six feet tall, it had a spiral twist to its two-toned wood, was topped by an exquisite carving of a teddy bear, with bells embedded in the bear's ears. Jean told him the bells were to alert bears that walkers were on the path. Nick was pretty sure she had had them added to make sure she could get out of the way when she heard him coming. His proclivity for falling was still an issue. It was, in fact, an issue that was keeping him in the rehab facility way longer than he wanted. Between the feds insisting that he remain available to them, and his ongoing health issues, he was terrified of leaving the facility. Either he'd wig out and wind up in a mental institution, or the feds would spirit him off to some facility where they interrogated terrorists and vanish him from public view.

It seemed that his extensive travel to nations where Islamic terror groups thrived had thrown him into the spotlight. He knew there was a threat in the Philippines, but when they started dragging out surveillance information about his travels around the country and asking him about the other engineers he'd met and travelled with, he started to wonder how long he'd been under their magnifying glass. Nick knew he was innocent, but it sure seemed like the government invested a lot of time and effort in watching him.

The mental health issues were more troublesome. Nick was still having visions and dreams of the tortured little girl. He caught a glimpse of her, or dreamt about her, at least every other day, and it was as though they were beginning to know each other through these visits. He didn't know her name, but she seemed to want to comfort him. He often dreamt of her watching over him while he slept, her small hand caressing his face and smoothing away his worries. In his dreams, he held the shivering child close and shielded her from an icy cold climate that contained a dark assailant that he could never quite visualize.

The rehab facility continued to serve as a sort of mini-prison where the herds of investigators could question him about the accident and his background. His sister Jean allowed them limited access to Nicholas during the last two weeks. On the days she couldn't be there, she had a friend who practiced law in Salt Lake City sit in for her. Between the two lawyers, they gave the investigators just enough to satisfy their curiosity. It was a brutal, contentious time, with accusations of obstruction on one side and badgering on the other. Today had gone in circles; nothing accomplished. Nicholas just kept moving toward the dining room, every step easing his breathing and lessening the anxiety he felt when he was around the investigators. This session had been a double helping of miserable as none of the clothes he picked out fit — all of them were too tight. He was back to wearing sweat clothes, and even those were snug. Unless he missed his guess, they were going to come to a decision of some kind today. Either he was going to get sprung, or they were hauling him off to a cell.

That was fine with Nick. He had had it with being in limbo. A cell or his freedom: easy choice. The thing that truly haunted him was whether the little girl was going to follow him to his destination, or would she stay behind in Utah with the souls that perished on the aircraft?

CHAPTER SEVEN
Salt Lake City, Utah
March 03

"Larry, that's the problem: I can't go home. They're camped on my front lawn waiting for me. I don't want to talk to the press. I just want to get out of here tomorrow and hide from the world for a while."

Larry gave a blank smile. Nick knew that smile: it could mean "I'm so proud of you I could cry;" or "I had a bad piece of fish for lunch." He was beyond enigmatic when he chose to be. Larry closed his eyes and stood very still for twenty seconds before he said, "Nick, I'm just glad you're alive. I wouldn't want to go back and face those vultures either. I can put you up in a hotel or hide you at my cabin, but your face is — well, you're going to stick out and attract attention until everyone forgets what you look like. Keep growing the beard. It makes you look old, but until all the burns quit sloughing skin, you'll be a bit less painful to look at. Is all your hair white, or just the stuff I can see?"

Nick spewed cola all over the bedspread in his room. This rehab facility was a hotel with nursing care. They wouldn't appreciate his wrecking the comforter. Jumping off the bed bought him a minute while he hobbled to the bathroom and grabbed a towel to mop up the mess. Life was still a bit confusing to him at times, and all his hair turning white freaked him out. Now he was upset that someone knew his hair color. Duh, it was right there on his head.

"Larry, don't you have some subsidiary where you can stash me until this blows over?" Larry Timmons was not just Nick's boss; he was one of the wealthiest men in the United States. He owned dozens of companies that Nick knew about, and many more besides. He had to have an office in India, or Siberia, or Brazil, even Cleveland, where Nick could be out of the reach of the American media.

Larry shifted from bemused to serious in an instant. "No, Nick. I don't have any place to stash you while you're this hot. You'd have to trek out past the last settled village in some Third World…"

Larry's eyes took on a sharpened brilliance, focused far outside the room. He shook his head in dismissal before a disturbing grin crossed his visage. "Nick, how do you feel about living in a dorm room with three other guys?"

"I outgrew that about twenty years ago, Larry. It was called being a poor graduate student."

"No, not at a college. I've got a place to stash you, but it won't have room service, and you'll have to help out with some manual labor. Interested?"

"In what, some copper mine you own in Chile? If you hadn't looked lately, I'm not exactly "shovel ready.""

Larry snickered. "I'm not even going to dignify that with an answer. No, it's a kind of religious retreat where nobody will bug you."

Nick looked like he swallowed a spider at the thought of chanting with monks every morning before dawn. "Larry, I'll take the copper mine over some monastery up in the north woods. I'll even bring my own pick and shovel. That whole vow of silence thing doesn't work for me."

"Not a monastery, but a mission house in Haiti. I'm headed down there tomorrow with a planeload of medical equipment. I'll be gone for three weeks, and you can stay there for as long as you want. The accommodations aren't the Hilton, but they're not much worse than this place. You have to share a room with a few other men, but the press will never find you there. The staff won't even be aware of who you are. If they do figure it out, they'll protect your privacy."

Nick thought about it. Haiti was a rough place from what he'd heard. "I don't speak the language. What good could I do for those people?"

Now Larry's smile turned to a broad grin. "Nothing and everything. We're a Hands-and-Feet outfit. You'll find out what that means with time, but for now trust me when I say most of the people you'll meet speak English. You still need to heal up, and this is a good time to go there with me. My whole crew on this trip consists of doctors and nurses. You'll get better care in Haiti than around here. How about it?"

Nick was out of options. His sister warned him not to show up in Minneapolis without a mask. He was still big news months after the crash. He didn't have the resources to hide out on his own, and even going to Europe couldn't give him anonymity in the age of the internet.

"How do we do it? I don't have my passport here, and no clothes for the weather. What about shots? I'm not ..."

"Slow down. First, I just need to get you to the airport and put you on my private jet without any fuss. The aircraft we're taking to Haiti is being prepped in Minneapolis right now. All the stuff is sitting in a warehouse, crated up and ready to go. We'll just sit tight for another day and once they're in the air, we'll book out of here and meet them at a small airfield in the middle of Iowa somewhere. The jet I took down here can land on short runways, and the plane for Haiti is designed for that kind of thing. Your sister's back in Minnesota. She can pack your stuff, can't she?"

Nick grabbed his phone and then paused. "Larry, I like the offer, but again, what can I do for those people? I don't want to be a fifth wheel and burden you and your medical team."

Larry grew sombre for a moment. "Nick, if you put your trust in me, and I trust God, we'll be okay. Now, call your sister and get the stuff you need. Your shots are current enough since you just got back from Manila last fall. A doctor here can get you anything else you need. Get that passport and I'll give you a ride on my airplane.

"We're going to Haiti, Nick. It'll be the experience of a lifetime."

CHAPTER EIGHT
Across Haiti
March 03

The landscape was unchanged since the last major earthquake. The still, warm air of the night was filled with a gauzy smoke that was ephemeral as the children's dreams across the Haitian half of the island of Hispaniola. The usual denizens of the night were astir.

This night, however, there was a restlessness in hovels and mansions alike. It was the children known in Creole as Resteveks – English speakers called them slaves. Throughout the night, one at a time, they were disturbed in their dreams. It was an instant's nudge to their minds. A small trifle that didn't awaken most of them.

For those that were awake, and praying for rescue, it was as clear as if God Himself had spoken the words: "I am sending a friend. You will find comfort with him. Have hope, my child."

Violene rolled over and sniffled. He had to be the one she saw in her dreams. The burned man who grew stronger in his appearance and his impact on her soul. He must be the one who could give her respite from slavery. She didn't know how she knew it, but she knew his name.

She whispered it over and over until she fell asleep.

"Papa Noel. Papa Noel. Papa Noel."

CHAPTER NINE
Port-au-Prince, Haiti
March 04

The chirp of tires as the plane touched down was followed by the roar of the engines as they clawed at the thick air in a furious attempt to slow the aircraft. Nick eyed the boxes around him, an irrational fear of shifting cargo dampening his face with beads of greasy sweat. Those X-ray machines would leave a nasty mark if they came loose.

The L-100 came to a crawl amidst the rumbling of turboprops in full reverse, burning kerosene enveloping the airframe. Once they hit ten knots, they turned on a taxiway toward the cargo handling area. A civilian version of the C-130, this L-100 was customized as a personal transport for Larry when he was moving relief supplies around the world. As Nick suspected, Larry was one of the largest philanthropists in Haiti. He just kept it low key: it was about the mission, not the glory. But a great aircraft made it easier to deal with travelling to remote locations.

Bumping along like a dolphin in front of an invisible ship, the pilot guided his charge over a few seams and dips in the taxiway and stopped with such grace that nobody noticed at first. Looking out the window next to his seat, Nick couldn't believe they made it down the narrow path. Not much wider than a city street, the wings hung out over lush grass. If they waddled off the path, the ground looked soft enough to swallow up the landing gear.

The four turbo-prop engines wound down, and the tail of the aircraft opened with a whine of electric motors. The back hatch yawned open to reveal a heat-shimmered slab of concrete and a half-dozen aircraft in various states of disrepair. A large man, skin as dark as the day was bright, bounded up the ramp once it hit the cement. "Larry, Bondye beni ou!"

Larry embraced the man in what passed for a bear hug when you're a good foot shorter than the recipient. "Andre, it's so good to be back. Are they ready to unload us and do customs?"

Andre's grin lit up the inside of the aircraft. "Oui, Larry. I brought two helpers along in the tap-tap. They'll stick around and inspect the cargo as it's unloaded. I made sure we got the most honest ones in all of Haiti. Which means you will have gifts for the customs men?"

Larry pointed at a large canvas bag tied to the seat of a dental chair. "It's the usual stuff; please make sure they don't hand it to Louis until they're done securing the load in the warehouse. Are they going to do customs for people as well, or do we have to go to the terminal?"

Andre looked around him, "They said that they are to do cargo out here, and we have to go inside to check the people through. It's a game. Perhaps you can talk them into changing their minds?"

Larry shook his head. "Nope. Once we start that we'll never get a break again. I'll walk my people through the terminal. They should see the place like everyone else. It's the best way of understanding what's happening. Are the tap-taps outside?"

Andre pointed through the wall of the airplane. Larry addressed his team, "We're going to get off the aircraft now and go through customs. We talked about it before, but the answers are 'No, I don't have anything to declare. I'm here as a tourist. I am not here to work and earn money; I am here to do God's work.' The Haitians accept that as tourism for our purposes. You filled out the forms on the flight, just have them in your hand with your passport. We'll get into those two bus things with cages in the back. You old-timers know that we call those tap-taps. They have roll cages and are much stronger than they look. It's cheaper than air conditioning, but we are on display in a mobile cage. The roof keeps the sun off of you. But we'll talk about that on our ride.

"This big dude is Andre. He's one of our minders and a great fellow. He'll make sure we stay out of trouble. We all just need to be aboveboard and honest with Andre and the authorities and we'll be fine."

"If everyone will please come with me and bring your bags, we'll get you through this, so we can get to the mission houses. Stick near Larry, or me, and it will be fine."

Andre waited at the bottom of the ramp and pointed to where they could carry their bags. Nick was the last one off the plane and Andre burst into laughter at Nick's still-red face and white beard. "Papa Noel! You are early for Christmas, but we welcome you to Haiti and seek your help in loading the sleigh."

Nick looked across the group to see that the Haitians were now laughing and pointing at him, repeating cries of "Papa Noel." In a moment, they started singing Christmas carols to him in Creole. Larry was being more helpful than usual; he pulled out a camera and started recording the fiasco.

Larry lowered the camera and his smile vanished like a popsicle in a microwave when he saw the stricken look on Nick's face. "You're being honored! Nothing to worry about."

"All I want is to vanish into the woodwork for a while. I don't need this attention. Please, don't encourage it, Larry. You know how hard this is for me."

Larry's smile came back. "You're not Nicholas Bacon down here as of a minute ago. You're Father Christmas. Andre did you a favor with that little joke. Nick, you have changed in profound ways since the disaster. You don't even look like yourself. Every hour you look more like Santa. Give it a couple of days in the sun, let all that white shag on your face grow out, and your own sister won't recognize you. I have no doubt that the people of Haiti will love you for who you've become, not who you were when that plane exploded."

Nick was skeptical, but he trusted Larry with his life. He had to: he felt alone in a strange and distant land.

CHAPTER TEN
Port-au-Prince, Haiti
March 04

Nick had experienced many things in his travels for his employer over the past 17 years, but the terminal in Port-au-Prince's airport was still a shock in many ways.

The disturbing roar of hundreds of voices trying to out-shout each other in a marble room is daunting, but when it is in a strange language, combined with the close confines, the experience put Nick at the edge of panic. Most of the other members of the mission team had travelled to Haiti before, and they were aware of what awaited them inside the building. Nick flinched as the roaring howl of naked sound smashed him in the face when the door to the terminal was opened a few feet from their tap-tap. It was dark inside the airport compared to the pounding sunshine on the ramp, and the thrum coming out of the door drowned out a small plane taxiing just a hundred yards away.

While others in the group smiled and exchanged chatter in Creole with the locals, Nick withdrew from the reality of the crush that filled the hallways and stumbled along in a paralytic state to the customs area. There was a Dixie-land jazz band, several dozen vendors with liquor and jewellery, and more than a few touts for local hotels. The group was warned not to let go of their bags or to show any interest in the merchandise. Nick had no problem there; it was the largest crowd since his plane crashed over a month ago. He was clinging to Larry like a four-year-old in an amusement park haunted house.

Bouncing like a string of pinballs off the bumpers of human flesh in the corridor, the group cascaded into customs. The public was banned from this area and a sense of casual fear, common to all customs halls, settled over the room. Handing his documents to the clerk, Nick realized he fit the classic smuggler's profile: he was nervous; appeared to be evading direct eye contact; and having a heck of a time understanding the official, forcing her to repeat the questions several times. Larry glided up to his side and spoke a few words in Creole to the frowning woman, transforming her face into a platform for gleaming eyes and soft laughter.

31

A few more questions were asked, with Larry translating, and they were off. Her final words were, "Enjoy your stay, Papa Noel."

Larry was chuckling as they moved over to have the bags inspected. "Get used to it; Andre had nothing to do with her response. You do look like Papa Noel. You'll be called Santa Claus, Pere Noel, and Nikolas. It's an honor. He's a beloved saint, and every child you meet will see him in your face. Do you know why?"

"Not really. I mean, when I look in the mirror, I don't see the resemblance."

"We never do see the good in ourselves, Nick. Aside from the fact that Christopher Columbus landed in Haiti on Saint Nicholas day, and Nicholas plays a huge role in Haitian history and culture, you have a personal link to the Saint. You have kind eyes. The eyes of a man who has seen too much and yet lives to love others. There is a hint of the real Saint Nicholas in your soul, coming out through your eyes. Now that your hair is totally white, and your beard is thick enough to hide the burns on your face, you look like the man who brings gifts on Christ's birthday. That's pretty cool for anyone. I'd embrace it, myself."

The line shuffled forward while Nick considered his new position. He could slide into this comedic role of Kris Kringle, but the soul of Saint Nicholas? Must be more to the guy than just toys and reindeer if Larry was so hyped about the job. Something to consider.

One by one they put their bags on the counter, and as rapidly as one could imagine it happening, the bags went on a cart unopened. The whole team of missionaries wore shirts touting the organization, and the customs folks knew that the organization policed itself with the rigor of inspecting drill sergeants. No weapons, drugs, or contraband came in with this group. Maybe a few dozen cans of canned food, or some bandages, but nothing against the law. They trusted them because they were Christians following Christ.

Nick didn't understand the whole import of that philosophy of life, but he did realize that just beyond the door there were dozens of shouting men pushing each other out of the way and being pushed right back. His vision was acting up again and parts of the crowd were shrouded in shadow. He tensed up and got close to Andre, who seemed to be the brightest figure in the room despite his dark skin.

Andre gave him a grin. "Papa, just stick close, and I will get you to our tap-tap safely." Andre seemed to grow to twice his size and tower over the crowd, breaking a path toward their vehicles. After opening the back of the cage on the first tap-tap, he started slinging bags with two tough looking fellows. He must have caught Nick's look, for he said, "My helpers. They are good boys. They work with us at the mission."

One at a time the missionaries climbed into the shielded cage in the back of the tap-tap and grabbed a spot on the bench seats running along the sides from front to back. That way, they could have their backs to the one side and look out the mesh on the other. Iron pipes were welded in overhead with subway straps every few feet. Some would stand, some would sit, but all would fit.

Once Larry hopped in the back, Andre told him to bolt the door and headed up to ride with the driver. They were locked in. Nick's stomach started to twist in upset at the realization he'd fled one trap in Salt Lake City and exchanged it for another mounted on the bed of a truck. When was he going to be free again?

The trip from the airport to the mission houses was right out of one of the dystopian movies he'd watched as a teenager. At every intersection, the rules went out the window and the biggest or fastest vehicle gained right of way, leaving behind a cloud of diesel smoke, shaking fists, and raised voices from other drivers. Corners were taken at multiple g-forces, without a doubt up on two wheels, if Nick were brave enough to open his eyes. This was a Third-World nightmare to Nick, who tried to pray, a habit he was picking up bit by bit after the airliner explosion.

After a few minutes, someone handed him a cold bottle of water. The others were all laughing and pointing out places of interest as they roared down the streets. Following one memorable and violent left turn, they slowed to a crawl and headed up a rutted road that not even goats should attempt. It had been paved at some point, but that was two or three changes of government ago. Some of his wounds from the plane crash were calling out for attention by the time the tap-tap sounded its back-up alarms and waddled in reverse into a gated compound on the dusty side street. The team remained in their places until the vehicle moved into the courtyard, the gate was rolled shut, and a set of steps was produced. The last one off, Nick exited the vehicle under his own steam inside the mission compound. All the bouncing, twisting, and turning of the vehicle stretched his tender neck and hand skin as well as put pressure on his ankle. He needed a rest and a dozen ibuprofen.

The chaotic streets of Port-au-Prince were replaced by a quiet courtyard in front of a large building. People streamed out of the building to help unload the tap-tap and carry the luggage inside. One young woman directed traffic and stopped everyone at the door to remove their shoes. She assigned each of the missionaries to their room with a point of her index finger and a smile, all done from memory. She knew all of the names without a clipboard, and when Nick approached her at the doorway her face began to glow. "Byenveni nan Ayiti, Papa Noel. Welcome to your new home."

The clappering bell of her laughter cracked Nick's gloom over the nickname. It was the most unusual laugh he'd ever heard: it came from deep inside her soul. "Thanks. I guess I'm stuck for the duration with that name. I hope it grows on me."

"It will. It's a term of endearment here. Andre called ahead and said Papa Noel was with him. When I saw you get off the tap-tap, I recognized you right off. Are you a mall Santa back in Minnesota? I come from the Twin Cities but I'm down here on a five-year mission. You know, seeking out new life, new civilizations, to boldly go…"

Nick liked her on the spot. She wasn't just cute, but she had that borderline insane quality that Nick cherished in his friends. He was pretty sure she knew a line or two from Monty Python as well. But if she was down here on a five-year commitment, she must be a serious Bible-thumper, something that Nick without a doubt was not. He never made it through the Bible and wasn't much interested in doing so.

"No, no mall work. I wasn't even aware that I looked anything but dishevelled until this afternoon. I was in an accident…"

She took his forearm with the grace of an animal handler trying to calm an anxious puppy, and led him back into the courtyard, out of hearing range from the others. "I know all about it, but I don't think the others realize it. The missionaries know, they were there for the news, but the staff here won't equate you with the miracle. So, if you wish to protect your privacy, don't mention it to them. They guard the teams here, and don't gossip, but most are poor and if a cameraman were to find out where you are and bribe them for access, it would be very chaotic. We want to avoid that."

34

"That won't be a problem. I just want to vanish for a while and get my act together. Larry said I'd be safe here and I trust him."

"Nick, we will take care of you here, and make sure your wounds heal. All of us love you as a brother, and if you want, we will pray over you to speed your healing. We also want you to be well regarding your mental and spiritual health. You can always talk to me or one of the doctors for counselling. I'm a licensed psychotherapist. No charge while you're in Haiti."

Nick took that in and drew a deep breath. He never expected to be covered in so much support. Larry made it sound like he'd be kept out of sight in a darkened room until his skin healed, and his ankle was stronger. He stood there leaning on the wooden walking stick his sister gave him, feeling the love of these people surround him like a jacket. He was weary, but content with where he was.

The winter sun of Haiti was doing something for Nick as he stood there with the house-mother. He felt the tension from the airport and the ride in the tap-tap drain away as his hands began to sweat. It was good to be alive and in the bright light after weeks in the hospital and rehab. He looked across the courtyard and saw the little girl with the scars and wounds peeking at him from the shadows of the little building that sheltered the water supply. He took a step toward her, and the lights went out in his head.

"...with me? Andre, grab a chair for Papa Noel." Nick felt gentle hands supporting him as a chair was placed in the shade of a tree in the courtyard for him to rest. "I'm okay. Didn't mean to scare anyone. Where did the little girl go? Could I just sit here for a couple of minutes and enjoy the sunshine?"

Andre's liquid baritone rumbled in response, "Papa, we have no children in the compound. However, you can do anything you want. We do not eat for an hour. Would you like a beer? I am going to have one."

Beer. That sounded wonderful, but Nick knew some of his medications would conflict. "No, thanks for the offer. Just some water or coffee."

Andre smiled with the brightness of a nuclear flash. "Papa Noel, Haitian coffee is the best you will ever have. I will make it myself. You just rest out here, but please put your hat on. Your skin already is burning." The house-mother gave Andre a thumbs-up from the porch and beckoned him into the mission house.

Standing inside the doorway, they peered out at Nicholas as he petted one of the guard dogs that roamed the compound. The dogs were pleasant and fawning during the day, but at night they would tear an intruder to pieces. This one strolled over to sit with him under the tree near the gate as though they were old friends.

Andre did not make eye contact with her as he spoke, his attention focused on Nicholas in the courtyard. "He's very sick. I don't think he should go out for a couple of days until he is strong enough. Should I put his bag upstairs in the guest quarters?"

The house-mother stared at the back of Nick's head for another moment and made her decision. "No. Let's keep him in the room with the other missionaries, but you're right about going out into the city. He needs a few days to acclimate. He is Larry's friend. There are no time limits on his stay, so we don't need to rush into anything. Let's get his coffee and a piece of that cake from yesterday's party. We'll just have to make sure he doesn't take a fall. Can the guys help out watching over him?"

Andre shook his head. "There will be no need: he's my project now. If he is out of the compound, I will be at his side. You mother him here, I'll guard him out there. D'accord?"

She smiled and hugged Andre. "You're the biggest teddy bear I know, Andre. Between us, we'll make sure he heals and doesn't get into any trouble while he's in Haiti."

Both turned to look as the courtyard grew dark. The shadow of a dense layer of clouds (unheard of this time of year) was blocking the late afternoon sun. Nick stood up as though sprung from a trampoline and toppled over into the dirt of the courtyard. He landed face first and began a violent seizure as the doctors of the mission team rushed to his side. Everyone tried dodging fat drops of hot rain that threw miniature geysers of mud into the air as they exploded across the dust and gravel of the courtyard. The guard dogs circled Nicholas, heads upturned, growling at an unseen threat in the sky.

A loud crack of thunder rent the air as the doctors lugged a muddy, bleeding Nick into the house using the lawnchair he had been sitting in a few minutes before. The shade tree he'd been under erupted into pulpy shrapnel as a bolt of lightning coursed through its center, boiling all the liquid inside and unleashing a cloud of steam that left a nauseating film in the nostrils of the stunned mission team. The hair on their arms was as stiff as needles.

CHAPTER ELEVEN
Port-au-Prince, Haiti
March 04

Violene took stock of her teeth. Her tongue, swollen from the blow, probed the tender spots along her left jaw like a rattler striking a rabbit. Nothing appeared to be broken, but no fragments did not rule out cracked teeth.

She had been eating a biscuit the cook had given her when her owners came into the kitchen. They never set foot in the kitchen; it was the sole purview of Cook and the Restevek children in the compound. Two of them had been in the kitchen, laughing with Cook about some nonsense thing. Violene was a worker in the house, and the boy was the gardener's assistant. Responsible for more than the grounds, he was the one who also washed the cars. He didn't enter the kitchen except on rare occasions. He was a year older than Violene and treated her as though she were his younger sister. He had just left the kitchen when the owners threw the door open, hitting Violene in the head and bashing her jaw.

They wanted to know what was going on in the kitchen — they heard laughter, and seen the boy walking back toward the gardens eating something. It was not mealtime for the Resteveks, and they were angry that their food was being shared with the slaves.

Violene stared up from the floor where she fell, biscuit clutched in her hand. She must have passed out for a second when the door clobbered her. The owner took the biscuit from her hand and threw it at Cook. Shrieking like a tormented soul, he slapped the grey-haired cook across the face and lectured her about letting animals eat in the kitchen. Turning on his heel, he kicked Violene as he went back out the door.

Cook, through a clenched jaw of her own, filled a towel with ice and pressed it against Violene's face with the utmost of tenderness. "Go to your room, child. If he comes back, he will do more and worse. I will call you when your supper is ready. But do not be surprised if I do not. It may not be safe."

Violene nodded through tears of pain and went to the shed off the main house. One of the older Resteveks ran away that morning, and the house

38

was in turmoil. The worst of her day was not that she had been hit with the door, but that she was going to have to move into the house and take up the escapee's duties in the morning. All of them.

She'd rather die in the shed than live in the house. She prayed that the hero of her dreams would rescue her soon.

CHAPTER TWELVE
Port-au-Prince, Haiti
March 06

Larry knocked three times on the bedroom door before it opened. Eric, one of the doctors on the mission, invited him inside the four-man bunk room. All the beds were made with great precision, and empty except for Nick's, the others having gone into the main room to set the table and get breakfast ready.

"Hey, buddy. Feeling a little better today?"

Nick eased his feet out of the lower bunk and sat on its edge. "Yeah. Sorry about all the panic. They warned me that I might have some seizures with that head trauma and the induced coma. That was supposed to be over and done with weeks ago. Eric tells me that you guys treated me here at the mission house. I'm lucky these docs are here."

"I don't know about lucky, Nick. Seems to me that God might have arranged for you to have nursing care. Eric stayed with you yesterday to make sure you were stable, but the rest of the crew got some serious work done out at the clinic without him. I'm glad we were able to be there for you. You had a rare rainy day to get some sleep. That never happens this time of year."

Doctor Eric shut off the room air conditioner and started to leave the room. "Nick, I think you ought to get up and eat breakfast with us this morning. Just take it easy today, stay here at the compound, and we'll check you over tonight. Andre has a cell phone. He can get hold of us if something happens. I'm heading out with the team today. I'm sure that your electrolytes were out of whack with the heat and travel. You were dehydrated, so we got you balanced with IV fluid while you slept. But you need to get out of bed today."

Larry helped Nick stand up and then handed him his walking stick. "Don't leave home without it."

Laughing, the men walked through the common area and arrived at the table just in time for the blessing over the food. A nurse practitioner on the team pointed to a couple of empty chairs. "Good to see you guys. Nick, glad you're up and about. Do you want to say the blessing?"

Nick fixed his eyes on the plate in front of him. He hadn't said grace over a meal in his life. He couldn't remember the words of the prayers his friend's mothers always said, not all of them anyway. "I'm out of practice doing this, sorry."

Larry reached over and took Nick's left hand in his, and the nurse to Nick's right took the other — everyone at the table joined hands. "Nick, just say what's on your heart this morning. That's all God wants anyway."

Nick took a deep breath and said, "God, I'm glad to be alive this morning. Thank You for taking care of me when I got sick. Thank You for Doctor Eric and all the others. Please bless this food, and the cooks who made it. That good enough, Larry?"

Larry was grinning. "Yeah, Nick. That does it nicely. Amen."

Plates were passed and soon everyone feasted on pancakes, Nutella, avocadoes, juice, coffee, scrambled eggs, oatmeal, and hot sauce. Some of the missionaries seemed to be competing to see who could put the most enormous quantity of hot sauce on their breakfast. Larry was so far in front of the competition that Nick didn't see how anyone could even try to catch him. He clinched first place when he put hot sauce on his oatmeal.

Once the meal was finished, they bussed their dishes to the kitchen, and a few of the team wiped down the table and shook the placemats in the courtyard. The cooks shooed them out of the kitchen, sending the team back for a morning prayer before they left. Sitting in the common room, they formed the chairs in a loose circle while Larry read some passages from the Bible. Nick didn't know what to do. Some were taking notes, some sat with eyes closed, and a few were reading along with Larry. Nick never imagined that "normal" people memorized the words like a preacher would and couldn't imagine putting all that work in for nothing.

One of the drivers stuck his head in the door and called the group to get in the tap-tap. Bibles snapped shut, chairs were pushed back in place, and everyone filed outside, leaving their personal possessions on table tops in the room. Even though he knew it was a safety precaution so that nobody robbed the missionaries out in town, Nick gazed at the valuables left behind with a thought: the trust level was high in this place.

Following along in their wake, walking stick thumping on the tile floor, Nick stopped at the end of the dining room. He stood in the doorway, squinting against the merciless sunshine, and waved to them as the compound gates opened. As the tap-tap pulled out, shouts of "Papa Noel"

41

rang from the roadway where a dozen children kicking a soccer ball had spotted him. Nick broke into a grin and waved back at them as the gate closed with a bang of heavy steel.

Sitting at the table next to the door of the mission house and staring out into the courtyard sounded like a solid plan for the day. Andre joined him at the table and pushed a cup of dark Haitian coffee towards him. "I put in some honey; you looked to be in need of a sweet, Papa Noel." Concern was scrawled across his broad face.

"I'm okay Andre. Thanks for the coffee. I was going to get another cup after I helped with the dishes."

Andre poked a thumb over his shoulder at the kitchen, "The ladies do the dishes in the morning. The missionaries get up early and help with the cooking and serving, but they leave so soon that they don't have time for dishes. The cooks take the evening off, so once the meal is ready, we serve ourselves and do the dishes. Lunch is out in the field. Usually energy bars and water."

After the calorie-laden breakfast, that made sense. Two meals at the mission house to bookend the day, and a quick, light meal for energy out in the hot sun. It also meant you didn't have to find a toilet in the middle of the day. Nick hoped that Larry brought spare energy bars for him, because he had nothing but his medications and a few items of clothing that were suitable for a warm climate. His sister didn't know that it was a bring-your-own-lunch excursion and had not included any snacks. Perhaps it was a less-than-subtle hint about his weight gain over the last months.

Andre read his mind: "Don't worry, Papa, you will eat lunch with us in the house. The staff makes up something around noon. It is often soup or sandwiches, but we eat well — it pays to be friends with the cooks. And the laundry team. And the translators. You see, we have a very busy place here when the missionaries are out in the field."

"Why aren't you out with them, Andre? You seem like the guy in charge. You're big and smart and speak at least two languages. Don't they need you to drive and translate?"

"Not today. They have two of my assistants with them. They are not going into Cite Soleil until the day after tomorrow. We have two mission houses here, and another group comes tomorrow afternoon. This group does medical work at the clinic. The other group is people like you. We have them go into the city and do God's work with the people. Today the medical team will go to the clinic at Titanyen just outside Mercy Orphanage. The staff there will take care of them. They have my phone number if they should need me. Today I stay with you and make sure you are all right. The house-mother went to meetings in Port-au-Prince today, so I am the logical choice to be your minder." His laughter filled the courtyard with rebounding echoes of pure joy and mirth.

"Thanks, Andre. But I plan on sleeping today if I can."

Andre wagged his finger: "No, Papa. Doctor Eric said you must be awake. We will play cards or chess. If you feel up to it, we can walk to the hotel down the road and swim in the pool. I have sunscreen and I'm sure some missionary left behind a swimsuit that will fit you. You need to be up and on your feet for at least a few hours. If you want to get out of the sun when it gets hot, we can go inside and talk, or pray. However, no sleep. Doctor Eric was quite insistent."

Andre reached to his left and dragged a scabrous looking chessboard toward him. A grungy plastic bag held the pieces. He assembled the board in moments and gave Nicholas the white pieces.

"Don't you draw for white, Andre?"

The face of confidence in front of Nick said, "Papa, if you still want to draw after this game, I certainly will. But for now, I think you may need the edge."

Ten minutes later, Nick accepted white for the second game. He needed the edge.

CHAPTER THIRTEEN
Port-au-Prince, Haiti
March 08

Breakfast was over, and the medical team had left for the day when Andre came for Nick. The two of them strolled to the lower part of the missions' compound and met up with the group that arrived the night before. Nick was looking forward to a fresh set of faces after being confined to the mission house the last couple of days.

Along with twelve pasty, winter-weary missionaries, Nick was crammed into the rear of the tap-tap. Two staff members leading the team that day were in the driver's compartment. Andre stood in the rear of the passenger area, hanging from a red subway strap. There were no windows on the vehicle, as a layer of mesh grating kept birds, larger insects, and stop-light muggers out of the passenger compartment. This allowed the sights, sounds, and smells of Haiti to roll through the mobile people cage as they went along. A mixture of fried plantains, diesel exhaust, trash fires, and rotting vegetation were very foreign scents to everyone except Nick. Nick had experienced similar places in the Third World, but none quite as vibrant as Port-au-Prince.

"Andre, what's the deal with the soldiers everywhere?"

"They are from the United Nations, Papa. After the earthquake in 2010 they came to keep order and never left. The Americans came for a time, but once their mission was done, they went home. We joke that the UN stands for "Until Never" which is when we think they will go away: never. They show no interest in leaving Haiti and nobody knows what they do that helps. But you see, they have lots of guns, armoured vehicles, money, and fancy berets. We don't. So, they stay."

The tap-tap jogged through the city, banging along the pot-holed thoroughfares before meeting a decent stretch of open road at the outskirts. In Haiti, that meant that drivers began passing them every few seconds, even when oncoming traffic was mere inches from a head-on collision. It was the worst game of road-chicken that Nick ever saw, and after a massive burst of anxiety, he shrugged it off and waited to meet his fate.

Well clear of Port-au-Prince, the mission team met a water truck bearing their logo at the filling centre. A line of trucks snaked around the huge parking area, and one-by-one, they trundled under the giant pipe that filled them in just minutes. After the clanging of the upper filling hatch, the drivers hopped down to their cabs and departed in a cloud of thick diesel smoke and groaning springs.

Nick was fascinated by the trucks and the water on a professional level. His whole life was water filtration. While they waited in the shade for their truck to take on water, Nick and Andre walked closer to watch.

"Is there anything else in the bags besides powdered chlorine, Andre?"

"No, Papa. They all use a bag of chlorine that they buy from the water people. We get our water free; God has arranged for that gift. All the others pay not just for the water but also for the chlorine. We bring our own that we buy by the shipping container. You put it into the tank before the water so that it is evenly distributed."

"Is the water filtered before it goes into the tank?

"No, Papa. But it is very clean water from a deep well. Very few places in Haiti have a well such as this one. The other trucks go throughout the city and fill cisterns in neighborhoods and pump tanks in taller buildings. With the chlorine, it is safe to drink. But please, stick to the bottled water we brought with us today."

"Deal. Where did all these trucks come from, Andre? They all look to be pretty similar but it's a bunch of different paint jobs."

Andre smiled and said, "Moooo."

Nick stood there, jaw agape. Andre made a sound so much like a bellowing dairy cow, right down to the decibel level, that it would attract every lonely bull for miles.

"Oh, Papa, you should see your face. They are all milk trucks from the United States. Brokers go to Florida, buy used milk trucks, and bring them back on sea-going barges. The plumbing is perfect for what we do, and they can be rebuilt when they start to wear out. Water tankers are too long for some of the streets, but the milk trucks are the right length. Our two trucks were donated by dairy farmers in Minnesota. We took them apart and shipped them here, so they could be refurbished. But they are beautiful! The suspensions are much tougher when we finish. The roads are too rough for the original equipment."

Their truck pulled under the giant pipe in the center of the lot. It was filled with sparkling water in ten minutes, the driver hopping up and clamping the lid down in a flash. As he pulled the truck away, the next was lined up and ready for its load.

As the dripping truck trundled down the rutted road, the tap-tap followed close behind. The tanker was sending up a spray of water with each dip in the road as the vents caught a wave from the unbaffled tank. Andre spoke up to make sure everyone heard him in the back of the vehicle: "Please check yourselves again for jewelry or things in your pockets. The little ones will pick you clean like a chicken if you have anything on you. That includes wedding rings and necklaces. Please, take all of it off and hand it to me right now. They will also grab at sunglasses and hats, so make sure you keep track of them. They are so poor that anything is more than they have. Remember to respond with love and concern: you are the hands and feet of Jesus today. Honor Jezi and represent Him. Forget yourself for this day."

Driving toward Cite Soleil, Nick started to get nervous. He'd been in tough parts of the world before, but this was beyond anything you would expect in the West. Dust was thick in the heat-shimmered air, and the smell of burning trash threatened to choke him. The water truck incited chaos on the side streets as it went by. The people in this dismal area had no source of running water. Other than the trucks that the mission team brought in each day, every drop of life-giving water was paid for with funds that were close to non-existent. Life and death hinged on the contents of a former milk truck and whether it took a right, or a left, into your neighbourhood, when you were a resident of Cite Soleil.

The tap-tap came to a halt as the tanker made a turn into a side street, backed out, and then pulled past them in the other direction. It came to a stop in an open area just before an intersection. The tap-tap followed suit and pulled up just ahead of the tanker.

Nick asked, "Andre, why do we turn around like that?"

Andre was no longer smiling. His matter-of-fact tones frightened Nick: "If there is a riot, or something goes wrong, the tanker will block for us as we escape. We never leave the vehicles pointing deeper into the neighborhood. We are always ready to flee.

Andre shouted to the mission team as dozens of children came running toward the water truck and surrounded the tap-tap. "Do not get of out line of sight of the tanker unless a staff person is with you. If you hear the horn, set down your bucket and return to the tap-tap right away. Do not delay if I call you, and do not argue with the staff. We have your safety in mind and cannot always explain what is happening. Okay?"

There was an acknowledgement from the group and Andre unlocked the door, swinging it wide and shooing the children back. Over his shoulder he shouted, "Do not let the children into the tap-tap. Make sure the door stays closed. Papa, you come out last and stick with me."

The missionaries climbed down the ladder at the rear of the vehicle and waded out into the crowd like surfers from a beach seeking a promising wave. Around them, instead of whitecaps, there was a sea of small children crying out to be picked up. Most of the team grabbed a child, or two, and moved toward the back of the tanker truck. The children under five were either naked, or close to it. Pants were a rare commodity.

The crowd flowed away from the tap-tap until Nick emerged from the shadows. A chorus of shouts arose from children and adults alike. "Papa Noel! Pere Noel!" As Nick got to the bottom of the ladder something strange began to caress his ears: hundreds of voices singing "Here Comes Santa Claus" in Haitian Creole. He looked out over the crowd and saw a glow of light surrounding each of the little ones. A few that were older, and then some of the adults appeared to stand in the shadows, even though there was nothing between them and the sun.

Andre was laughing and directing the chorus as though he were Leonard Bernstein in front of the Boston Pops. People came from the surrounding alleys and homes to see what all the commotion was about and joined in the song. Nick was baffled. Sure, he was a good 30 pounds overweight, caused by his stay in the gourmet restaurant that disguised itself as a rehab center, but he didn't think he looked that much like Santa. It was at that moment that he caught his reflection in Andre's mirrored sunglasses: Santa Claus with a walking stick dropped right in the middle of Cite Soleil. His breath was sucked from his lungs at this transformation. How could he not have seen it himself?

The answer was simple: Nick was a humble man who never looked in a mirror with any concern about his appearance. Since the accident he'd grown used to the facial hair and a fresh crop of fuzz where his brush-cut had been burned off in the explosion. But he'd never *seen* the

47

transformation from doughy engineer to patron saint of children before this moment.

Andre grabbed him by the arm and spoke in his ear, "Papa, you don't look so well. Do you want to get back in the shade of the tap-tap?"

Nick straightened up, latched onto his walking stick with an iron grip, and shook his head. "I'm okay, Andre, the Christmas carols just freaked me out a little. What do we do next?"

Andre surveyed the hundreds of smiling, singing faces that surrounded them. "I suggest we go to the water hose and use this pleasant miracle to speed things along. Nobody will argue with Papa Noel if he keeps order on the water line. Come with me and I'll show you what we do."

Andre scooped up two toddlers like a bird of prey, and carried them under his arms, joyous squeals escaping from them. Nick used his right hand on the walking stick, its bells jingling with each step, and his left hand and forearm were grasped by dozens of tiny hands in the blink of an eye. Within seconds, they were holding on to his arm right up to his shoulder, each one entreating him for something he didn't understand.

"Andre, what are the kids saying?"

"They want to know where their presents are, Papa."

"How do I tell them I didn't bring any?"

"Papa, you do not need to tell them that, they expect to be disappointed. Just enjoy the time with them."

Nick took a moment to wrap his mind around a life where disappointment was the norm. How would he deal with a life like these kids lived? His thoughts were interrupted as Andre came to halt 20 feet from the back of the water tanker. "Papa, we will stay here and make sure the line is good. "No" is the best word, and you will need it often. If you see someone cutting into the line, admonish them with your most stern voice. If they come back, I will take their bucket and remove them from the line. Just let five-gallon buckets in the line, nothing smaller. It wastes too much water trying to fill the little ones with our hose."

Andre pointed to the end of the hose where two missionaries were struggling to fill buckets. Four inches in diameter, the hose put out a steady stream of cold, clear water. The children raced in line to fill their buckets, while other missionaries pulled the full ones off to the side. Children as young as eight years old picked up the thirty-pound buckets, balanced them on their heads, and staggered off into the depths of the slum.

One by one, the missionaries were captured by smaller children who otherwise just dragged their heavy buckets to their homes. The missionaries each took a bucket, or two, and carried them for the children. This saved wear and tear on the buckets and spilled far less water. The staff followed along as the children skipped alongside or held the pail by the other side of the handle. Small black hands were worn and calloused in a way these white people from Minnesota had never seen.

"Andre, how come the parents send these little guys out here when they know the buckets are too heavy? All those dads are just sitting watching. Why don't they help?"

Andre turned to look at the men. "Papa, those children are Resteveks. You call them slaves in English. Those men bought the children from their parents. They must do as they are told."

Nick lost track of the line in front of him. Slaves? Ninety minutes from Miami? Child slaves?

"Seriously, Andre. What's the deal?"

"I am serious Papa. The parents cannot feed their children. Rather than let them starve, they sell them. At least as a slave, they are given food. Some go back home when the parents can buy them back, others when they get too old to be trusted. But most never see their families again."

"Andre, these people are dirt poor! How can they afford slaves?"

"Papa, it is all relative. They have enough money to afford a child or two to do the work. They are fed a little bit, and they wear rags. It has been so all my life in Haiti."

Nick grabbed the handle on a filled bucket, a child held the other. Off they wobbled along the street, walking stick clutched in the other hand as the Restevek child led him to his owner's residence. Andre tailed along close behind with dozens of other children who gazed with rapt attention at Nicholas.

"I can't fix slavery, but I can help a couple of them."

Nick made two more trips before his efforts in the hot sun started to sap his energy.

"Last trip, Andre. I'm about shot."

Nick followed the child down a different path this time, between the tight rows of hovels. They emerged on another main street and continued deeper into Cite Soleil.

"Papa, we are too far, we need to go back. Just set the bucket down and let her carry it the rest of the way."

Ten feet away, half-a-dozen young men hiding in the shadows mocked Andre. "Oui, Pere Noel. Abandon the child and go back to your little truck."

"You can't help anyway, old man. Flee while you can."

Andre gave the group the stink eye. While the mission group had a good relationship with the gangs in Cite Soleil, Andre had never seen this bunch before. They had a rougher look than the other young men Nick passed on the streets of the slum. As they got out of their chairs and started toward Papa Noel, Andre put a hand on his shoulder: "We must leave now, Papa. They are dangerous."

Nick looked for the child and her bucket, but the little girl was no longer there. How did she vanish that fast? Looking up again, Nick saw not a bunch of young men approaching, but a pack of demons, complete with swishing tails and horns, shrouded in darkness.

Andre tightened his grip on Papa's shoulder when Nick began shouting. "Stand back! I call on all the Saints and powers of Heaven to defeat your darkness. Be gone, demons!"

Nick's walking stick transformed into a giant copper-headed serpent that hissed and spat venom at the approaching demons. A brilliant light surrounded the head of the snake – bright as the noonday sun. Andre stood transfixed behind Nick. Rooted to the spot himself, Nick felt time spin around him like a whirlwind.

The demons began to taunt Nick. "You have no authority. You don't even believe what you say. You're a fake. The kind of fake that caused deaths on your airplane. Come, be with us. You can be powerful on our side. Our master will rule this world. He rules this place."

Nick thrust the serpent/staff at the demons and a deep rumble emerged from his mouth, "I command you in the name of Jesus Christ to relinquish your hold on this neighborhood. I banish you in the name of the Nazarene. You are the ones without power. I call on our Lord to cast you from our midst. Be gone!"

The demons shrieked and split, backed up a few paces, and then fled the street. Complete quiet fell on the quarter of the city, interrupted a moment later by the repeated blaring of the air horn on the tanker truck.

Andre grabbed Nick by the collar and hustled him toward the tap-tap. Ahead of them, they saw two more missionaries and one of the other drivers running away at full speed.

Emerging from the narrow alleys onto the main street, the horns of the vehicles were an obscenity of decibels. Nick couldn't run with his bad ankle, but they made good time and clambered on board the tap-tap. The streets were empty; abandoned water buckets littering the roadway. Andre did a quick headcount and then pounded on the wall between the driver's compartment and the passenger area. The tap-tap roared to life and the bellow of the tanker's diesel engine followed in their wake. "Take us back to the compound. Do not stop for anything."

The streets of Cite Soleil were as empty as a ghost town as the mini-convoy sped down the streets. Nick looked out through the mesh side of the vehicle and saw demons in some of the doorways, gesturing obscenely toward the tap-tap. Once they hit the main road that led toward Port-au-Prince, and away from Cite Soleil, people were out in their usual numbers. Looking back, Nick could see dark clouds boiling over the slum, lightning crashing back and forth between the clouds and the earth, on an otherwise clear day. Nick's heart spasmed as though lightning struck him. He watched the world swirl to blackness, slumping over on the bench seat and rolling to the floor. The tap-tap accelerated toward the mission house.

CHAPTER FOURTEEN
Port-au-Prince, Haiti
March 08

The missionaries had just hosed off their feet in the outer compound of the mission house when there was a blaring horn at the massive gate. One of the security people looked up at the television screen and unlocked the chain holding the gate shut. Larry's car squirted through the gate the instant it was wide enough to admit him. He wheeled up into the parking area and sat with his head against the wheel for a minute, composing himself for the ordeal to come. Once his breathing was under control, he opened the door and waved to the team that had just fled Cite Soleil.

"We need to talk. Please grab something to drink and meet me in the common room in fifteen minutes. Andre and Nick, I need to speak to you in private. Please come upstairs."

Nick was weak from the events of the day, leaning on his walking staff like it was a young tree in a hurricane. He was drained in ways never experienced. His focus was wandering, and he staggered a little as the trio climbed the stairs. Andre wrapped an arm around his shoulders and said, "It is all good, Papa. I will take care of you."

They went into Larry's office, cool shade enveloping them as they crossed the threshold. Larry flicked on the ceiling fan, glancing up to make sure there was power. Walking around his desk, he stooped and opened a small refrigerator, offering his two guests cold cans of soda. It seemed like a total luxury after being in the dusty streets of Cite Soleil.

Andre took Nick's can from him as he seemed befuddled by what to do with it. Pressing the cold can on the back of Nick's neck; he pushed Nick's head closer to his knees like a yoga coach, easing his sense of disorientation and nausea. Andre faced Larry. "Perhaps you should let him rest. I can answer the questions you have."

Larry took a sip and said, "Does he need a doctor, Andre? I can get one of the mission doctors at the clinic to come back and tend to him."

Andre shook his head. "He is just upset over what happened at the water stop. He will be fine in a bit."

"What did happen, Andre? I was in the office of the port director arranging for our containers to be delivered when the mayor called me. He said Nick started a riot by challenging some gang members. Where were you?"

Andre continued to hold the cold can on Nick's neck and leaned back in his chair. "I was with Papa Noel, Larry. He didn't start any riots. The gang was taunting him, and I told him we must leave; they looked dangerous. We were leaving the alley when we heard the horns of the trucks honking. They summoned us, and we came running."

Larry pondered that for a moment. "Andre, I talked to Charles on the phone — he said he heard you shouting out to him and told him to honk the horn and bring everyone back. He was positive that it was your voice, said he saw you at the corner of that alleyway before you ducked back in. Which is it?"

Andre shrugged his massive shoulders. "I was there to protect the missionaries, Larry. I would have called Charles if I could have, but I was busy taking care of Papa Noel."

Nick was confused by that exchange. He didn't remember Andre calling out to anyone or leaving his side. He was having a hard time believing his own recollection. Demons? That was beyond insane. He sat up straight in the chair and drew a deep breath. "Thanks, Andre. I feel better."

Andre handed him the soda, a fruit champagne of some sort. It was without question what Nick needed. He drank half the can in a go. "I don't remember things very clearly, Larry. But Andre is my hero. He got me out of there when those guys turned into – trouble. I owe him."

Andre patted him on his back as though he were a frightened child. "You are welcome, Papa. I would do it for anyone."

Larry rubbed his chin. "That still leaves us with the problem of what to do tomorrow. We can't send any mission teams back into the area, but I don't want them to be without water. Andre, can your guys take the trucks in and be safe?"

"Let me check with my friends, Larry. They will know what is happening now that we have left. I've never seen that gang before; it must be new."

"You may be right. Why don't you guys go downstairs and wait for me. I've got to call the mayor back and let him know what happened."

Andre and Nick left the office and returned to the courtyard, taking a seat under a shade tree.

Nick realized he was as tense as a piece of thread holding up a boulder. What if everyone else was thinking like he was – that he was nuts? They must all be convinced he'd lost his mind in the crash, because it sure seemed that way to him. That bump on the head when he got blown out of the plane must have done more damage than the doctors told him.

The two men just sat in the shade of a tree until Larry came outside the building. While it was designed to host missionary teams, it served many functions. A two-story adobe structure that looked like an upscale motel, it was complete with a balcony for evening worship services. Larry's office was in the middle of the staff rooms on the second floor, and the residence area for the visiting missionaries was on the ground floor.

"Let's go talk to the others. We need to straighten this out for the whole group."

Leaving the sunshine of the courtyard, the men entered the much darker mission house. To their left was a large kitchen where all the meals for the team were prepared. Straight ahead was the set of rooms for women, while to the right was the community room. On the other side were the men's quarters.

Larry went to the far end of the room, sat in a deep cushioned chair and said, "I'm glad you're all here and nobody was hurt. Anyone like to talk about what happened in Cite Soleil?"

A couple of hands shot up and Larry pointed at the youngest member of the team who just graduated high school at Christmas.

"It was weird; one minute we're filling buckets for a long line of people, and the next minute they all ran away. I saw two or three young guys run into the line and start shouting, and they all took off. Next thing we know the horn starts honking and we hopped into the tap-tap and locked the door. The rest of the team came running down the street and we took off. Other than the young men shouting, I didn't see anything. But it felt really creepy. I can't define it, but my skin crawled when it started happening. I felt better once we got back on the main road and left Cite Soleil."

The rest of the group nodded with one exception, an older man in the back of the crowd. Larry noticed the look on his face and said, "You want to tell us what you saw, sir?"

54

The man gathered himself and spoke in a voice reserved for sacred places.

"I was on a side street carrying a bucket of water for a young girl. I heard shouting up ahead and like the young lady said, my skin crawled. A cold front washed over the street I was on, and everything went very quiet. A moment later we heard the horns honking. All I saw was a bright glow from the center of the small square ahead. But the shouting. I never heard anything like that in my life outside of school."

Larry waited for a full minute before talking. "You said you never heard shouting like that before. What was so unique about it?"

The man shook his head. "No, when I said I never heard anything like it in my life outside of school, I meant the words. They were old. I'm not sure of the language, but I am a professor at Northwestern University in the history department. It sounded like a proto-Turkish variant. I detected some hints of Greek in the shouting, but there was one actual word that was distinguishable. The rest was just a feeling that the words were very old, Eastern Mediterranean in origin."

"What was the word you recognized?"

"I am fairly sure it was "Christos." I couldn't see beyond the glare ahead of me. Something was reflecting directly back at me as brightly as the sun in the sky. But that word stuck out. When I heard it, things seemed to change dramatically. That's when I felt conflict. Like just before I got out of the helicopter with my squad in Viet Nam. I haven't been that terrified since 1969. I never wish to be again."

Silence settled over the room and was broken when one of the missionaries began to pray out loud: "Father, please protect us from Satan. Today, I think, we came up against something very dark on our path. Please lift us up in Your hands and guide us, Father, as we are Your representatives in a failed world. We are strong only through You, and Your Son. His name protected us today, and we call on You to cover us with grace in the coming days. I pray this in Your Son's name, Yeshua Christos. Amen."

The rest of the assembled crowd chorused the amen. Larry sat stone still in his chair for a moment, then said, "Andre, let's get some lunch put together for these people. Some of you folks help Andre in the kitchen. I'll be in my office."

Larry got up and was almost out the door before he froze in his tracks. He turned and beckoned to Nick. "Hey, Nick, will you come with me upstairs. I need to talk to you."

Nick gathered himself with great apprehension, then moved as though under a death sentence toward the door. He heard Larry talking to someone outside. It was the house-mother. "...Eric back from the clinic. Have him come see me. Tell him to be discreet and just come to my office."

She nodded her affirmation and fished out her cell phone. Nick trudged behind Larry up the stairs, sure that he was going to have to leave Haiti after this morning. He also was sure, for the first time in his life, that wasn't what God planned for him.

"He's fine as far as I can tell. Just got stressed hotfooting it out of that alley on his bad ankle. If you want, I'll haul him to the clinic in the morning and x-ray his skull. But given what he's been through, nothing short of a CAT scan will really tell us much. I'd gladly escort him to Miami if need be, just let me know so I can organize my work at the village and hand it off to someone else."

"Hey, Doc, I'm right here. Don't I get a say in what happens to me?"

Eric smiled and then grew stern, "You've got a say in it, Nick, but it sounds like things got pretty ugly this morning. I don't think we need to evacuate you, but it wouldn't hurt if you came to the clinic with me and hung out tomorrow. That way the medical staff can monitor you and make sure you're properly hydrated and rested. I've got plenty of stuff you can help me with, and it won't put much stress on your body. Besides, the nursing staff has things they have to do, and an untrained assistant can do a lot of what I need help with in the clinic. How about it, Larry?"

"Is there going to be a place for him to sit on the job? If that ankle's a problem, he should probably get on tomorrow's plane. I checked and there are seats available. I'll be glad to buy him a ticket. I just need a trusty doctor to sign off on it for insurance purposes." Nick was growing tired of others determining his fate.

"My ankle is fine. I've continued to use the stick because I'm worried it might get twisted up on those rough streets. If you hadn't noticed, there's not a lot of even pavement in Cite Soleil. See, it's just fine."

Nick stood up and hopped on his left foot until both Doctor Eric and Larry were laughing at him. "He looks like a demented cross between Santa Claus and the Easter Bunny. You can quit jumping, Nick. I see your ankle is just fine. It's between you and Eric if you want to go with him tomorrow. I just can't have you go back to Cite Soleil until Andre and the other guys tell us it's okay. We're still trying to piece together what happened today. The United Nations sent troops to patrol tonight. It's pretty weird in there right now: nobody moving around and lots of wailing and moaning. Nobody understands what – well, we have an idea, but it's kind of crazy."

Nick knew what he meant but wasn't going to talk about his personal experience quite yet. "You mean that missionary's prayer about Satan being loose in Cite Soleil? Isn't that kind of a reach, even for the U.N.?"

"You're not a church kinda guy, are you, Nick?"

Nick wasn't sure whether to be offended by that statement or not. "No, I'm not really, Eric. My family never did the weekly church thing, and I only go if it's a wedding or something like that. But I don't attend every week. I'm more spiritual than religious."

Eric's snort was more disgust than anything. "I've heard that before. I don't want to rain on your parade, so I'll just wander off and get my supplies ready for tomorrow. Bring any meds you need with you, and don't worry about water. Water we have plenty of at the clinic."

Nick leaned back in his chair. "Can we talk about this without it getting nasty or judgmental? What do you mean? I hate murky waters when I'm going swimming."

Doctor Eric's face indicated that he'd gotten a sign from Larry to go ahead. "Nick, I wasn't always a man of faith, but the fact is that once my eyes were opened, I realized that I was just like you – neither hot nor cold. Lukewarm. If you read the Bible, you'll see why that doesn't work. There's evil in the world, and there's God. I chose, and I'm glad I did. I was just deluding myself over spirituality. That's what Satan wants us to do: straddle the fence. Because when the test comes, we likely will fall on his side of the fence."

Nick started to say something and then snapped his mouth shut like a turtle that just scored a minnow.

"Looks like that started the hamster turning on the wheel for you. If what I heard described downstairs over dinner was accurate, you guys ran into evil today. You can justify it, you can explain it away, but you can't ignore it or condone it if you don't want to be consumed by it. I'm beat, and I'm crabby. It was a long day and a couple of kids we're treating aren't doing very well with post-operative infections. I apologize if I've been rude. I should say goodnight. I'll see you guys at breakfast."

Eric got up, waved over his shoulder and walked out into the warm night air.

Larry sighed and scrubbed his face with his hands. He looked like a man carrying a million burdens, all of them heavy.

"Hey, Larry, I'm sorry that I set him off. I-I don't know what I know. But he seems firm about where he's at. Do I need to apologize?"

"No. He'll be fine by morning, Nick. You didn't do anything wrong. We're just worried about you if there's going to be spiritual warfare here in Haiti."

Nick looked puzzled. "Spiritual warfare? Like gangs fighting it out or something? I'm even more lost."

Larry took a sip from his coffee and swallowed with a grimace. "Lukewarm. Just like Doctor Eric was talking about. Spiritual warfare, Nick, is when believers in Jesus find themselves under attack by the forces of evil. Haiti is a land of both deep faith in Christianity, and equally strong voodoo practices. There is constant spiritual warfare here: people's souls are up for grabs. You're not a believer in anything and that makes you a target for the dark forces. Jesus is famous for standing at the door and waiting for you to open it for Him. Satan, on the other hand, likes to knock loud and lay out incentives for you to come through the door to his side. You've got people in that room below us praying for you right now. Maybe we ought to join them?"

"Isn't it the same if you guys are pressuring me as well? What's the difference if you both use the same tactics?"

Larry got up and headed for the doorway. "The difference is, Nick, that we'll be sad if you don't join us in our beliefs. But we won't force you. The other side? They'll try to destroy you if you don't join them. We invite you to join us. They will kidnap you and force you if you waver. That's the difference between good and evil."

Larry stepped onto the upstairs patio and then returned within a few seconds. "Hey, if it's okay with you, I'm going downstairs to pray with the others. We do that every night. I want to lock the office. You can stay up on the balcony if you like."

"Thanks. It's nice out. I'll just sit here and watch the stars for a few minutes."

Larry reached over to the desktop and grabbed a spray can. He motioned for Nick to join him outside. "Last thing you need is malaria, or dengue fever. Hold still while I spray you down with repellent." Larry hit Nick with enough insecticide to frighten off every mosquito south of

Florida and north of the Antarctic. He tossed the can back on his desk, shut off the lights, and locked the door.

"See you in the morning, Nick. Don't stay here too late; it freaks out the security staff when they see people up here after we turn off the lights. Too many ghost stories in Haiti, I guess."

"Good night, Larry." Nick stared up at the night sky and wondered about ghosts, evil, and what he'd seen that morning. The warm air covered him like a blanket and soon he was sound asleep. He didn't hear the coyote that came up the stairs and approached his chair.

CHAPTER SIXTEEN
Port-au-Prince, Haiti
March 09

As he dozed, demons were swirling all around Nick in his dream, tugging at his clothing and knocking him from the chair. He hit the patio with a thud, chair overturned on its side.

The blow to his body as the chair went over dragged him like a tow truck into the real world. Or was it? He thought he saw an enormous black shape lunge toward his face. The lights were out on the balcony, but the moonlight must have reflected in the animal's eyes, turning them a glowing red. Nick raised his arms to shield his face just as the coyote locked onto his neck with yellow, stinking fangs. The teeth penetrated his skin and started to crush his windpipe when Nick heard a yelp, followed by sounds of a violent struggle. He lowered his hands and sucked in a breath just as Andre snapped the creature's neck and threw it over the balcony. It travelled the length of the courtyard, hitting the steel gate over 60 feet away with a ringing blow that brought everyone out of the mission houses.

"Papa, are you all right? Where did it bite you?"

Nick reached down for his left ankle. He thought it hurt and felt sticky, but he wasn't sure: he still didn't have his full wits about him. He did know that his neck was hurt; it was hard to breathe. His hands came back clean as he searched for torn flesh, and his breathing eased as Andre picked him up and set him in his chair.

Lights went on in the compound and on the balcony. A crowd of missionaries gathered around a dead dog in the courtyard, voices raised but unintelligible to Nick.

Nick checked his ankle again but in the bright light, there didn't appear to be any damage, just a frayed strap on his sandal. His neck throbbed with every hard-to-come-by breath for a few moments. He had gotten lucky this time. There was no damage in spite of his certainty that the creature had been trying to tear his throat out when Andre grabbed it.

Andre, who was watching the events below, turned toward Nick and stopped cold. In an instant, Andre seemed to expand in size until he was at least eight feet tall. He pointed at the roofline behind Nick: "Be gone, agents of Satan. Leave this place and these people. You are cast out in the name of Jesus."

Nick looked to where Andre was pointing and saw hundreds of bats lined up on the edge of the roof just a few feet above and behind him. The sky churned with a swirling motion, hundreds more bats as thick as fog swooped down into the lights of the courtyard, flying over the heads of the people examining the animal near the gate.

The bats on the roofline rustled for a moment then hissed as Andre approached them and began to luminesce. A moment was suspended in time as Nick's mind tried to compute what he saw and heard. The spell was broken as the bats exploded into the night sky, darkening the face of the full moon for a moment as they flew to the west.

Larry and three of the other men bounded up the stairs and burst onto the balcony. "Andre, what's going on up here?"

Andre pointed to the body in the courtyard, "I was coming up to get Papa Noel and it ran at us. I was surprised. I knew it wasn't one of our dogs, and when I grabbed for its collar it tried to bite me. I just flung it over the balcony. Is it all right?"

Larry gave Andre a very strange look. "No, it's dead. Andre. That's at least a sixty-pound dog and that gate, is a good distance away. You're telling me you picked it up and threw it 60 feet? What are you doing here after midnight?"

Andre spread his hands in supplication, "Larry, what can I say? It is so. I can't explain except that I was surprised. Surprised men do strong things, no? I was doing maintenance on the tap-tap and found a broken fuel pump. I just finished working on it and wondered if Nick was still sleeping up here. I saw him a few hours ago when he came up here. Never saw him come down again."

Nick said, "I'm glad Andre was here. It was biting down on my throat when he grabbed it off me."

Doctor Eric pulled out a small flashlight and shined it on Nick's face and neck. Pulling him closer, he probed around Nick's windpipe.

"No bite marks that I can see. No trauma at all, as a matter of fact. Sure, that you didn't dream that part, Nick?"

Shaking his head like a wet dog, Nick pointed to the roofline, "I didn't imagine the coyote or the bats. They were all there. Andre saw them, too."

Andre gave a sheepish grin and shook his head. "I saw the dog, Papa, but no bats. Larry, I am sorry about the dog, but it was attacking him and I …"

Larry looked back and forth between the two of them, confusion and scepticism writ large upon his face. There was no way anyone but Andre and Nick could know what had happened. The courtyard lights blinded everyone below from seeing what transpired on the upper balcony outside Larry's office.

"Let's all go in and go to bed. There's been too much upset around here today and Andre should be home with his family. Andre, you need a ride?"

"No, Larry. I have my moto. I'll see you in the morning."

"I want you to go with the large group tomorrow, Andre. Let's visit the hospice in Port-au-Prince. I want all the translators and staff with that one group. I'll head out to the clinic with the other group. We'll need one driver, so please assign someone. I'll ride with him in the front. We'll leave a little later, everyone needs sleep tonight. Goodnight, Andre."

Andre started to leave and turned around. "Papa Noel; it has been a long day. I hope you have an untroubled sleep. I will see you in a day or two. Be blessed, Papa."

"You as well, Andre. I'm beat, Larry. Let's go to bed. After a day like today, tomorrow hopefully will be…"

The final words were consumed by a blast of thunder that rattled the windows and drew everyone's attention to a brilliant bolt of lightning that crossed the clouds a hundred yards overhead. All of them ran for cover as a veritable wall of water pounded from the sky for the third night in a row, turning the darkness silver with lightning and rain.

CHAPTER SEVENTEEN
Port-au-Prince, Haiti
March 09

The post-dawn quiet of the house was broken by the tintinnabulation of a vegetable peeler on the side of a chipped ceramic bowl. Cook was preparing dinner already, better done in the lazy cool of the morning. Later, once the sun rose high in the blue skies of Port-au-Prince, it would be too hot to sit outside and peel vegetables. The heat was almost devastating from the humidity the last few days of rain had brought. The air conditioning in the master's rooms didn't extend to the kitchen.

Violene helped Cook with her tasks, hoping for some of the produce that wasn't good enough to feed the master. The food she was allocated was not enough to keep her growing and healthy. Cook played the game of hiding some of the master's food for the Restevek children. She had been a slave herself and knew that such small mercies made the difference between life and death. This morning Cook had another task placed in front of her: fatten Violene up as the master commanded.

"Violene, you trust me, do you not?"

"Of course! You are like my mother. Why wouldn't I trust you?"

Cook continued to peel carrots for a few minutes. "Today we must talk about what will happen. If the master finds out, I will be fired and blacklisted, unable to find work. You can never talk about this morning to anyone. Agreed?"

"Of course. But why do you look so sad? It is as though your heart is leaking."

Cook's heart was indeed leaking an unending river of tears. She was lucky, if such a thing could be said, that she had been a homely child. She was spared sexual abuse. But both her brother and older sister were handsome children and suffered brutal treatment at the hands, and other parts, of their owners.

"Violene, you must listen and not speak for a time. You will be getting more food, better food, beginning this morning. The master wants you to grow taller and gain pounds on your skinny bones. Violene, do you know what men do to women?

Violene turned her eyes away. Yes, she knew.

"You do. The master wants that with you. But not until you are more like a woman. I do not know how long that will take, but today we begin. I tell you this, so you can prepare. You have two choices now: you can stay and be his woman, or you can plan your escape. How? You must think about where you will flee and who will take you if you leave. If you stay, you must pray to God that He will protect you. The master is — brutal. He is very rough with the girls he selects. I do not want that for you, Violene."

The two sat for a while longer. Thoughts of flight or abuse rocketing about their heads faster than the vegetable peelings fell into the bowls.

Violene was going to have to grow up now, whether it was her wish to do so, or just another burden imposed upon her by a very cruel world. Her time as a child was short unless her friend in the dreams came to rescue her before she was turned over to her master.

CHAPTER EIGHTEEN
Road to Titanyen, Haiti
March 09

Larry turned and looked at Andre at the wheel. No expression intruded upon his face, but he was wondering how he'd got conned into Andre driving the team around today. Glancing through the rear window, he spied Nick in the back of the tap-tap with the medical team. They were headed to the clinic outside of town at Mercy Orphanage. After the late-night repairs to the vehicle, and the encounter with the coyote, tremendous thunderstorms swept the island until dawn. Andre convinced Larry that he needed to be along in case there was a problem with washed out roads on the way to the orphanage. Larry dragged his feet and complained, but ultimately agreed, and changed the driver line-up for the teams.

In the back of the tap-tap, Nick spent the trip to the clinic staring out the sides of the vehicle. Unlike their trip deep into the slums of Cite Soleil the day before, today they were heading out into the countryside. Nick had little hope of anything improving for him in traveling out to the remote location. He didn't think of too many things more depressing than a group of children in an orphanage. The clinic was another story, it sounded like some modern equipment already was installed, and more being trucked up from the airport once it cleared customs. He wondered how that was going but didn't give it much thought. That was Larry's bailiwick.

Looking through the steel mesh sides of the vehicle, Nick knew he was missing more than he was seeing. The feeling nagged at him for a quarter of an hour before he asked one of the nurses. "What's wrong with that picture?" He pointed a finger at a large slab of concrete in an empty field as they roared by a donkey cart, giving a honk for good measure.

She looked back at the slab and the empty field and gave Nick a shrug. "I don't understand, Nick. It's just a slab from the earthquake." A bulb went on in Nick's head. Sure, the buildings fell during the earthquake in 2010 but the foundations were still there. They had nowhere to fall.

"Every one of those concrete pads used to have a building on it?"

She nodded, getting his point. "Yup. Some were homes, some were stores, a few factories, a few barns. What you're not seeing is the hundreds

66

of structures that didn't have a concrete base. The ones on packed earth left no trace when they were cleared away. Nick, a quarter-of-a-million people died in that earthquake. Most of the wreckage has been cleared away, but even a couple of years ago, there were still buildings tipped over along this stretch. Those pads are the last visible remnants of the structures."

There were hundreds of vacant lots that they passed on the way out of town. Nick was in shock at the enormity of the damage. The reports on the news couldn't begin to convey the extent of the devastation the earthquake brought to Haiti. "Where did the people go? Who cleaned up the bodies?"

"You'll see one of the biggest mass graves in history in a little bit. After the earthquake, there was a real fear of contagion. The authorities had a huge problem on their hands: there were miraculous rescues going on for weeks. They had to go with the greatest of care and try to save people trapped in all sorts of buildings. The flip side was that they were slow getting to the bodies and it — it got pretty bad.

"Instead of trying to bury all those people in proper graves, they dug a giant one outside of town and brought over 200,000 bodies to the site. You can talk to the staff about it; all of them lost a family member in the quake. Most of them never found out what happened to their loved ones. It's kind of fitting that the rich and the poor were buried in the same place. That way everyone knows where his or her relatives are located."

Nick watched the concrete pads thin as they got further from the city centre. After a few miles they faded out altogether. He didn't realize the enormity of what happened until that moment. "Doesn't it upset them to talk about it?"

"No, Nick, the entire island has some wound from that day. Most of them are happy to talk about it: it reminds them of their loved ones. He'll never talk about it, but Andre was on a rescue team that found a lot of survivors. No training, no nothing, but he sure had a nose for finding the living ones. Geez, that's kind of a bad word to use under the circumstances. But a woman I met down here talked about him taking crazy risks to get into collapsed buildings to pull out the living. You'd never know it to talk to him, but he's a real hero to a lot of people."

Nick looked at the back of Andre's head as he drove along, laughing at something Larry said. Andre had been there for him twice. He didn't even flinch when he picked up that dog on the balcony. He just — what did he

67

do? It seemed kind of blurry both times Andre saved him. Nick had some real questions about what he'd seen and heard last night. He must have hit his head again when the chair toppled over.

The nurse leaned forward and knocked on the back of the cab and spoke to Larry through the mesh. Larry nodded agreement to whatever it was and talked to Andre.

She sat back on the bench. "Nick, we'll go and visit the grave site before we head out to the orphanage. It's pretty humbling. I can't explain it, but you'll get a better understanding of this country when you see the monument at Saint Christophe, outside Titanyen."

Twenty miles outside of Port-au-Prince the tap-tap turned up a hillside road that led nowhere. There were no homes, no structures of permanence at the top, just the usual Haitian assortment of shanties and shacks. Turning into a parking area, the tap-tap was enshrouded in a funereal quiet. Nick noticed the decreasing volume with every mile they travelled. It was a reverential silence. The reason was simple: they were parked on the edge of one of the largest mass graves in history. There were an estimated 200,000 people buried in the flat, sun-blasted plateau in front of them. A shimmer of heat rose from the white stone and dust even though the day was still very young. In the center of the site was a single boulder. Doffing hats, the missionary doctors and nurses got down from the tap-tap with solemnity and assembled in a circle, reaching out to hold hands. Larry told them the story of this being selected as the site for the grave because it was the least valuable land in all of Haiti. Nothing of worth had ever been here, nor could any crop grow on this hillside, a site used for generations to dispose of the bodies of the government's political enemies. In the wake of the earthquake, authorities needed a quick way to dispose of hundreds of thousands of bodies before disease ravaged the capital. Dump trucks were filled with the dead and dumped in pits created by earthmovers. The trucks came around the clock for weeks, until most of the bodies had been removed from Port-au-Prince. Some were never found, crushed by building rubble during demolition. They formed part of the foundation of the new Haiti that was rising today.

Ending his history lesson, Larry said, "Nick, do you want to offer a prayer for these people and their families?"

Nick twitched as though an electric current ran from his fingertips to his toes. He realized that he was staring at the solitary boulder in the middle of the grave and contemplating all of the sadness and death that it represented. Larry must have picked up on his expression. Why was Nick being asked to pray at every opportunity?

"Sure. God, please bless the families of the people surrounding that rock. Give them solace, let them know You're taking care of their children now. Please protect the rest of the people here, God – they've suffered so much already. Help Haiti heal; help them find a way to be happy. Amen."

The group spent another ten minutes in silence, praying at the site before getting into the tap-tap and continuing to the clinic and the orphanage. Nick was in a spiritual pit after what he'd seen. He couldn't quite wrap his head around a quarter of a million people being buried together in such a desolate place.

After joining the traffic on the main coastal highway, the tap-tap headed northwest toward their destination. For the first time since he'd come to Haiti, Nick had lungs full of fresh air. The sea breeze cut away the rancid smoke of burning trash and kerosene that permeated every other public place he'd been thus far. It was also twenty degrees cooler with the moist air blowing in off the Caribbean. Saddened as he was by the mass grave, he knew a bit of serenity. The ocean reflected light in a glistening shimmer and relaxed him.

Three miles down the road, the tap-tap entered a village that straddled the coastal road. Slowing to mingle with the traffic, pedestrians, and assorted livestock, Nick got a good look at a rural area for the first time. Poverty, goats and pigs running loose, children by the dozens, and shanties crowded in on each other at the edge of the road. The whole scene contrasted with the smiles displayed by so many people they bounced past.

Just beyond the village, they came across a mangled car being pushed to the edge of the road. The crowd one would expect around the wreck was instead gathered around a raging stream a dozen yards away. Just visible above the surface were the rear tires and bumper of a bright yellow SUV, a mission compound sticker visible on the corner of the bumper. Without warning, Andre yanked the wheel and brought the tap-tap to a sudden stop next to the crowd, leaping out of his seat and running toward the stream.

Larry piled out of the vehicle in pursuit of Andre. Grabbing him by the arm, Andre pointed at the stream and then motioned to the tap-tap. Larry ran to the back door and opened it while Andre prowled along the bank looking for something. One of the nurses shouted, "What's wrong?"

"It's Madeleine's truck. She was coming out to the clinic for a check-up and she's not in that crowd. I need that rope on the shelf, so we can drag the vehicle out."

Doctor Eric grabbed the heavy tow rope and passed it to Larry while everyone else ran toward the bank. A police pickup truck was on the verge of the road, and two Haitian police officers directed traffic. Sticky sheets covered in blood shrouded three bodies next to a large area of broken glass and spilled gasoline. A local man was sweeping the mess toward the shoulder of the road, a neat pile forming next to the first corpse.

Larry motioned for one of the officers to back his pickup truck up to the stream so that they could tow the vehicle out. The officer just shook his head and said that the vehicle had been underwater for thirty minutes: there could be no survivors. He told Larry to wait; a tow-truck was on the way and would remove the vehicle, and any bodies, from the stream.

Larry turned and walked toward the missionaries on the bank just in time to see Nick dive into the turbulent water upstream of the wreck. Before Larry realized what was happening, Andre dove in a few feet away and vanished beneath the surface.

Hitting bottom didn't help Nick's damaged head at all, but he popped back up to the surface like a cork. In the next moment, he was slammed against the driver's door by the force of rain-swollen stream. Holding onto the frame with one hand, he pushed below the surface and tried to open the door, but the angles were all wrong. The vehicle was upside down and too close to the bank. Struggling to keep from being pinned between the bank and the vehicle, he pulled himself down and reached inside. Moving his hand from side to side, he found the steering wheel and then the body trapped inside the passenger compartment. There was no response to his touch.

After hooking his foot inside the window frame, he came up and took two deep gulps of air. Nick dove down into the narrow space between the door and the bank, the violent flow of water battering him against the wreckage like an angry bully interrupted while mugging an old woman.

Upside down and working by sense of touch alone, he reached across the driver's lap and unbuckled the seatbelt just as the dome light went on. Too muddy to see much of anything, Nick felt the driver being swept away from him through the front seat. Grabbing onto the victim's clothing, he was sucked through the window and ejected out the open passenger door as the current created a vortex around the car.

With the air in his lungs all used up, Nick went to the surface. Knowing the stream was shallow; he tightened his grip on the victim's garments and pushed off the bottom. Like a bobber held under water, he reached the surface and found himself on the bank next to the limp body of Madeleine, one of the managers at the mission house. On her other side, Andre was gasping for air just like Nick.

The team ran across the bridge to where the three of them lay. By the time they got there, Nick and Andre had already started CPR. Refusing to give up their places, they continued for ten minutes, covered in debris and mud from the torrent raging just a few feet away.

Nick reared his head and spit out a mouthful of dirty water just as Madeleine rolled on her side and vomited, grabbing her enormous belly. Within seconds the team took over and covered her with a blanket. The crowd surrounding them erupted in cheers and began to sing a Haitian hymn. Nick rolled on his side and threw up as well. God alone knew what he swallowed in that stream. He let Larry and Doctor Eric help him sit up again, the contents of his stomach strewn across the muddy earth. Andre was lying on his side, panting, but smiling as though he won every lottery and raffle on the planet with one ticket.

"What in the name of Heaven prompted you to do that? You could have drowned. I'd have two dead people on my hands. Three with Andre jumping in to save you. Nick are you nuts?"

"I heard a baby crying. I knew I could save her. I'm just sorry I got pulled from the car before I could find her. Is that so wrong?"

"Madeleine doesn't have a baby – yet. There was nobody else in the car; I saw her leave the compound this morning. She was going to get gas and meet us at the clinic. Nobody else was with her."

Gazing across the ground toward the rest of the group, Nick wondered what he had heard. Positive that he had heard a baby crying from the car, he had jumped in without hesitation. But what had he heard, if not an infant?

The activity around Madeleine drew his attention. A nurse was pushing Madeleine's legs wide apart and two of the doctors were holding her hands. A moment later the chaos on the bank of the stream reached new

71

heights as a baby's cry split the morning air and rang across the scene. It was the same sound Nick heard just before he dove into the torrential waters.

Another cheer shattered the air as the crowd applauded and sang. They gave the mother and child some room and formed a dancing parade to where Nick was, reaching down and lifting him into the air and onto their shoulders. Andre and Larry got them to set Nick down. Andre helped Nick to his feet and put his arm around him. "Papa Noel, I think you will have many friends in this village for all your life."

The three of them, surrounded by the jubilant crowd, walked to where the mother and child were cuddled. A nurse hovered over the two like a guardian angel.

"Anyone want to guess her name? It is a girl, you know."

Heads shook in wonder. Madeleine, in a voice raw with mud and emotion pointed at a very soggy Nick.

"Her name is Noel. For Papa Noel."

CHAPTER NINETEEN
Titanyen, Haiti
March 09

The market at the side of the road was no different than dozens of others that Nick had experienced in his travels. The big difference was that when the tap-tap stopped to pick up some vegetables, they were not swarmed. It was too hot and sticky this morning to do that kind of thing in Haiti; the vendors instead greeted them with smiles and small waves. Both styles of sales pitch worked well, for the missionaries spread out throughout the market to make their selections, more inclined to buy from someone without pressure. Nick and Andre, still wet from their rescue in the river, didn't venture into the market with the others, but instead walked to the edge of the road.

"Don't eat any of it until the kitchen staff cleans it and checks it, Papa. Much of it is grown in our own waste. No melons at all, but fruit from trees is almost always safe."

Nick smiled at Andre. "Okay, mom. I won't eat any poopy potatoes until you wash them."

Andre slapped him on the back, a fine mist launched itself into the air: the wet clothes made a strange noise. "You are truly trouble, Papa. If I didn't watch over you, there would be riots everywhere and submarines in our rivers. I'm not sure Larry could stand the excitement."

At the mention of Larry and riots, Nick looked around the market and spotted his boss, relieved that he was nearby. Nick evaluated every set of eyes looking his way. Most were open and welcoming, some imploring, some sad, and some hostile. Why hostile? He'd done nothing. Perhaps it was his white skin. The legacy of foreign rulers and invaders left a deep scar on the island that lasted hundreds of years since they gained their freedom from France. Perhaps Nick was a reminder of that bloody and larcenous past.

On the other hand, clusters of men moved around the periphery of the market, all of them dedicated to some unknown mission, and all watching Nick – they didn't seem to even notice the other mission team members. It was too soon for word of the rescue in the stream to have spread to this village, and they weren't approving stares in any event. Every single person staring at Nick was shrouded in darkness. Nick rubbed his eyes and wondered what was going to happen, since the last time he'd seen that many "shadow people" it had turned out to be a band of demons in Cite Soleil.

Looking at Andre, he realized both were tracking the same three groups of men. Nick started to move toward the carpentry shop where they were making coffins when he heard the horn of the tap-tap.

Returning with their packages, the group found Larry pacing back and forth. "Let's go, folks. I forgot about a meeting this morning, and I'm later than usual with our long stop at the accident. Everybody on board!"

It took just a moment to load the produce and climb into the compartment. With a clang of the back gate, and a cloud of smoky exhaust, they were on their way up the hill toward the clinic and orphanage. The road was steep, and as they climbed away from the coast, the land became as arid and barren as the surface of the moon. Even with heavy rains the previous three nights soaking the island; this area was still parched and brown. The sole plants to survive the extreme climate were cacti and thorn bushes. There was almost no ground cover and a few immature trees scattered around the hillsides. Mature trees were found in just a few spots, most within the walled yards of small clusters of homes on either side of the road.

Troubled by the landscape, Nick beleaguered his favourite nurse with another question: "You seem to know the history around here better than anyone else. Is there something wrong with the soil around here? I don't see any crops or any trees except the ones shading the houses in the little villages."

"They chopped them all down for fuel, Nick. Nothing grows on the hillsides because once the trees were gone the soil erosion really got going. There's not a lot of rain most of the year, and until three years ago, things were so desperate that tree after tree was chopped down. People can't afford kerosene or other fuels. They turned everything that grew into charcoal. It's starting to change, but agricultural programs haven't hit this area yet. It's called Titanyen for a reason."

Nick searched the hills around him for signs of life and came away empty. "What's that mean, Titanyen? Never heard it before this week."

"Titanyen is the name of this area. It means "less than nothing" in Creole. Pretty apt. They have no real resources, no money, no farmland, and no jobs. Larry is trying to give them one thing that will lead to the others: hope. But it takes a long time, Nick, and it won't happen until we prove to these people that we aren't trying to cheat them like so many others before us."

"This couldn't have started with the earthquake; I remember Haiti being a shambles back in the 1980s when I was a kid. Didn't AIDS almost wipe out a generation here? Was that the root of it all?"

The nurse gave her answer some deep thought. "I'll give you chapter and verse if you want, but it comes down to their founding. Haiti was a French possession populated mainly by slaves. Long before our American Civil War, around 1800, the slaves overthrew the French and sent them packing.

"France didn't take well to that, so they sent their fleet to sit off the coast. The deal was simple: pay us back for the property you took, or we'll come back and kill you, or enslave you, and it will be ten times worse than before. The Haitians weren't strong enough to beat the French, so they agreed. They paid giant reparations to the French until after World War II. So, all the money that every other nation in the region used to build roads, schools, factories, resorts, and everything else, went to France to pay off a debt of $21 billion. Once they paid off the French, a couple of dictators in a row stole the rest of the money from the people. It stinks, but that's it in a nutshell. They can't get a break. It's almost like God's teaching them a lesson that nobody understands."

The tap-tap took a turn off the main road, which was little better than a rocky trail, and started to climb toward a long, stone-and-block wall. As they approached the gate in the wall, Nick realized the entire wall was at least 10 feet high. It appeared to surround the compound, continuing to follow the folds of the hillside until it dipped out of sight. The gate rolled open without a hitch and two men greeted Andre and Larry. Slapping the side of the vehicle they shouted to the occupants in Creole when it rolled through the gate, "Good morning, Doctors!" The vehicle ground up the slope of the parking lot until it was next to a pastel-colored block building. Bright, pleasing shades of coral and rose covered the building, with beige and purple highlights. Large verandas and a shiny steel roof gave the immediate feeling of openness and light. While there was plenty of shade, it didn't have that look of impending doom like so many structures in Haiti. This was a building of life. A group of children from the school were outside playing when the medical staff climbed down from the tap-tap. Mobbed by smiling little faces, they sought nothing material, just a moment with the strangers in their midst. Cries of "Papa Noel" greeted Nick, who was getting used to the name by now. A dozen children surrounded Nick and tugged at him to play. He smiled and held onto his walking stick, making his way toward the clinic.

Grabbing their equipment and the day's supplies from the storage areas under the tap tap's bench seats, the team was led up to the clinic by the children, who then peeled off and resumed their play nearby.

Once inside the main room of the clinic, Nick was confronted by dozens of Haitian children and adults who were suffering from an assortment of maladies, most ensconced in pain. Moving with the team, he nodded back and smiled at the patients who were waiting. Doctor Eric grabbed his attention and beckoned him to follow down a long hallway. "We're setting up a wound clinic down here, Nick. I heard a nurse tell you about gangrene on the ride up here. That's our number one problem today. Everyone gets a tetanus update or a shot, no exceptions. Are you current?"

Nick was sure of very little since he came to Haiti, but he knew he was current on tetanus. Eric accepted that and pointed at a set of shelves and a nearby sink. "Why don't you strip out of your wet clothes and put on a pair of scrubs? There's got to be some in your size. Our Haitian pediatrician is about your height."

Nick rummaged through the pile until he found a pair of scrubs in a cartoon pattern. Seemed that a certain spongy fellow was popular in Haiti as well. Eric directed him to a room down the hall that had a shower so that he could get rid of the mud in his beard and change in privacy. Nick closed the door to the exam room and stripped off his dirty clothes. The shower was the perfect temperature, and there was a bar of gritty soap ideal for scrubbing away whatever lived in that stream. Nick was pink and fresh when he finished towelling off and put on his scrubs. Padding down the hall in a pair of surgical slippers Eric had given him, he was feeling more than a bit conspicuous in his new outfit. And fat. Definitely fat. The doctor might be the same height, but he was no doubt lean like most Haitian men. Nicholas Bacon was no longer able to claim that status as proved by the bulging seams that gave testimony with each breath.

76

Waiting at the door, Eric handed him a small cup filled with pills. "You better take these. I'm sure you either swallowed some water or it got down your nose. Sit down on the bench and I'll check your ears and nostrils for debris."

After a thorough exam, Doctor Eric slapped Nick on the back and said, "Can you unload that case we brought in here? Just lay the contents out on the counter over there by the table. Put one of each item on the counter and stash the spares on the shelves. But wash your hands after you get the case open, it's dirty. You won't be touching the sterile stuff, but you don't want to cross contaminate anything we brought in after your little dip with Andre."

Nick lugged in the case and wiped it down with some wet paper towels before opening it. The thing gained weight in the last hour: it was much heavier than it seemed before. The morning's excitement was catching up with him. Grabbing a bar of soap, he scrubbed his hands as he'd seen on television all his life. Eric came over and put a hand on his shoulder. "You aren't involved in any procedures today, Nick. Just get the dirt off and store the supplies. I appreciate the effort, but you're not doing surgery."

Nick chuckled. "Overboard, eh?"

The two men busied themselves readying the room and making sure that everything was available for their patients. After a few minutes Eric said, "I have to go down to the refrigeration room and get some ampoules we might need. We'll put them on ice down here, but backup batteries are so expensive that we make them available for just the one unit in the main storage room. Even if the power goes out, that fridge by the shelves will keep cool for a few hours. Can you check and make sure the freezer has ice inside?"

Nick opened the door and saw at least 20 pounds of ice and a stash of frozen flavored ice sticks. Laughing, he pointed at them: "Therapeutic value, Doc, or personal stash?"

"Both. I love those things and it seems to ease the visit for some of the kids. We give them anaesthetic when we clean the wounds, but grape ice seems to do more for their well-being. It's a rough world for these kids, Nick. Any kindness we do is right from God in my opinion. We call this a Hands-and-Feet ministry: Jesus isn't here to do it with His own limbs, so we are those hands and feet. Sometimes that means we do surgery.

Sometimes it means we clean wounds. Sometimes we can't do much except give them a frozen ice. It's all part of His plan."

Nick had been watching, but not participating, in the prayer sessions of the two groups in the mission houses. While he considered himself a believer in God, he had deep reservations about the merit of the church on this earth. To him, it seemed the refuge of scoundrels and bigots. These folks with him in Haiti believed in their hearts; they walked the walk and didn't do much talking.

"Doctor Eric, do you think that you make any difference down here? I know you come to help, but isn't it a drop in the ocean? There's so much that's screwed up about this place that ten or twenty, or two hundred for that matter, can't possibly make a difference down here each year."

"That's up to God, Nick. The number is actually a lot larger. You're seeing our group, but there are forty-seven weeks each year when new teams come here to work. It's almost a thousand volunteers each year on the ground with just our organization. There are lots of other mission groups scattered all over Haiti. Probably talking about ten to twenty thousand people a year that come here to help. That's not a drop in the bucket."

"But you could just send the money you spent on airfare and the mission houses, and let the Haitians do the work. They're capable of it. Isn't it kind of paternalistic to come into their country and tell them how to fix it? Feels a bit like the 1950s and advisors to the colonies of Africa or something."

Eric turned dark red and busied himself with scrubbing the exam table with a sterile cloth. Once he obliterated any germs that survived a cloud of bleach and a flurry of cloth snapping, he was ready to talk. "Yes, Nick, we could just send money. Experience tells us that it would make things worse. Are you familiar with the term "kleptocracy?""

Nick nodded as Eric continued. "Well, my friend, that's what Haiti has been for decades. The average person you meet is a magnificent person. People all over Haiti want to improve their lot in life. However, some of the powerful ones, the ones with weapons, and influence, and power — they're the kleptocrats. They have, and will continue, to steal anything not bolted down in the foreign aid department. What happens to those kids out in the courtyard, or the old lady in that village down the hill doesn't bother them in the least.

"Haiti has received enough foreign aid over the last five years to fix most things to some survival level. But the money, most of it, just vanishes into various government accounts which then winds up in people's pockets. Money that should buy bulldozers buys a couple of new limousines. Vaccines for the kids? Turns into a resort in the Dominican Republic. The list is endless, Nick. That's why we come down."

"Okay, they steal the money. But why aren't you training doctors to replace you? Or engineers to help with the roads? Heck, after that drive up here I'd settle for a couple of ambulance drivers and paramedics. All of those things need money but could be protected from theft."

Doctor Eric turned on the lights in the overhead lamp and checked the focus of the bulbs. Satisfied he returned to the conversation. "All of those things are being done. I contribute to a scholarship fund for training doctors through my alma mater. But it takes time to build it up to where it can run on its own. In the meantime, we make a difference. Out in the courtyard there's a herd of kids. One of those kids in five wouldn't have made it to adulthood five years ago. I'm pretty sure all of them will make it now.

"More importantly, and getting back to your original point, we come as the hands and feet of Jesus. It's not that we do so much physically, but we show that someone cares. That someone loves these people. Nick, we bring a message of hope and concern to people who feel like the whole world has abandoned them. Just like Jesus. Some of us might be phonies, but the phonies never come on a second trip to Haiti. They move on to a different kick. My team, every one of them except you, has been here at least twice. That's the difference, Nick: we come back in spite of what we see and what happens to us. We wouldn't have it any other way."

Throwing the door open, Eric pointed to the courtyard. "Nick, I need you to be my helper with getting the sick in here today. If you would be so kind as to help the mothers carry the kids in here, we've got work to do. Like it or not, ready or not, today you are the hands and feet of Christ."

CHAPTER TWENTY
Port-au-Prince, Haiti
March 09

The ride back to the mission house in Port-au-Prince was a raucous series of practical jokes, silly songs, and water fights. After a day of dealing with sick villagers, almost all of them young children, the medical team was about to burst. Except for Nick.

Most of the team experienced fulfilment, even joy in their work that day. One doctor scored a victory over death during the day, catching an infection before it ran wild in a child's abdomen. All were seasoned professionals in their fields, and each of them had seen much worse cases during their previous visits to Haiti. Nick, an engineer by trade, hadn't spent much time around children with missing and deformed limbs. Open wounds, skin disease, cleft palate, blind eyes, and a dozen other maladies, got him down in the dumps. It was worse than any culture shock he'd ever experienced. Even the rescue on the way to the clinic paled in the shadow of the misery that paraded past him as the day crept by with agonizing slowness.

Halfway back to the mission house, they stopped at a new grocery store. One of the few luxuries they all enjoyed were the amazing sweets the Haitians started to make in the last few years. A good indicator of the recovering economy was a new ice cream factory that opened near the grocery store. Between the fresh-baked cookies in the bakery, and the sugared sodas in the cooler, there was a case filled with unique flavors of ice cream that you could not find anywhere but in Haiti. Such delights as Mango Curry, Cherry Vanilla Rum, and Cayenne & Caramel, met the approval of the doctors, technicians, and nurses in the tap-tap. The store was the testing grounds for new batches, and it was like shooting craps in Vegas: you either went home big or went home broke. The medical team was intent on rolling the dice and sweeping the tables tonight.

The group dismounted and headed into the store, looking more like a kindergarten field trip than a medical mission team. Andre came around to the back to close the door and saw Nick sitting up against the front wall of the passenger cage. "Papa, don't you want to pick a flavor for tonight? If you let them pick, you will get Vanilla Clam Chowdah or something."

Nick looked up to see Andre grinning at him. "Clam Chowdah? You say that like a native of Boston, Andre. When did you go to Boston?"

Andre hauled himself up into the cage and sat opposite Nick. "You'd be surprised where I have been and what I have seen, Papa Noel. We have teams come from many places, and I have visited some of them in their homes during our weeks of rest. I like Omaha best."

Omaha? Nick had a hard time believing that one. Nothing against Omaha, but it was Omaha. "All right, I'll bite: why Omaha."

Andre rubbed his stomach, "They have enormous steaks, fresh corn, salads, and apple pie. I have eaten many things, Papa, but nothing tops that menu for me."

Nick smiled. Hours had passed since he thought about anything that pleased him. He felt his funk lifting just being around Andre. It dawned on him that every time Andre came around things got better for him. More than that, Andre had saved his life on at least three occasions. Something off-the-charts good was going on with this guy.

"Are you a Christian, Andre?"

"Certainly, Papa. All the staff are Christians. You do not have to be, but all of us have seen the light. Aren't you?"

"Not officially. I believe in God, but…"

"You are more of a spiritual than a religious man."

Nick stared at Andre. He said those exact words to Doctor Eric when the topic came up last night. But Andre wasn't in the room. How did he know that?

"Were you outside when we were talking last night?"

"No. I was working down below on the tap-tap, Papa. But I have talked to many good men who were unsure in my life. You are no different. You seek God, but you do not want to admit you have questions. You question yourself and wonder if you are good enough to be with Jezi. And you hate yourself for your answer, no?"

Nick shivered as though he was back in the rain-swollen stream trying to rescue the woman and her baby this very morning. His core felt cold. The kind of cold experienced by corpses in morgues. It was painful beyond his experience, and he wanted to curl up in the late afternoon sun of the tropics to conserve body heat.

81

Andre put a hand on his shoulder and tipped his head back so that Nick had to look him in the eyes. "You are a man at a crossroads, Papa. You saw what happens in Haiti when you linger in the road: you get killed. But now it will be a spiritual death you suffer, not just your body. I will pray for you. I will pray with you, if you like. But you must pray to the God you are not sure about and ask Him to show Himself, Papa."

Andre stood and swung out of the door, landing on the ground with a puff of dust in the unpaved parking lot. Nick sat in the back, by himself, under the watchful protection of his new friend Andre.

He felt the need to decide as well. Moreover, he dreaded the approach of another spiritual cold front. Each time the feeling got stronger, and it made him fearful of what might be worse than this ache in his soul.

CHAPTER TWENTY-ONE
Port-au-Prince, Haiti
March 09

Nick was sitting in the corner of the common room when Larry motioned him out on to the patio. Pointing at the cell phone on the table he said, "It's your sister."

"Jeanie! What's up?"

"You're boiling in a pot of liquid money, big brother. There's a herd of media people who are throwing gold at me like it has no value. That's how I view it anyhow, because all of them want to buy an interview with you. They're also a bit angry about your slipping away from them in Salt Lake."

Nick twitched a little. The rehab center was supposed to carry him on the books for another few weeks before his secret was out. Larry paid them a nice sum for that. "Do they know where I am?"

Jean snorted. "No, your prison break was so hackneyed that they never figured out how you escaped. Whoever ratted you out wasn't on duty when you vanished. Seems the press even grilled the guy who drives the laundry truck. As if you hid under a pile of dirty sheets. They've seen too many movies. But, once they find someone who saw your parka and scrubs exit, they'll start tracking you. It's just a matter of time."

That was fine with Nick. Time was something he had plenty of, as Larry was paying him full salary while he was in Haiti. "Tell me about the interview thing. How much are they offering?"

Jean rustled a piece of paper and started reading, "Let's just do the legitimate media. I've got six offers from assorted talking heads. All of them are offering you a prime-time special with four minutes of advertising time for your use at no fee. That translates to about $250,000 for each at the high end, $150,000 at the low end. The tabloids are offering about $50,000 on average. One internet movie channel is offering you a cool million bucks for the rights to your story, but you have to let them put a few product placements in the thing. Movie studios are going even higher, but they all want to make it a tie-in with book royalties. They'll just cheat you out of all that money, so I'm not even talking to them in any serious way. That answer your question?"

Nick pointed at Larry's soda can and motioned taking a drink. His throat was as dry and tight as a wormhole in the desert. After a lukewarm sip, he managed a few words. "I can't even make sense of that kind of money. What should we do?"

"If you want, I'll negotiate and find out who's serious. I still think the big money is in a book. What I recommend, brother dear, is that you work on a manuscript while you're down there. Get about 30,000 words done and I'll get my friend Julie to flesh it out and work as the editor. I've already talked to her, and she's fine with flying down, and hammering it out with you at one of those new resorts Haiti is throwing up every month. She'll come back here with it ready to publish.

"Type it up fast — borrow a computer and get busy. If we form our own production company and package it properly, I'm thinking we'll clear at least five million on the combined rights. All the major publishers have been bugging me, but if we can roll a total package, it's that much better. You've got a good voice, we can have you do the audiobook yourself and pocket that money. But you must have a book first. Are you up to doing that? If you are, I'll get the rest to work out."

"Heck, yes. You've got my power of attorney from last year, is that still good?"

"Two more years. It's a general power of attorney, so it ought to cover most things that might come up. I won't sign anything until you green light it, Nick. If we can wait, I prefer you were in the room when we do that kind of thing. Speaking of which, what are your return plans?"

That was a question for the ages. Too much was going on in Nick's corner of the universe to even think about going back and facing the press. He needed to sort out his own feelings before he tried to explain them to anyone else. "I'm content to hang out here until summer. Haiti's a lot better than Minnesota in March. They don't even know what road salt is down here. Nice people, good meals, decent bunk. How about you come down here with your friend Julie and we can talk?

"No way. The vultures would follow me to the airport and sniff you out. Last thing you need is them descending on wherever you are. Can you get a computer to use? If you can't, I can ship one down to you. You need to get this done while the iron is still hot. I can't stress that enough."

84

Nick put his hand over the mouthpiece of the phone. "Larry, do you have a computer I can use while I'm here? I lost my laptop in the luggage bin of the plane that blew up."

Larry leaned back in his chair. "Sure. We have a computer you can use. Can you let the others use it at night for a while? We keep a mission blog and people like to talk to their kids back home. Emails, videocalls, that kind of thing. But you can have it about 21 hours a day."

"Thanks. I appreciate it."

Nick returned to his call, "Jean, I can use one of Larry's computers. I've never written a book, but you know what: where do I start?"

"At the beginning, Nick. Start at the beginning."

CHAPTER TWENTY-TWO
Minneapolis, Minnesota
March 10

"Sit down, Schimmler. And put your cell phones on my desk."

Special Agent Schimmler gave a quizzical look, but he did nothing in this life better than take orders. He produced three different phones and set them on the desktop.

Sweeping the three phones into an odd-shaped metallic container and closing the lid, Deputy Director Blokhin punched a six-digit code into the panel on the top of the box and walked it over to an open file cabinet. The cabinet, rated for Top Secret material, shut with a grinding thud, clear indication that it wasn't used very often. Rounding the desk, he took his seat. Staring at Schimmler for what seemed a very long time he said, "I'm more than disappointed that you've failed to find anything that allows us to discredit this idiot. He was involved in this bombing in some way. I'm not accepting the excuse that he was a victim of circumstance. Recap the evidence you have for me, and let's see what it is that you've bungled."

Schimmler was starting to perspire. The mystery man kept the office warm to torment his minions. While Schimmler was in the Denver regional office on the organizational chart, he'd been sent to Minneapolis to report to Deputy Director Blokhin late last night. Dragged out of his apartment and thrust in the back of a police cruiser, he only had time to pack a single change of clothes before being dropped off at the airport. The ticket waiting for him was at the back of the jet, closest to the restroom in a seat that couldn't recline. Delayed on the ground for over three hours by an accident on the taxiway, he had arrived in Minneapolis at almost one in the morning. This seven o'clock meeting was hard to wake up for, and his face reflected a botched attempt at a clean shave. The saving grace was the fact that his third wife was insufferable, and he knew he'd have a chance to roam the bars in Minneapolis before heading back to her. He might even get lucky.

"Schimmler!"

His wool gathering ended with a bang. "Sorry. I was just thinking the sequence through. None of the forensic evidence leads us to believe he ever handled the bomb. There is no trace of explosives in his house, the extended stay motel where he'd been the past six weeks, nor did we find any trace in the research facility where he was working.

"None of his credit records indicate any transfers of cash or securities; he's been checked very thoroughly after all of his trips. We got good intel on him from two of the three Muslim nations where he's worked in the last three years. He's not a part of any known group involved in terrorism.

"Frankly, he's just a loser engineer. The explosive residue we found on his coat, and on his skin, was already burned, so it was post-detonation. The microscopic amounts that were not burned are typical of a bomb that had a weak spot and blew out before full brisance was reached. That's the pressure associated with a blast wave through…"

Blokhin slammed his hand on the desktop. "I know what brisance is, you moron. You, however, obviously looked it up at some point in this investigation. It simply means that he didn't place the device properly, in my opinion."

"I wouldn't say that, Sir. It might mean that he got very lucky and the pressure wave bounced off something first, like —."

"Enough. This is not open for discussion. It won't make a difference in court. So, here's what you need to do, Schimmler: make the evidence fit. I want a black bag done on his attorney's office, so we know what they're doing and where he is. I know he's gone, but I want to find out where we can grab him and extradite him."

Schimmler looked puzzled. "You want us to fabricate evidence and burgle her office?"

He pointed at the file cabinet. "Good thing none of your recorders can catch anything in there, Schimmler. Because nobody but a dummy conspires in a room where he personally hadn't checked for listening devices. Yes, that's exactly what I want. And once you figure out where he's staying, our people are going to bring him in for rendition."

Schimmler sat with his face frozen. "Our people? I have to go wherever he's hiding out?"

"Yes, idiot. Odds are he's in Haiti with his boss. We have some former Tonton Macoute who will provide for his transport to a facility in a friendly nation. But they are even more incompetent than you, Schimmler. This whole thing, from the very beginning, has been populated by morons who can't seem to get the job done. Simple stuff like putting a bag in the checked luggage instead of the overhead bin. This particular group of twits keep saying that they can't find him. I also want a second search done of his house. I suggest you look in the sump pump in his basement for explosives. I'd rate it as a 100% chance that there are tools there that match the marks on the fragments that the ATF and FAA recovered from the bombing."

The bulb went on for Schimmler. Someone connected with Blohkin had placed the bomb in the aircraft and was framing Bacon. Why was irrelevant. While the deaths of over 100 innocents didn't really bother Schimmler, it made it clear that it was best just to follow orders from anyone as well placed as Deputy Director Blohkin. Not doing so could be very hazardous to your health.

"Yes, Sir. I'll get right on that. It will take a day or so to arrange. Do we have any local people who can provide things off the books?"

"I don't want any of this written down. I'll give you two names and numbers."

Blohkin repeated the information six times until Schimmler could recite it without error. Both names were false but would suffice.

Schimmler realized that the evidence he sought was already in the sump pump well, but the eavesdropping devices had to come from people who left government service for more lucrative ventures.

"Schimmler, you're not looking very sharp. Go and get yourself cleaned up. You're going to be here until you find what I need. Don't drag it out to keep away from that shrew you married. I'll know if you do. That won't go well. Now get out of here and make sure you bring back results."

Blohkin opened the safe, produced the Faraday cage box containing the cell phones and removed them as though they were covered in Ebola strands.

Schimmler didn't have the guts to grin, but he left the office free of the leash of legality that had kept his instincts in check far too long. Now it was time to see what he could do without any rules hampering him. That appealed to every dark instinct he'd suppressed all of his life. Nicholas Bacon was as good as dead. But first, Schimmler was going to deal with that miserable sister of his, Jean Silver.

CHAPTER TWENTY-THREE
Port-au-Prince, Haiti
March 10

After breakfast, the medical team headed out for another orphanage on the far side of the city. With no permanent medical facilities on site, this new orphanage was run by a team of missionaries from Arkansas. The two groups collaborated on different projects, and shared medical teams when they visited. Restricted by the sparse resources on site, Doctor Eric's team brought more than the usual amount of stuff with them.

Larry enlisted the other team to join them so that they could carry meal packs with them designed to deliver the maximum amount of protein, calories, vitamins, and electrolytes in the smallest bulk. Designed and crafted for the unique needs of malnourished children, they would be a treat for kids who barely survived, much less thrived, on their daily rations. While the medical team treated the children, the other team would play games with them and sing songs. Two guitars were included among the medical supplies.

Larry still didn't want Nick out and about in the town, but he seemed to be clear of medical danger. Nick spent the previous evening in the commons room with the medical team while they read through the Bible, talked about their day in the clinic, and prayed together about the rest of the trip and what they might accomplish.

He might have been physically in the room with them, but Nick was still outside the circle. Invited to join the others, he politely declined and just listened. Nick prayed by himself to a God who was just emerging in his life. Not a lot, but to the best of his ability. He wasn't even sure how to seek what he needed.

He was too embarrassed to ask for help. His upbringing lacked any emphasis on religion, and what little there had been, was left behind in his parents' home when he was still a small child. He was an engineer; he'd figure it out on his own. There was no problem that couldn't be fixed if you applied the right laws of physics and chemistry to the issue at hand. Or explosives. Lots of high explosives sometimes fixed problems. At least that's what his old boss told him when he first started as an engineer. But that man was a Green Beret and thought high explosives could fix most problems.

Twenty minutes after the teams left for the orphanage, Nick and Larry were helping clean up the kitchen. Andre was supposed to pick them up with a heavy truck. Today they were going to head to Mercy Orphanage and clinic and install some of the equipment that came down on the cargo plane with them. Larry had gotten a call the night before that half of it cleared customs and was ready for release. After hanging up the phone, Larry mumbled that he wasn't paying any more customs fees to get his stuff, and that the bribery had to stop some place. Corruption was endemic to every Third World bureaucracy, and Larry believed Haiti was at an even higher level: a kleptocracy. If he didn't put up a fight, he'd lose a little bit of his soul with every payment he made to the criminals who infested the government.

There was a thunderous blast of an air horn from outside the gates just as they finished a third cup of coffee and the last of the dishes. The two men spritzed themselves with sun spray and bug repellent and headed for the gate where Andre was laughing with one of the security guys.

"Come along, my friends. I have the biggest truck I can drive just waiting for us to have an adventure. First to the airport, Larry?"

"Yes, Andre. My God, where did you get this thing?"

Outside the gate, filling the road was an old Soviet Army heavy truck that somehow made its way to Haiti from nearby Cuba. Spewing black diesel exhaust into the morning air, it could haul a tank on its short low-boy trailer. "My friend has a cousin whose wife's uncle moves things for a living. He couldn't drive for us, but it's not terribly complex. I have driven it before, so you have no worries, Larry."

Nick and Larry both looked at the truck, and each other, and at Andre. His sincere expression caused the two of them to burst out laughing. Once they composed themselves, Larry took a sip of water. "Andre, you have the tool kit to install that stuff?"

Andre pointed to a large box behind the cab. "I've got the heavy tools in there, Larry. There are tools for the electrical and plumbing up at the village in the tool shed. I checked yesterday, they are all there and waiting for us."

Satisfied that they didn't need anything else, the three clambered up into the cab of the old relic and belched off in a cloud of inky smoke.

Cornering in the narrow confines of the city was tricky, but they were lucky that they ran into trouble at only one intersection. Larry and Nick hopped out and guided Andre around the offending telephone pole. Planted on the very edge of the road, it restricted the swing of the back wheels of the trailer. It took a bit of backing and filling, but they cleared the "T" intersection in under ten minutes with no damage to the pole or the truck.

Arriving at the airport, they drove around the perimeter to the customs shed adjacent to Larry's private L-100. The customs agents had the paperwork in their lavishly-furnished office, which was cooled to a very brisk 73 degrees Fahrenheit. The 60" big screen on the wall was running a bootleg copy of a Disney movie that had hit the theaters just a week previously. The aroma of Haitian coffee filled the air with a tang, and cigarette smoke watered Larry's eyes as he closed the door behind him.

Larry put the bills of lading down on the counter and greeted the head of the office. "Louis, good to see you. I understand you have our equipment cleared for transport. Where should we go to load it?"

"Larry. Good to see you as well. Have you the documents for the clearance payments?"

Larry's smile vanished as fast as most bribes did under the counter of this office. "Louis, I have talked to the Mayor, who spoke to the President: there are no fees on this equipment. It's not for sale: it's going to be installed in the clinic we operate. No patient is charged for our help, so there is no money to pay bribes."

"So, you say, Larry. We have been through this before. I never check your mission's people and their baggage, yet your staff seem to always have the latest shoes, sunglasses, and foods from the United States. These things are not sold, but by dodging the import duties, they take away from Haitian businesses. I thought you were trying to help us rebuild Haiti?"

Larry found a smile somewhere and pasted it on his face. "Louis, we have often talked about this topic. My missionaries bring things for their stay and leave the extras here rather than take them back home. I cannot curb their love of the Haitian people, nor their Christian impulse to help others. I make sure they keep it reasonable, no more than gratuities."

"And computers, Larry? Are new laptops mere tokens? I know from my sources that you smuggled twenty of them into the country last week. I let it go, but they should have paid for those crossing the border."

Larry maintained his smile. The computers came into the country, but it was two of them, not twenty. Furthermore, they were left at the mission houses for the use of the teams. There was no smuggling. They came in with two of the people on one team, and there was no effort to elude proper taxes. The Haitian officers at the customs counter in the terminal noted them on the forms and said that they must not be sold to the public, but there were no other restrictions placed on the computers.

"Louis, I want to claim my machines and get them installed. If there is a question about them, we can call the President. I have him on my speed dialler if you want me to place the call."

Louis should have been nervous at the escalation of the game, but he wasn't. Instead, he was ignoring Larry and inspecting his manicure. "I doubt he's available to talk right now. He's in Cuba for trade talks. I wished him well this morning when his plane left. But perchance you want to wait for him to return and talk about it next week?"

Larry sensed something different in the air. He had put an end to this nonsense in the past by threatening to call the Mayor or the President, as both were honest men at heart. In any event, they didn't expect him to pay bribes when he was doing everything he could on behalf of the Haitian people. Today, on the other hand, Louis wasn't worried about the phone. The power had shifted somehow, and he was making it clear that tribute must be paid. Larry knew that if he didn't pay, the equipment would spend months in a warehouse near the airport, bits and pieces of it stolen or wrecked until it was worthless. Today he had to pay. The question was: how much?

Louis was nibbling at a croissant while he sipped coffee. He had all the time in the world, Larry did not. "Louis, I apologize for the misunderstanding on those two (he held up two fingers) laptops. Perhaps we should have declared them officially and paid tax on them. I didn't think they were an issue. What is an appropriate fee for the import of two small computers?"

"Don't worry, Larry. I am a forgiving man. I will forgive the fees today as well. Our friendship is important. How will you be removing the equipment?"

Larry didn't get the question. He must have missed something in the give and take. "I've got a truck, Louis. I'll just put it on with a forklift and drive away."

"Good. Where are your truck and forklift?"

"Outside. Wait, forklift?"

"Yes. We no longer provide a forklift for moving your goods. But, you knew that, Larry. I am sure we discussed it the last time you were here."

Larry did not remember that conversation. He had a sick feeling about what Louis was doing. "Since I have no forklift with me, and you no longer provide the service, how am I going to remove the crates from the warehouse and put them on the truck?"

Louis flipped open the gate in the counter and walked toward the doorway. "We can see if one of the cargo companies will rent you their forklift for an hour or two. That's really all I can do for you. Would you like me to take care of that?"

Larry knew that he had lost this round. Whatever bribe Louis intended to get out of releasing the shipment of his medical equipment had at least doubled this morning. Larry wasn't going to drive all the way out to Mercy Orphanage to get his forklift. It wouldn't fit on the truck after he loaded the crates and he'd have to jockey back and forth at least four times to get this done. God knew what Louis could do to the medical equipment if he left it in his charge for all that time. "That would be nice, Louis. I am sure you can convince them to bill me? I don't carry much cash with me."

Louis lifted his sunglasses just far enough for Larry to see his jaundiced and bloodshot eyes. "No need to bill you, my friend. They take credit cards. You can pay them right now. It seems when you bill people, the fee is always much higher when the paperwork is done."

Larry fished out his card as they walked toward the warehouse. Andre and Nick were in the truck, and Larry's gesture sent them heading across the perimeter of the field to the warehouse by the service road. Once they were out of earshot of the building, and any witnesses, Louis stopped, took off his sunglasses and gave Larry a glare that would stun a rhino. "Larry, my humor about your calling the President is through. If you ever threaten me like that again, you will find that things vanish. It is terrible how quickly fires start. The watchman we have misses intruders from time to time. I hate to think something as valuable as your digital x-ray machine would be lost to theft or fire. Today I am being reasonable. In the future, I expect you to pay fees like the rest of our importers. Am I clear?"

Larry was rooted to the spot. This wasn't the Louis he'd dealt with for almost a decade. That Louis was a small-time thief. This was outright extortion by a mobster. "Louis, I am sure we can avoid any unpleasantness, but you must remember that we are simply poor missionaries trying to help the people of Haiti."

Louis rumbled with a phlegmatic laugh that spoke of countless cigarettes and immeasurable draughts of whiskey consumed late into the night. "You are rich, Larry. I know that you own that plane. Nobody leaves a leased plane in Haiti for weeks at a time. You think I didn't look you up on the internet? Be reasonable. My reach extends far past the airport. You will find it very difficult to get medicine, machines, and people into Haiti without my help. It will be almost impossible if I'm standing in your way. So be like the rest, pay what I ask, and don't threaten me with phone calls to the Palace, if your safety and that of your people means anything to you. What happened in Cite Soleil can happen again, and in places that would surprise you. It would be tragic if any of those precious children at your orphanage were harmed."

Louis turned and walked toward the warehouse. Larry stood in the shadow of an abandoned airplane and wondered who he had just been talking to for only a moment. The answer came quickly enough: a demon who threatened missionaries and children.

CHAPTER TWENTY-FOUR
Titanyen, Haiti
March 10

Andre ground the gears one final time before he parked the truck in what he must have thought was the single possible spot in the vast compound that would suffice. Larry stared out the window during the trip from the airport, the etch-a-sketch of his features writing out a message of anger, depression, and confusion. Andre's attempts to engage him in conversation left the cab of the truck one of the most uncomfortable places in the Western Hemisphere that morning.

Once the truck's engine chuffed to a halt with an ashy belch that hung in the air, Larry jumped out without a word and headed toward the church located next to the clinic.

Andre and Nick exchanged glances of confusion. Larry was always voluble, never reticent when faced with a difficult situation. He was the type to discuss almost any problem in hopes that someone else saw the answer even if he didn't. Neither man had any idea of what Larry was thinking or planning. He left them without direction, and a growing sense that something terrible was confronting them in their mission.

A swarm of children from the orphanage took their undivided attention as they were transformed into living jungle gyms, with two or three children hanging on each of them. They couldn't do much without Larry directing them, so they chose to wait and play with the kids instead. Nothing bad ever came from hanging out with these kids, each one of them acting as an amplifier for love given and returning it ten-fold.

An hour passed before Larry, looking much better, walked over to the veranda of the clinic where Andre and Nick were enjoying a cold bottle of cola. "Sorry about that. Needed some time with the Boss before we got going. Andre, you ready to fire up the forklift and get those crates down?"

"Yes, Larry. Where do you want them when I bring them down?"

Larry pointed at the railing in front of them. "If you'll unbolt this, we can set the crates right here. That way we can put a hand fork under them and roll them right into the rooms where they belong. I'm thinking we'll just uncrate them out here, inspect them, and then prep the rooms. Wait.

Let's make that prep the rooms first. No point in uncrating them until we know the power and plumbing are ready to go. Nick, that's where you come in: I need you to do that engineer magic of yours on the set-up side of things. I've got the manuals for this equipment in my briefcase. Can you get tools from Andre and help me?"

"I'd love to. Haven't turned a wrench in a long time. Which room for which piece?"

Larry handed Nick the satchel with the manuals and pointed out the appropriate rooms for each crate. "There's a set of bolts already in the floor for each machine. First room on the left is the digital dental x-ray machine. There's a dentist chair that's still at the warehouse, they didn't release that yet. So that one can wait. The next room over we've got a new surgical table. Power connections for that one, it goes into the center of the room. The last crate is for teleconferencing equipment and computers. Some of it's wall-mounted. All the hardware is in a crate with the monitors, camera pod, and a combination conference table/desk with light panels, image scanners, cameras, and room for keyboards. That equipment will require power and satellite cables. We'll have a direct link to a satellite when we need it; communications gear is part of the desk. That way we don't have to rely on the phones around here, and we can conference specialists from all over the world. It'll really help the doctors with the tougher cases."

Nick whistled. "You're state of the art with that gear. Even with Andre helping, it will take a day or two to do each room. Is there anyone who can help us with lifting? My ankle feels good today, but I don't want to push it. I like my walking stick; I don't like needing it to get around."

"Yeah. We've got guys here at the aquaponics farm who can come up and help when we're installing the gear. Just get everything prepped and ready before you drag them away from their usual work. I don't want them to get behind on that project."

Nick shook his head. "You have more irons in the fire than any three people should. How do you keep all the balls in the air?"

"I have help from above. Andre, let's start out with the railing and then we should have lunch. I didn't realize we wasted so much time at the airport. The kids will be eating pretty soon, and we can have lunch with them."

Nick grabbed a wrench from Andre's toolbox and started at one end with Andre undoing bolts at the other. Larry held the railing steady, and in less than fifty minutes they cleared the railing away and opened the veranda for the forklift.

Dripping sweat evaporated in seconds in the late morning sun, leaving each of the men covered in a fine patina of salt. They stood in the opening they created and watched the children from the school swarm toward the dining hall across the courtyard. "I think we'll be okay to leave this open while we eat. Nobody is using the clinic until late afternoon. Let's go get some lunch with the kids."

Walking across the dusty ground, they could hear sounds of laughter, clinking silverware, and singing as they approached the dining hall. It was dark inside after the walk across the courtyard, and there was a cooling swirl of air from the ceiling fans as they entered the room. Taking a moment for their eyes to adjust, Larry and Andre headed for an open table, a chorus of children shouting out Larry's name as he went down the row of tables. Nick took up the rear and waved at a table of children greeting him in Creole, "Bonjou, Papa Noel."

They sat with a group of four- and five-year-old boys. The children smiled shyly and stared at Nick. After a moment, it became uncomfortable for him. "Okay, I give, why are they staring?"

Larry looked at his face. "It's the beard. Geez, I didn't realize it was that long. Haitian men don't grow that kind of thatch on their faces. You're an anomaly."

Larry turned to the children and spoke to them in Creole for a moment. One little boy pointed at Nick and seemed to ask a question. Larry laughed and said, "Oui!"

A dozen small hands reached for Nick's face at the same instant. Gentle fingers ran through his beard and touched the hair on his head as well. One youngster plucked a hair from the beard and the rest followed suit. Nick flinched but held steady while they collected keepsakes. Andre and Larry laughed until there were tears in their eyes while the little boys held up their trophies: long white hairs that by all rights belonged on Nick's chin.

Larry spoke to the boys in Creole again and they all laughed. "I warned them not to pluck you like a chicken. They won't do it again."

In a moment, large bowls landed on the table in front of Nick. Filled with a thick stew of beans, there was a medley of vegetables and vibrant

97

spice in the mix. Nick grabbed a piece of dark bread from the platter in the middle of the table, placed it on a plate, and ladled a bowl full of the stew. Passing them both to the little boy next to him, he served the others at the table before helping himself.

Larry sat smiling and watched as Nick bit into his bread while the others sat waiting on him. Once he swallowed his bite, he asked, "What are you waiting on?"

"You showed a servant's heart by dishing up for the rest of us. The boys expect you to say a blessing over the food. They don't just like your beard, Nick, they seem to respect you as an elder. A man of substance. Perhaps as a man of good deeds. I get the feeling they've been waiting for you all their lives. These little guys rarely meet anyone, especially someone that looks like you, who takes care of their needs before his own. You're being honored with their waiting. I'm impressed."

Nick felt something sweep through his body, a palpable presence like he'd felt in Cite Soleil. This time though, it was good. Abundantly good. Nick knew deep in his soul that he was being shown an opportunity that he had never had before in his life. An opportunity to live outside of himself and his own petty concerns. He merely had to accept this invitation and go through the doorway that opened.

"I-God, please bless these boys, and these men, who share their table with me. Let this food give us energy and bless us in our work. Amen."

A chorus of "amen" and a flurry of spoons met the end of the prayer. Nick didn't touch his food. Instead he closed his eyes. "God, I get it. Finally. Help me understand what You want from me. I'm ready to do Your work."

When he opened his eyes, he saw the smiles on the faces of Andre and Larry. "There's hope for you yet, Nicholas."

"Oui, Papa. Welcome. I think you have made a choice for the better."

It was the best meal that Nicholas Bacon ever ate, surrounded by friends in an orphanage in Haiti. Born again over a bowl of stew.

And to those who could see, a small tongue of flame flickered over the head of Nicholas of Haiti in the dim light of the dining hall.

CHAPTER TWENTY-FIVE
Titanyen/St. Medard/St. Archaie, Haiti
March 12

Nicholas was once again at the clinic in Titanyen, finishing up the activation of the new equipment. The past two days were spent installing and testing all the equipment they hauled out from the airport. In between turns of the wrench and voltage checks, Nicholas quizzed Larry and Andre about their faith. He was coming to accept his new life in Christ, but still didn't know the details that he needed to feel comfortable.

Larry set down his tools and shuffled up from the floor. Stretching to relieve the kink in his back, he shook his head. "Nicholas, that's not what I'm saying. Everyone has their own understanding of God, even of Jesus. Being a Christian doesn't mean you have to belong to a specific church to be legitimate. This mission is a great example: we have all sorts of people involved who range from Missionary Baptists to Latin Rite Roman Catholics. It's a sad fact that the church is divided here on earth. It keeps us from truly doing the work of God.

"What I am saying, is that you have to find your faith rooted in His word. The Bible is like the owner's manual for Christians. Just like the diagrams and instructions with the machines in this room, we look to the Bible for our answers. You need to read the book to get it. Start with the New Testament, and then read the Old Testament. You don't have to have read it to believe in Christ, but it will give you an understanding that you need to live a good life."

Andre chimed in, "I've got it in an audio book. If you like, I will loan you the player and you can listen. It was read by Johnny Cash. A great voice for the Bible. It is like God is reading it Himself, sometimes. I should think."

Larry started laughing. "Cash would love that, Andre. John R. Cash was a believer, but he covered most of the sin bases as well. That is a good start, Nicholas. It's a little easier to consume in that format. I've got a spare player or twenty that we can put it on, and you can keep it. You'd be amazed at the stuff people leave behind when they return to the States."

When lunchtime came, the three of them piled into Larry's S.U.V.. The former Red Army truck was returned to its owner after hauling the gear earlier in the week. It didn't look like they'd need it for a while; Louis was holding out for a major bribe before releasing the next load. He named his price as they loaded the first truck earlier in the week. Larry was hoping to take his case to the President of Haiti when he returned from Cuba the following week. In the meantime, there were other items the men could tackle at the clinic.

Heading down the hillside, Larry directed Andre to continue west along the coast. Nicholas hadn't seen this part of the island before, and he was surprised by the number of villages that hugged the sides of the road, and the green fields extending toward the mountains and the sea. They were in stark contrast to the barren wasteland around Titanyen.

In the small village of St. Medard, Andre turned off on a side street and pulled up next to a restaurant with an outdoor patio. The three got out and found seats in the shade of an awning. A young girl, perhaps ten, came out and greeted them. She took orders for drinks and went back inside, returning a minute later with condensation-beaded bottles of a local soda. She handed them a card with a handwritten menu on it and gave them their privacy.

"Is she a slave? Shouldn't she be in school?"

"No, her grandparents own the restaurant. I have known them both for years. They can't afford school, but they do home-school her. She's not missing out by any means. Her parents were killed in the earthquake. They both worked in Port-au-Prince during the week to support the family, and the building where they worked collapsed. There aren't many people who didn't lose someone dear in the quake. Andre is one of the few I know who came out unscathed."

"It is true, Papa. I had no family here, so I could lose no one. It is a mixed blessing. But most of my friends suffered greatly in the earthquake. Poor Haiti, it was yet another blow against her soul."

Nicholas sipped at the straw. "Why did you bring me here, Larry?"

Larry continued to watch the events in the street when he replied. "Because you have seen the worst extremes of Haiti, and I have this feeling that you need to get to know the Haitian people better. That it needed to happen soon. This village is a typical one. People, even those who lost so much in the earthquake, continue to live their lives. There are

100

no tent cities here, no buildings left to raze, nor are there orphans begging in the road. This is what life should be like in Haiti. It can be, again, once some time has passed. God is working here, and He has plans for you to help in that work."

Nicholas didn't know how to react to that statement. "Larry, I'm just a guy hiding out from the media. I'm nothing special."

Andre laughed from the belly. "I'm just a guy..." He slapped the table and then got up and walked inside the restaurant, still laughing until he was lost from sight in the back.

"What's so funny?"

Larry's face took on the appearance of old, acid-washed bricks. It had to be a trick of the light, but he seemed to age ten years in just moments. As quickly as it came, it was gone. "Nicholas, you're not just some guy. You say that every time your gifts come into the spotlight, but it's not true. Doctor Eric and I talked about this the other night, and while I can't pin Andre down, I heard things from others who were with you in Cite Soleil. You have led a life in the last three months that speaks to the protection of God. It's biblical in its scope, Nicholas.

"You get sucked out of a jetliner that explodes, plummet 10,000 feet to the ground without a parachute, ride an avalanche to the bottom of a mountain, and have no life-threatening injuries? I bring you to Haiti, and the first time you head out into town you confront a group of demons and start commanding them to flee in some ancient language you couldn't possibly know.

"Everywhere you've gone, everything you've done since Christmas, has resulted in an attack on your person that would crush most people into crumbly little bits under the wheels of an infernal machine. Instead, you have healed, prospered, and inspired.

"Those kids at Mercy Orphanage are telling tales about you and your beard. You're a mythical figure to them. Most of all, you opened your heart and let Jesus in over a bowl of stew and some bread. I saw flames of the Holy Spirit over your head two days ago, Nicholas. You're anointed. God needs you here, now, for some very specific reason. Andre and I both agree that Satan is fighting you at every turn. We want to help you. There is very little in this world that is more dangerous than an immature spirit stepping into conflict with Satan. Let us be your guides, Nicholas."

101

Nicholas couldn't believe his ears. He knew Larry took his faith as the bedrock of his persona, but this was stark-raving-nuts. "I'm flattered that you think God has picked me for some mission, Larry, but I don't — I can't — I'm not able to buy that. No disrespect, but I'm just a guy with a bunch of burn scars and a mechanical aptitude. I'm no saint. Far from it, Larry. I'm not even much of a believer."

Andre was standing in the darkness of the doorway. "I beg to disagree, Papa. Have you looked in a mirror lately?"

"Yeah, when I brushed my teeth this morning. Why?"

"Did you not notice that your hair has grown several inches and all of your scars have healed since you got here just a week ago? Your beard as well. You are not the man who I met at the airplane. God is changing you. I agree with Larry. He is planning something big for you, Papa Noel. You gave your soul to Him, why not give Him your heart today and find out what His plans are?"

"I don't know."

The girl came back to take the order. Nicholas didn't feel like eating so Andre ordered something for each of them in Creole. Larry nodded his approval, so Nicholas figured it was good.

They sat in silence, waiting for the food. A gentle breeze cooled the space under the awning and brought the smell of fresh laundry and dust from the street. Time passed in contemplation; Nicholas was lost to the rest of the table.

Once they had eaten their lunch, Larry ordered coffee. Sipping the rich blend of the island, the silence assumed the comfortable feeling that lifelong friends know. Nicholas reached a conclusion that he needed to share with the others.

"Andre, you said I gave my soul but not my heart to God. You're right. I said the words because they were true, but I didn't want to put it all on the line. Larry, you're right as well. Something is going on. I'm still fuzzy about exactly what happened in Cite Soleil, but I did see demons. They didn't start out that way, but the gang that was taunting me turned into creatures from Hell. I don't know any other way to describe it.

"The other thing, the thing that bothers me most, is that I can sense that same evil on occasion. It's swirling around me sometimes. The other morning at the airport, it was strong. That guy you walked out of the office with? He was a demon. I saw him just like the others in the slum. I know you guys will pack me off to an asylum for saying that, but it's destroying me to keep it inside. Laugh if you want, but I know what I saw."

Larry put his hand on Nicholas'. "You're wrong. That's part of what Andre and I were talking about with your being new in faith. There's a biblical precedent for seeing demons. I'm a member of the club that thinks miracles, saints, angels, and demons are all around us in this age. People feel like that's all behind us, that it ended thousands of years ago and is no longer believable in our era. That's nonsense. I feel that evil myself. I don't see demons, but then I don't see much difference between green and red, Nicholas. It's a gift from God that you can sense that in people. Embrace it."

"Okay, I'll embrace it: I don't have much of a choice. But I'm going to be young in the faith for a long time to come. You guys all have a serious head start in the religion thing. How do I avoid mistakes? How do I protect myself from this evil? Larry, I have the feeling it's out to get me. If Andre hadn't stopped that dog the other night, it would have torn my throat out. He can't be with me all the time."

Larry sipped at his coffee and maintained a silence that was broken by the gears turning in his head. After a couple of minutes, he spoke at such a low volume that nobody could overhear him past the table. "You're wrong about Andre. He can be with you all the time. Andre, if you're up to it I want you to move in the mission house and stay with Nicholas. Andre is churched, and he can answer most of your questions. Listen to that Bible he gave you and think about it. Talk about it. Join us for prayer in the common room. And get baptized."

"I was baptized as a baby, Larry. We can skip that one."

"You probably were, Nicholas. But there's a different look on baptism that some Protestants share: we view it as being born again. The baptism was more your parents dedicating you to God. Now, at a mature age, you can give your life to God willingly. It's one of the most important items of faith, Nicholas. It shows you're willing to let the you of today die so that you can be reborn as a follower of Jesus. It is one of the things that God asks of us. Even Jesus was baptized by John the Baptist."

Nicholas realized he had heard those stories in church and never gave them an iota of thought when he was young. It was all locked away in some part of his brain, but it wasn't real to him. The rest of these people, most of all Larry, Doctor Eric, and Andre, lived it every day. That's what they were asking of him. His heart skipped a beat. That quiet voice he'd been hearing since lunch with the children let him know it was important.

"Let's do it. Can we use the church at the orphanage?"

Larry looked at Andre. "Do you feel the threat to Nicholas as strongly as I do, Andre?"

Andre nodded. "We should not wait. I do not want him assaulted by evil before he can finish layering on that armor of God. We can go to the beach at St. Archaie. It's just a few kilometers from here. There is a strip by the fishing boats where the water comes up on a small beach."

Larry threw a generous pile of dollars on the table and drained his cup. "No time like the present, Nicholas. Let's go baptize you."

"Don't we need a preacher?"

Andre pointed at Larry, "We call him the Bishop behind his back. He has the faith of most clerics and then some. But he smokes cigars and looks bad in a priest's collar with that hair."

Larry shook his fist at Andre as he climbed in the passenger seat of the vehicle. Andre held the door open for Nicholas. "Come on, Nicholas. God is waiting for you to join His kingdom."

Andre pressed shut the door behind Nicholas and climbed into the driver's seat. They pulled away from the restaurant as clouds started to gather overhead. Before they reached the coastal highway, a thunderstorm rolled over them and started to wash away the dirt road they were traveling on.

"Larry, I have that feeling right now. There is something evil surrounding us."

Andre seemed unperturbed. "Jesus walked out on the water during a storm like this to instruct the apostles. Perhaps it is part of the faith? We will be at the beach in a few minutes and it will be fine."

Andre turned onto National Route 1 and headed toward the site of the baptism. Traffic continued to blast past them, heedless of the weather. Now Larry looked concerned as well, but Andre remained calm. There was no traffic in the town. There was nobody to be seen; everyone took refuge from the storm. The men pulled up a hundred yards short of the beach and got out into the maelstrom. They could go no further in the SUV; the rain and the spray flooded the end of the road.

Lightning struck the surface of the sea in front of them while slimy grey mud sucked at their feet. As they passed a small plaza, dogs began to gather from every direction and follow in their wake. One by one the dogs darted in closer as the men splashed through the puddles. The dogs made no noise but bared their teeth and snapped at the air as they closed in around the points of the compass. Nicholas felt moved to act in his own defense but was at a loss: would the dogs understand English? Would they pick up on his body language? Andre seemed confident in the face of this danger, but both Nicholas and Larry cast their glances at the dogs in fear.

Nicholas felt a strength well up in the arm holding his walking staff. The power, for there was no other word that could describe it, spread to his chest and then the rest of his body. Drawing himself up to his full height, he turned and pointed the staff at the animals. He said not a word but by force of will commanded them to back away as he turned in a circle, rain pelting his skin and wind tearing at his beard and hair.

Looking like Moses in a Cecil B. DeMille production, Nicholas glared at the dogs, who cowered in fear and plopped down in the muddy road. More confident, Nicholas turned toward the beach again, and swept the dogs aside with a wave of his staff. They moved to the brush on the sides of the road and turned their faces away from the trio as they stepped over the gate that signaled the end of the road and the beginning of the sand. Unsure of what he'd just done, or why, he was jarred by the slow dawning of a simple fact: his impact on evil was taking root in his consciousness, and he was willing to use it to protect others.

Heavy surf rolled on what should have been a placid beach; there should be no surf in this part of the bay. God and geology deigned gentle ripples to this body of water. Breaking on the shore, it crashed in a deafening cacophony. Stopping at the railing, Larry instructed the others to take all their stuff out of their pockets. He picked up a piece of plastic bag and wrapped it around their phones and keys, wedging the bag in the latch of the gate.

Larry took Nicholas' right hand and Andre took his left. They walked out to their knees in the surf. Larry held his free hand high in the air and said, "Lord Jesus, we're here in a storm just like the one You calmed on the Sea of Galilee."

Glancing over his shoulder, Larry was timing his words to something that Nicholas couldn't see. "Father, we baptize our brother, Nicholas, in the name of the Father, the Son, and the Holy Spirit. Nicholas do you accept Jesus as your Lord and Saviour, and renounce your sins, renounce Satan, and embrace this life as a newborn child of Christ?"

"I do!"

The rogue wave Larry waited for washed over the three of them, plunging them under water, tumbling them across the rocky bottom and spitting them out on the shore.

Nicholas took stock as the water drew back toward the ocean and realized that it was now quiet around them. The rain and wind stopped as though a switch were thrown in Heaven. He shook the water from his head, brushed his eyes, and looked up to see the clouds parting. The waves, angry and as tall as a house just a minute before, were glassy calm. The rain lasted just long enough to wash the salt water off their skin, and then it followed the angry sea into the past.

Nicholas stared at Larry and Andre. "I'm ready to accept my role, whatever it is. If that wasn't a sign, I don't know what would be. Let's get back and start work. I've got a lot to learn."

CHAPTER TWENTY-SIX
Across Haiti
March 14

Across the countryside, the Restevek children sensed a change coming with an urgency and purpose that frightened and encouraged them at the same time. Their owners took a harsher tone in dealing with them, and the dreams were coming almost every night of the one called Papa Noel. Resteveks don't have social clubs, don't have social media, or even have time to talk at their random encounters at the market and water truck. What Restevek children have is an abundance of fear. Fear of their owner, fear of hunger, fear of the future.

Until now: now there was hope. Some of them began to prepare for their escape. The older ones put away small bits of food and containers for water. They made sure that the things they could not hoard could be stolen from their owners as they escaped. The sense of impending upset was becoming palpable to those in tune with God's word for them. Children, most importantly abused and enslaved children, were His special concern, and He made His presence felt even to those who did not yet believe.

But for now, they waited. They could not secure what they needed too far in advance for it might be discovered or stolen. While they waited, they prayed. Even if they did not know that is what it was called, it was still prayer. Across the nation of Haiti, the prayers of children flew out of windows and entered the heavens in a pitiful torrent of misery.

It was heard as sweetly as the singing of angels when it reached His throne.

CHAPTER TWENTY-SEVEN
Minneapolis, Minnesota
March 14

"That's really nice. But he's not even in this country so it's problematic. You can call again next week, and I'll see if he's back."

The two federal agents looming over her desk didn't intimidate Jean Silver in the least. Bozos with credentials. Neither one was a member of MENSA, and both wore cheap suits.

"You realize, Ms. Silver, that if you are hiding your brother you can't claim attorney client privilege to avoid prosecution. We have a warrant for his arrest, and as his counsel, you're required to surrender him to us at the first opportunity."

"Special Agent Himmler, much as I want to pop open the door to my private washroom and produce my brother, I can't. I last saw him a month ago in Salt Lake City. He hasn't returned to Minnesota. Well, if he has, he hasn't bothered to drop by and say hello. My understanding is that he's traveling on business with his boss. Last time I discussed his job with him that could bring him to any place on the globe that needs water purification systems. Look at places with water, or lack of water, and you might find him. That may be difficult, but I'm sure you know some competent investigators who are able to do more than harass innocent victims of tragedy."

Schimmler wasn't having it: "Your phone records show a series of calls to a cellular number in Haiti. You've spoken to Larry Timmons, whom you just said is with your brother. Is that where your brother is?"

Jean sipped at her coffee, perturbed that her lipstick smeared on the edge of the cup. She slammed the cup down with an explosive tsunami of coffee rolling across the desk as it shattered. "Now you've torqued me off: show me the warrant that you got from some judge to tap my phone. It better not be signed by your idiot friend the judge in Salt Lake, either. If you like, I can revisit that issue with the bar association of Utah, and now Minnesota. You're past the thin ice zone on the lake, Himmler, you're out in open water."

Schimmler just smirked. "Metadata can be collected without a warrant, Ms. Silver. We aren't tapping your phone, we're merely monitoring for possible terrorist communications with foreign nationals."

Jean ground her teeth. This was what she'd railed against for years. Every time you gave a government any power over you, liberty was lost. "Gee, how much better I feel. If you two are done, you can leave. I will surrender my brother the minute I see him. Next time I hear from him, I'll let him know you clods are looking for him. By the way, that warrant is garbage. You took him into loose custody for a month after the crash while he was being treated in Salt Lake City. He was exonerated of any involvement in the explosion. Your crying wolf didn't help, because your lapdogs in the press wouldn't buy your story either. They like miracles like the people who watch their networks. What's the big rush to bring him into custody and grill him again?"

"That's classified, Ms. Silver. The warrant states he is to be taken into custody as a material witness. "Clods" like us aren't privy to the reasons for the judge's orders. Here's my card. Call me directly if you talk to your brother. In the meantime, have a lovely day, Ms. Silver."

Jean stood up and turned her back on Schimmler, choosing to stare at the late-winter landscape and ignoring the federal agents in her office. Footsteps sounding on the lobby tile let her know that Schimmler was retreating, and a click of the door acknowledgement that he'd left the office. A minute later the agents appeared in the parking lot four floors below. Schimmler turned and waved at her as he opened his car door. Jean gave him a salute of another sort in return.

Taking a moment to scribble something on a note pad, Jean walked to the outer office with her winter coat on, and her enormous purse slung over her shoulder. "Wendy, I'll be back in two hours. I'm taking a long lunch today. You can lock up and take one as well; we don't have any clients coming until three today."

Wendy read the note: "Meet me in the loading dock in five minutes. Don't say anything."

Ever the consummate professional, she grabbed her keys and said, "Sounds great. I'm dying to get some shopping done at the mall. I'll see you around 2; that'll give us plenty of time before your next appointment."

Three minutes later they met next to the dumpsters. "I don't trust those two feds. Have Lopez come in and sweep the office. That jerk Himmler has bugged us. He couldn't know I talked to Larry from metadata: he's listening in on the office. If he tapped my cell phone, he'd have heard both sides and know Nicholas is down there with Larry. Therefore, he couldn't hear the other side of the conversation, just mine, and that reeks of a bugged office. Tell Lopez he won't spot anything on the phones, but he's got to find any little presents those two left behind in the office. Nothing about my brother can be discussed here until Lopez comes in. Make sure you call him from a burner phone. Buy a half a dozen; get an international plan on all of them. Those Mexican places on Concord Street in Saint Paul have what we want, and make sure you use cash. I'm assuming you still have some left from the contingency fund?"

"I spent it on shoes. Of course, I have it. But I have to swing by my house to pick it up. Can this wait until after work? I don't want them following me and seeing what we're up to. If we wait, I can slip down there in my daughter's car."

"I like your evil mind, Wendy. Make sure Lopez puts in new alarm codes and verifies all the wiring. Have him put in a couple of nanny-cams. Those creeps will be back to black bag our office, unless I miss my guess, and I want it on video. Oh, and have him put a shaker on my windows. He'll know what I'm talking about. That'll mess with any laser listening devices they might try. Have the shaker play old Styx tunes on a loop. I hate those guys and I'm sure the feds will tire of "Lady" fast. It takes me about thirty seconds."

Wendy laughed. "Where did you learn about all that stuff? Did I miss something in your resume?"

Jean finished freshening her lipstick in her compact mirror and snapped it shut. "My husband was a spook with the Army Security Agency in his wretched youth. He's taught me all sorts of handy things. That's where I met Lopez: at one of their little reunions. He's good people. Grab the phones tonight. The rest of the day, we just can't talk about anything confidential in the office. When my client shows up, we'll head over to the pancake place across the drive and pig out there. God knows she'll say yes to banana chocolate chip pancakes."

"Get Lopez to come in with the cleaning crew like the last time. That will give him plenty of time to do his sweep and fix the office up while they clean the joint. Let him know he can expect the money in his account

110

tomorrow. Tell him to leave a note three sheets down on the pad with his billing amount."

Jean snuffed out her cigarette on the wall next to the NO SMOKING sign. "One other thing: if Lopez finds any listening devices, I want him to remove them without any fuss, and put them inside the entertainment cabinet where the DVD player is. Have him get the most disturbing video he can find, and have it run on a loop near the bugging device. I don't care if it's baby rabbits being eaten by snakes, or children's television with big purple beasties. But I want them to have to listen to it instead of me if those bugs are active. Just loud enough to obscure what we say, not loud enough for them to give up listening. Payback is sometimes unfair and horrible. He'll get the spirit of the thing."

"Yes, boss. Want anyone killed while we're at it?"

"Not yet. But if they mess with Nicholas, it just might be on the "to do" list."

***

The phone call interrupted a late-night skull-session and was an unwanted intrusion. He stared at the caller identification panel and smiled.

"I'd better take this one. Ernie wouldn't be calling so late unless it was a big deal."

Colene Abbott nodded her blessing, and he grabbed the handset: "Kurtz, what do you want, Lopez?"

For the next few minutes Kurtz took notes on a pad of paper so that they wouldn't be part of the official data base, and then asked Lopez a series of questions. Scanning his notes, he said, "Let me see if I can get permission. I'll call you either way, but if you don't hear from me in the next hour, it's probably a "no.""

Hanging up the phone, he turned to his boss. "That was Ernie Lopez. I'm sure you remember the name? He was not with me at the place where I wasn't in the country, we didn't do that stuff back in the day."

Abbott winked at Kurtz. "I love it when you talk like a spook. I presume you have a reason for this reference?"

"I learned to trust him, and that recommends him as a source, on that little expedition. He's also a pretty good friend and you know how picky I am. So that's a mighty small circle for me."

111

Abbott started twirling her finger in the "let's get to the point" motion.

"He's asking me to do a deep-pull on some F.B.I. agent that he thinks is framing an innocent guy. I know that's not in our area of authority. But this dude is trying to frame the guy for the airliner that went down over Utah at the first of the year. That is right in our bucket."

"Oh, I remember Lopez. Your taste in friends is colourful at the very least. So, you want me to bless this and let you help your un-cleared friend?"

Kurtz pushed back from his desk. "Yeah. Uncleared at the moment, but he's proven his bonafides in the past. He's given us some excellent stuff in the past year. Ernie is okay, but he knows a lot of people in the gutter. They tell him things, he passes them on to me. He's useful. More importantly, I trust him not to try and jam me up on something like this. My inclination is to get what he wants."

Abbott stared at the desk and replied. "If he just wants to know this guy's official evil deeds, fine. Nothing that puts the agent in danger. No family stuff, nothing classified. If the guy's bent and involved in that explosion, we want to know it as well. That case has gone nowhere if I recall, and it sure looks like we have a legitimate interest in solving it. Please remember that our law enforcement function is secondary to our other goals. Keep this on the unofficial side, and have the geeks hack the appropriate data bases. No footprints. If you find something, let me know before Lopez is notified."

Kurtz nodded. "There's something else that makes me want to look into this: the guy he's trying to frame is that Nick Bacon. I'm sure you saw the updates out of Haiti the last few days where the embassy reported on some miracle he performed. Some of the locals have started a rumor that he's possibly The Messiah. If nothing else, that makes him a point of interest. And, according to the profile I saw a couple of weeks ago, Bacon's been a regular traveller to the center of Islamic terrorism for years. I'm pretty sure we want to see if this is legit."

Abbott frowned. "One caveat: this conversation never took place. We didn't do this. If it pans out, we'll find another way to out this guy. But this is dark grey."

Kurtz smiled. "That makes it more fun. I like a challenge. I'll let him know I'll look. It'll probably take a couple of hours, but nothing that will impede what I'm already doing."

Kurtz was already back on the phone, digging, when Abbott gave up on the meeting and walked back to her office. She couldn't help smiling: Kurtz was a pit-bull when it came to this stuff, and he'd find out the truth.

CHAPTER TWENTY-EIGHT
Plymouth, Minnesota
March 16

Insomnia was driving her mad, and now Porkchop, her Teacup Yorkie, decided to hold a late-night bark-a-thon. At four pounds, she wasn't much good as a guard dog, but she made an excellent burglar alarm. Jean flicked on the computer screen next to her bed and checked the monitors. Her security system was still armed, but the exterior cameras were down hard. She ran the video back ten minutes and saw a hand appear with a spray can just before each camera went blank.

That was enough. She reached under the headboard where she kept her .38 snub-nosed revolver and pulled it free of the duct tape. Next, she dialled 911 on her cell phone and told the operator that someone was breaking in to her house. She left the line open and made her next move.

Already dressed in dark green pajamas, she got down on the floor and crawled into the hall. Porkchop was throwing herself against the front door, so Jean knew from where the threat was coming. The barking ratcheted up a notch and got closer to the stairs leading to Jean's room. Porkchop was retreating from whoever was in the entryway – they must be inside. A moment later she heard the little dog scream in agony and go silent. A tear formed in the corner of her eye as the lump swelled in her throat.

"I hear you, so leave now or I'll shoot. Don't come any closer; the police are on the way."

From the bottom of the stairs she heard a low chuckle. "They'll never get here in time. You're mine, Silver."

It was that moron Himmler. "Get out of here, Special Agent Schimmler. I know you don't have a no-knock warrant, so if you leave now you might live. If you come any closer, I'm assuming you want to kill me. Get out now."

"I'll just explain to the cops that you had a break in and I spotted it while I was looking for your brother. Too bad the burglar killed you. If the cops get here before that, I'm on a national security case and that story will keep me out of trouble. I know you haven't called them; your phone line has been shunted out of the network for the time being. Your alarm will not call for help, and you can't either."

The moron had never heard of cell phones? "Stay there, Himmler. Last warning."

Schimmler was so full of himself that he assumed she was bluffing. He found out just how serious Jean Silver was when he stepped on the fourth stair. His six-foot-three-inch height brought the upper half of his skull above the top stair. Against the light from the moon illuminating the cream-colored wall behind him, it was a perfect pop-up target. Hard to miss at less than 10 feet, even with a two-inch barrel.

Jean learned very well when her husband taught her how to shoot. She kept up her concealed carry permit and visited the range every month with an identical weapon she kept in her purse. Her heart was pounding, and the tears were flowing over the death of Porkchop, but fury steadied her hand and she pulled the trigger with a smooth, sweeping motion that would make any range instructor proud of her pupil. The blast from the end of the muzzle was the last thing Schimmler saw while stealing oxygen from decent humans. Jean was night-blind and deaf from the gunshot in the confines of the upstairs hallway, but she was sure that Himmler's head was no longer peeking up the stairs.

Two full minutes went by with no sign of him, and her night vision was starting to come back. The first thing she saw when her vision cleared was the blood spray on the wall of her living room. Where Himmler's silhouette appeared a few minutes before, his brains now ran down the wall with a mist of blood and bone fragments.

The Plymouth Police Department made a dramatic entry through the front door a moment later and found the dead dog and Schimmler's corpse. Next to the front door the glass panel was removed with a professional glass-cutting tool that leaned against the outside wall of the house. It was the one place the alarm couldn't be triggered and still make a hole big enough to get into the house without breaking down a wall.

Once they identified themselves, and the neighborhood was aglow in the disco storm of throbbing emergency lights, Jean threw her gun down the stairs and remained in the prone position where she'd taken the shot. Two officers handcuffed her and helped her sit up.

The dispatcher was talking to them on the radio, and when the sergeant walked in a moment later, he ordered the cuffs removed. Helping her to the side of the bed, he prompted one of the officers to bring her a bottle of water from the fridge.

"Mrs. Silver, what happened?"

Jean, through a haze of tears and mucus, put it very succinctly: "He killed my dog Porkchop. He needed to die."

The Sergeant smiled. He liked this woman.

CHAPTER TWENTY-NINE
Port-au-Prince, Haiti
March 17

Nicholas and Andre moved into their own room in the mission house and spent every minute together. As a rule, Nicholas liked to be on his own, but his friendship with Andre grew stronger with each passing day. They spent their time studying the Bible and discussing its meaning. Nicholas was a speed reader and he blasted through the New Testament in record time. The Old Testament was not as thoroughly examined; Andre suggested some books to read and some to skip until later. By the end of the week they had read the whole Bible, and Nicholas had some of his questions answered.

At night, when the teams returned to the mission houses, the two men joined them for the evening meeting and prayer. For the first time in his life, he enjoyed worship with others. All his life it had felt like a burden of some sort, but now it was as vital to him as breathing. He even learned a few of the Christian rock songs that Andre had on his player and found himself humming them in unguarded moments. He was developing a liking for Jamie Grace, Casting Crowns, and Chris Tomlin.

He wasn't struggling with the details, but his head was full-to-bursting with all these new stories and concepts. That was good, because there was space available after dismissing years of prejudice and preconceptions about religion. Not so much about faith, but about religion. He still didn't like a lot of the divisions he found in different faiths, but as a blank slate spiritually, he was forging his own views unencumbered by centuries of strife. There was so much in the Bible warning against that, and yet it happened despite "the manual" that Larry talked about.

As he was getting ready for bed, Larry strolled through the room and tossed him a licorice whip. Larry seemed to always have candy or soda with him since there was no smoking allowed in the mission house. "Nick, grab Andre and meet me upstairs. I want to talk before we call it a day."

Five minutes later they walked into the upstairs office. Larry was sitting with his feet up on the desk; head leaned back, little honks of noise coming from his nose as he was snoring away. The man did the work of a dozen and didn't sleep well at night because his brain never quit trying to resolve all the challenges he faced during the day. Sometimes that caused him to nod off when the odd moment of peace presented itself. Andre reached out with his left hand and knocked on the door using his fingertips. Larry pried an eye open before flopping his feet to the floor. Sitting up straight, he grabbed a stick of gum and started chewing. "Andre, is he ready for full-blown spiritual warfare?"

That didn't sound all that attractive to Nick, but he kept quiet. "Yes, he is, Larry. He could use more study, but he's a fast learner. God has made him receptive to the lessons he needs. But we should not provoke Satan. Let's see what happens if we go slow."

Larry snorted. "After the storm at his baptism, I think Satan is itching to take a slap at him. Sure, we won't go out of our way, but the hair on the back of my neck has been standing up for three days. It's coming; I just don't know what it will be.

"We've got a new medical team coming in tomorrow. Doctor Eric is staying over for another week, but the rest are going home. Let's stick around tomorrow until the new team gets in and brief them on the situation in Cite Soleil. We haven't been in there with a mission team now in almost two weeks. I don't want to keep sending in our drivers without help. It's like giving up ground in a battle. We'll send the new people in their first day but let them know what they're facing before it happens. Nicholas, you go to the clinic that day. Tomorrow I want you to eat good meals, sleep a bit, and pray. Once you leave this place, I'm afraid it's going to tear loose out in town. You need to be ready."

Nicholas nodded his understanding.

"One other thing, Nicholas. I got a call from your sister this morning when I was out in town. Somebody burned your house down. It's a complete loss. I'm sorry to have to be the one to tell you the news, but it seems to be a part of the attack I'm talking about. Part two: she shot an intruder and killed him. It was Special Agent Schimmler. But she's okay."

Nicholas' stomach spasmed as though he'd been kicked, and he lurched to stick his head in the wastebasket before losing his dinner.

"Nice. Well, it is Saint Patrick's Day, so now we've got our green for the day."

"Sorry, Larry. I'll take the bag to the trash." Nicholas wiped his mouth on his sleeve and took a deep breath.

118

"How did they burn my house down with news crews staked out? Nobody saw anything? Jean's okay? I mean, she's doing okay?"

"You can get the details from your sister if you like, but she said Schimmler broke in and killed her dog. He threatened to kill her as well. She shot him in self-defence. As for your house, there was a power outage in that area because a stolen truck knocked down a power pole a few blocks away. The news trucks all broke away to cover the accident and the search for the driver who'd run away after the crash. The news crews were gone from your house for about half an hour. With the power out, your neighbours didn't see anything until the house was fully involved. Nothing left, buddy. Anything in there you can't replace?"

Nicholas stared at the wall while he took mental inventory. "I'm homeless, my sister's going to be indicted for killing a federal agent, and all I have are the clothes on my back. If that's the luck of the Irish, I'm changing teams.

Andre put his arm around Nicholas's shoulder and said nothing. The unhappy soul slumped in his chair and took a couple of deep breaths. "Is this just paranoia, or are we in actual combat with Satan? Because if we are, it would be kind of nice if someone told me what we're fighting about or fighting for. I have no idea. To paraphrase myself, I'm just a guy with no place to live and nothing to wear."

Andre squeezed Nicholas's shoulder. "You are fighting the things that are dark, Nicholas Bacon. You are destined to play some big part in my country. God spared you on the airplane. You cast out demons in Cite Soleil. You spoke in a language I never heard spoken in Haiti, and they spoke back in the same language. But when they taunted you about the children in Creole, and told you to flee, you stood strong.

"When we drove away, I saw violent storms, like we saw the day of his baptism, hovering over Cite Soleil. None of the others commented on the storms, but I saw them."

Nicholas glanced between the two men. "Thank you, Andre. I thought I was nuts. I never mentioned the storms because it was part of a dream as far as I could tell. And, yes, they did taunt me about being a fake. About being unable to save anyone. I don't know who or how to save someone, but that's what they said."

Larry reached into his drawer for a cigar and then put it back; rules were rules, even for the boss.

119

"That pretty much ices the cake for me. It's happened twice, now. Storms which reveal conflict in Heaven. Biblical in their nature. The demons called him out as a fake, and challenged him to protect children? They must know his mission even if he doesn't. It involves children. We just have to figure it out. As for saving people, don't forget that wreck at the river, Nicholas. You saved her life and the life of her baby. In fact, you raised the dead. I count that as a part of the prophesy.

"I'll be gone for part of the day tomorrow. I want you two to pray hard all day. We'll meet here for supper tomorrow evening. Andre, watch over Papa Noel. You know, Saint Nicholas was a true protector of children, Nicholas. You share the name with a saint, demons have linked you to children, and there is a power growing about you each day in the spiritual realm. Perhaps you are the modern Nicholas of Myra. Wouldn't that be interesting?"

CHAPTER THIRTY
Saint Paul, Minnesota
March 17

Ernesto "Ernie" Lopez sat across from Jean Silver in a dive bar on Saint Paul's East Side. Both were dressed in the garb of the local low-life, but Jean's manicure and $200 haircut gave her away.

"You always know how to show a girl a good time, Lopez. Could we go upscale next time and just meet at the Union Gospel Mission?"

Lopez sipped his beer and watched the bar behind Jean. His back, as always, was pressed up against the farthest wall he could find; Lopez spent a lot of time in this bar over the last twenty-six years. Every person in the bar knew him. Every person in the bar except Jean attended his infamous Day-After-Christmas parties at some point. That translated to loyalty. Nobody looked his way, and the bartender was watching the monitors under the bar that covered the outside infrared cameras on the corners of the bar. Lopez had paid big money to have them installed in what looked like old hornets' nests on nearby structures to make sure nobody was watching them. Other deals were made in this joint from time to time and having unexpected guests could be inconvenient. Almost as inconvenient as being shot with the sawed off 12-gauge shotgun under the bar. Lopez loved the place.

"You were wired for sound in every way I've ever seen. Whoever did the work was top notch. That means I can't promise I found all the bugs. The only way you'll get your privacy back is to knock out all the walls and rebuild the space.

"I found a recording unit in the ceiling, all of it solid state. No tapes, no hard drives, just a full terabyte of the best memory system you can buy. You need a special code to download it. Which isn't a problem because it's set up on a cellular link and they can do it remotely. I left it right where it was. The bugs were another story: I moved a few of them as you requested. Right about now they're hearing about the great things that a gigantic purple-friggen dinosaur can do. Gotta hand it to you, that's some cruel stuff. Same thing with the window buzzers. I made it solid state like their toys and threw in a little Average White Band to compliment Styx. Hate both of them with a passion."

Jean traced a pattern on the scummy table top with a fingertip. "Who?"

"Has to be feds, Jean. Or former feds. I don't think you're up to anything illegal, not with the kind of practice you have. But somebody spent huge dough on you to find out what you know. Have you given away anything they can use against you? I mean, it doesn't have to be anything you've done, but they could do a "Martha Stewart" on you and get you with a perjury trap, or a conspiracy charge. That means you have to think very hard about what's gone on in your office this past week or so."

"Not me, but my brother. I think they're framing him. Guess I better get word to him. Interested in taking a vacation in Haiti?"

Lopez shook his head. "I'm on too many watch lists. I have some issues with TSA over the past year or two and don't think I could slink in and out without drawing undue attention. Jealous boyfriends are such a pain in the rear. No, they already know where he is if you've even mentioned it in passing. There's no way to know how long those bugs have been in place. My best guess is a day or two before you called me, but who's to say? Either call him or go down yourself. But playing it cute won't help."

"Thanks, Lopez. It's good having you on my side."

"You're absolutely right about that. I'm worth my fee just for this advice: Jean, don't mess with these guys. Anyone who spent that kind of money to bug your office is playing for keeps. Just play it straight. Report the bugs to the United States Attorney and the Bar Association. That way they have to back off."

"We might be a little bit late for that advice. I shot a guy last night."

Lopez didn't even bat an eye. "I wondered if you'd get around to that little gem. He was one of the feds chasing your brother. The story isn't getting any play in the news, but a friend tipped me off."

"He killed Porkchop and I was next. He cut the glass next to the front door and just stepped through the opening. He knew what my alarms covered, and that the motion detector was off because Porkchop has run of the house. I couldn't afford the fines if she set off the motion detectors every week."

She paused and snuffled a bit: Porkchop was gone and she didn't have to sweat the alarms anymore.

122

"Why didn't you call the cops and let them handle it?"

"I did call the cops. You know as well as I do that the cops are just minutes away when seconds matter. I grabbed my revolver and plopped down in the prone at the end of the hallway. I've never killed anyone before, Ernie. It isn't so hard when your back's against the wall."

"Good chance Schimmler was taking a little personal time to deal with you. I know how charming you can be when someone annoys you. I think your restraining order in Utah really ticked him off.

"It's probably a little late, but after you whacked him on the stairway, I got back the information I'd been looking for. I knew the dude was shady, but I didn't realize just how bad it was. Seems he got away with killing a fellow fed a few years back. Some ATF agent that got in his way on an undercover operation. He claimed he didn't know the guy was a cop, and during some illicit weapons buy, he got hinky. Schimmler blew his head off. The FBI covered his butt, because there's no love lost between them and the ATF. But my source is deep in the swamp, and he said it was a bad shoot, and that some evidence was missing when the case closed out. Schimmler managed to pin it on the dead ATF agent, which was really convenient with no eye-witness testimony as to what happened to the crate of grenades that was involved.

"At any rate, your complaint had the kids from the Office of Professional Responsibility sniffing around again, and I guess his chain of command was more than a bit nervous. It's good to have a bad boy for the occasional bag job, but not when he's tied to a complaint like yours."

"Great. You might have uncovered that little nugget before he visited my living room. But you're on the money about the restraining order. I made his professional life miserable when he came on too strong. I have a feeling the OPR was planning on talking to him about that, and if he were already dirty, it might have opened the can of worms again."

The two sipped at their drinks and thought about her near miss before Jean spoke again: "I never figured out what he wanted in my house. If he wanted to burgle my house, he already knew I don't keep any files there. Computers are wonderful, but I remote log in to my files over an encrypted link on the web. My hard drive is always pristine. That way they can't seize it at customs if one of my clients goes deep end and I happen to be with them. No, this was a message at a minimum; a full-blown hit is more like it. I'm just lucky I got the drop on him, or he'd have

123

really messed me up. I could feel it in his voice: he was up for fun and games before he killed me. Ernie, I'm in a mafia movie, but the last act is yet to come."

"Again, be careful with these guys. They won't be stopped by an encrypted file on the internet: they make up the codes. But your shooting Schimmler will back them off for a couple of days. I promise you, this is bigger than we know, and they'll try again, Jean."

Jean got up from the table and threw down a twenty. "Don't worry, Lopez. I have a pretty good idea on how to deal with any more idiots that come along in Schimmler's place. Life is about to get interesting."

CHAPTER THIRTY-ONE
Port-au-Prince, Haiti
March 18

Once her morning chores were done, Violene was summoned to the garage. The driver was waiting and told her to get in the car. Afraid to question anyone in authority over her, Violene got in the back of the car where she found the temperature to be cool and the air dry. The driver reached over and buckled her in for the ride. The first stop was to a doctor's office near the city's shopping district. A private clinic: the equipment was state of the art. Violene was poked and prodded in ways she never dreamed of, and several samples were taken. She was forced to answer the most private questions about her family, what little she knew of them.

The next stop was at a small clothing shop in a fashionable part of town. There she was measured in every dimension and fitted for several dresses. When she asked why all the measurements, the woman clerk said that special undergarments were to be made to fit her alone. How nice it would be to have things that fit was a glorious thought, not knowing what was in store.

The final stop was at a beauty spa. She was given a shower, manicure, pedicure, and a haircut. Her opinion was not asked in any regard of her appearance. An elderly, but very patient woman, made her up to look much older than she was. The woman explained the technique needed to give just the right look as each item was applied. Once she was done, Violene scrubbed her face free of the makeup and tried it herself. It took four tries, but by the end she was doing a good job on her own.

The woman, who seemed very kind, gave her a supply of all the makeup and when she was sure no one could overhear them, she asked if Violene saw a doctor that day. "Yes. It was our first stop. Why do you ask?"

"Because you will be given ointments and pills to take. The pills will stop any pregnancy and you must use them when you are told to do so. If you do not, you will have a child and be thrown out of the home. If you are lucky."

125

As though a battle raged within her, the older woman took some time before she said, "My child, you have not yet been — touched. It will happen soon. You cannot say who encouraged you to do so, but you must pick a moment and flee. If you stay in that house, nothing but sadness will be in your life. Leave as soon as you can. It doesn't matter where you go, but anything is better than what awaits you behind those walls."

CHAPTER THIRTY-TWO
Port-au-Prince, Haiti
March 18

With the first group of missionaries on their way to the airport, and the second group still in Miami, there was a gap of several hours when the mission house was empty.

Andre and Nicholas were sitting in the living room reading Psalms out loud and talking about the meaning when one of the kitchen staff asked if they'd like lunch. "Papa, what if we go in to town to get lunch. You've never been in Port-au-Prince, and there is someone I want you to meet. We can have lunch in a café downtown."

"Super! I'm feeling a little cooped up hanging around here this week. I'd love to see the city from some place other than the back of a tap-tap."

Andre thanked the cook and ran to grab his water bottle and wallet. Snagging the keys from the board on the wall, he was waiting for Nicholas when he came out of the bathroom. "We'll take the car." After scribbling a note for Larry, Andre walked into the brilliant sunshine of a late morning in Haiti.

Sunglasses fitted in place, and floppy hats covering their heads, they drove deep into an older part of the city and parked the car. Andre took a quick look around and was satisfied with whatever he was seeing. "I wanted to make sure there were no gang signs on the walls. This section of the city has been peaceful for many years, but it was very dangerous right after the earthquake. Do you mind walking a bit?"

Nicholas held up his walking staff. "I'm ready for a hike. Which direction?"

Andre pointed down a long, wide boulevard. "We'll head down Boulevard Jean-Jacques Dessalines and then we will meet my friend after we have lunch. There is a very nice French restaurant which will please you without a doubt."

"He was the leader of the revolution that kicked the French out, wasn't he?"

"Yes. A very revered man in Haiti. You have been studying Haiti's history, Papa?"

"I have. Figured I should if I were going to be here a while. I want to understand the place. It's kind of ironic. We walk down his boulevard and have lunch at a French restaurant. I wonder what he'd think of that?"

"Haiti is a land of many ironies, Papa."

The two ambled along, tempted at every step with offerings from hundreds of small vendors crowding the sidewalks outside lots still littered with rubble. Almost every structure along this road collapsed in the earthquake, and many that didn't fall down were damaged by fire in the aftermath. The variety of goods ranged from luxury radios and televisions to used tennis shoes. Dozens of small braziers were set up in impromptu sidewalk cafes. Nicholas knew better than to try the cuisine — his stomach could never survive the encounter — but the smells were buffeting him and weakening his resolve.

After a few blocks of enduring the stares of the residents, most of whom never saw a beard like Nicholas's in a book, much less in real life, Andre took a turn to the left and headed down a narrow road. Nicholas glanced up for a sign in the event they had to run for it and saw that they were on the Rue des Miracles: Avenue of Miracles. There were none of those in sight; most of the buildings along this road were still showing signs of damage from the earthquake, and shadowed people lurked in the background, not quite in the light but not the deep tones he'd visualized in others. Nicholas's senses were tingling with foreboding, but Andre seemed very comfortable as he walked along.

After six very dusty blocks, they came to a "T" intersection, the end of the Rue des Miracles. The road went left and right, but they could go no further to the east. Andre was undaunted and walked up to a door in a building remarkable for being upright and free of cracks in Port-au-Prince. A small brass sign next to the door proclaimed it: La Souvenance.

Andre knocked on the door as Nicholas tried to look in past the dusty panes. A woman straight off the front page of a fashion magazine smiled and waved as she trotted toward the door. "Bonjou, Andre! Welcome. Please come in and bring your friend."

Turning with the grace of a ballerina, the woman flicked a switch and illuminated the room. It took a moment for Nicholas' eyes to adjust, but he was rewarded with an exquisite restaurant consisting of creams and dark wood surrounding crystal and white linens. The woman embraced Andre and extended a wet hand to Nicholas. Realizing what she'd done, she wiped her hands on her apron. "I'm so sorry. I was cleaning pans when you knocked. I am Marie De Courte. My husband and I own the restaurant. Welcome to La Souvenance, the finest French restaurant outside of Petionville."

"What Marie does not tell you is that they are the single French restaurant outside of Petionville. But they will be the best anywhere in Haiti unless I am very wrong. Marie, this is my friend Nicholas. We call him Papa Noel for obvious reasons."

"Enchantee, Papa Noel. A friend of Andre is my friend too. Please, have a seat. Do you like coffee? I just made a pot. My husband won't be back for a while, but I would be glad to make lunch for you. We have a wonderful breast of chicken in a white sauce, and small potatoes. I have a beautiful wine to go with it; it will be our special tonight. You are here just in time to sample my portion, but there is plenty if you have some bread and a desert as well. I have some crème brulee made with a coffee extract and a lemon tart for you to try. What do you think?"

Nicholas's stomach audibly rumbled. Andre chuckled, "D'accord, Papa Noel."

Moments later she returned with coffee for the three of them, a bottle of white wine, and a bottle of sparkling water. Once the men were served, she vanished into the kitchen.

In less than five minutes she brought three steaming plates of food to the table and delivered them with a graceful flourish. Reaching out her hands, they completed a ring encompassing the table and Nicholas spoke for them: "Father God, thank You for the blessing of this food and this good woman who serves us so humbly. Bless this new business and bless us on our journey today. Amen."

Nicholas sampled the first bite and was transported to gastronomic heaven. There was even fresh heart of radish in florets on the plate. After trying a bit of everything, he let out a sigh of joy. "Marie, Andre said this is a new restaurant. Where do you know Andre from?"

Nicholas's syntax must have stumped her because it took her a minute to answer. "Andre saved me from a crumbled building after the earthquake. I was under a fallen roof near the National Palace. I was alone in the office when the quake struck. I was pinned and all I could do was shout. I was there two days before Andre found me. I almost lost my leg, but as you can see it has recovered so well you cannot imagine it."

Marie turned a smooth leg back and forth in the air, like a Folies Bergere dancer. There was a small scar along her calf, but no deformity. It was hard to believe it had been crushed.

"The doctors tell me that it was a close thing. Andre brought me out and a veterinarian helped me! I will take help from one who works with animals, anytime. He was quite skilled. He was also our one hope; all of the other medical people were quite busy. I think Andre is my angel. He stayed with me until I was able to get to the hospital. Besides, he found my husband for me. And this restaurant. Andre, were it not for my husband, I should marry you. You are handsome and kind."

For the first time since they met, Nicholas saw Andre squirm with discomfort. "Marie exaggerates. I did hear her, but I was not alone in saving her. Her husband? Well, he is my friend, and I told him of Marie's rescue. He already knew her from a time when he bought insurance from her agency for his taxi. He appreciates a beautiful woman and sought her out. I do take credit for the restaurant, of that I am very proud."

Nicholas looked at Marie. "Mr. Humble isn't going to tell me the story, would you?"

"It is simple enough. Andre knew my husband and I wanted to open a restaurant. We are both trained chefs but could not find a restaurant that paid enough for us to make it. This place had been here a long time with a fine reputation. Then the owners were arrested, and it closed. Andre found out we could buy it for a very low price from their lawyer, and he loaned us enough to open our doors."

"Isn't that risky? Buying a restaurant from criminals can't be good for your reputation."

Marie's laugh could only be compared with the tinkle of crystal chandelier droplets clashing in a light breeze. "We thought that as well. But it was so well publicized that they were kidnappers that there was no chance of their bad deeds being carried on any longer. We invited some people in for a big dinner and they spread the word. We do a lot of business dinners here. We have a parking lot with an armed guard, and it is quite safe to be here on the Rue des Miracles. God is watching over this place now."

Andre leaned in and made eye contact with Nicholas. "Papa, the previous owners were buying and selling slaves, little children. They also kidnapped wealthy people and held them for ransom. Some they sold into prostitution when their families refused to pay. But they are in prison forever, and God will no doubt punish them Himself one day. It is not all that rare here in Haiti. But it provided an opportunity for my friends."

The three finished a lunch fit for royalty and cleared the table in a group effort.

"Andre, bring more friends. If you call ahead I will make enough for all of us. I'm so sorry you missed my husband. I will give him your regards. Papa Noel, so nice to have met you. Please come back before you leave Haiti."

"I will if I can, Marie. Thank you for such a beautiful luncheon."

"Andre, take care of Papa Noel. He is a very special one. He is much like you."

"I will, Marie. He is in my charge until he leaves. I promise on my honor, he will be as safe as anyone in Haiti."

Walking toward the car, Nicholas puzzled over Andre's mood. Stopping at an intersection, Nicholas couldn't restrain his curiosity: "Why did we spend so much time with her? It seems you have a reason for me everywhere we go and with everything we do. I don't think I got anything out of that but a great lunch."

"Then the lesson was taught, Papa. Other than the day you were baptized, you have seen bitter, hard, and terrible things in most of Haiti. I wanted you to see that good people are bringing it back to life. That nice things can be found even in the midst of a crumbling city."

Nicholas looked at the fallen buildings that surrounded them. Andre was right. There was goodness and light all around him, but he was blinded to it by the darkness that swirled. He resolved to start looking toward the light in everything he did in Haiti from that moment on.

CHAPTER THIRTY-THREE
Port-au-Prince, Haiti
March 18

Leaving the restaurant, Andre headed back along Rue des Miracles for a few blocks and then turned to the right. Ahead a large open space in the skyline was framed by awnings and tents.

"What's up there, Andre?"

"It used to be called the Cathedral of Haiti, but it is officially Notre Dame de L'Assomption. It collapsed during the earthquake. Much of the country's religious history was in the building. There were frescoes, statues, paintings, and books that can never be replaced. My friend, who is the parish priest, is still there. He stays to minister the people of the neighborhood. He is a very strong man of God, Nicholas. You said you were raised Catholic, and I thought perhaps you would like to talk to a priest about what is happening. Larry and I are Christians of great faith, but the Father is a scholar and a brilliant soul. There is no translation in English for this concept, but he shines like you, Nicholas. There is something different about the two of you. I hope he can help you understand all that is happening."

Nicholas was honoured by Andre's words. He was beginning to grasp the fact that that he was a brilliant soul. He was fresh from the mint as a Christian, all the edges still rough and brittle like a shiny quarter. But if Andre thought it important, he would meet the man. A gardener approached and greeted Andre in Creole. Andre shook his hand and introduced him, "Nicholas, this is my friend Fritz. Fritz, my friend Nicholas. We call him Papa Noel."

Fritz shook his hand, pointed toward the remains of the church, and gestured toward a wall that was still standing. After a moment's chatter about the preservation team working to save a frescoed wall, he led Andre and Nicholas to one of the shaded areas under the open tents.

He pulled out a chair for Nicholas from a table and gestured for Andre to sit as well. Once they were seated, he walked to a nearby cooler and removed three bottles of orange soda. Offering each of them a bottle, he sat at the table and opened his own.

132

Andre and the gardener talked for a few more minutes in Creole while Nicholas spent his time staring out into the courtyard where workers were moving loose pieces of the fresco into boxes. He heard his nickname, Papa Noel, once or twice in the conversation but the rest was lost to him in the rapid-fire exchange of a language so far from French that Nicholas was useless as a participant. After watching for a while, it was obvious to Nicholas that it was a recovery process rather than a demolition. The men and women were handling the debris with great care. What a tragedy to lose your national heritage to an act of nature.

Andre brought him into the conversation after a long exchange, switching from Creole to English. "I'm sorry, Nicholas, that was rude not to include you, but I wanted to explain all that happened to Father Fritz, and while we all speak English, Creole is much stronger for the two of us. I want you to meet my brother in Christ, Father Fritz. We just call him "Fritz." I am sorry I did not make his title clear to you, I was just happy to see him. It has been a long time."

Father Fritz sized Nicholas up for a moment and then closed his eyes in prayer. He stayed that way, lips moving but no sound issuing forth for an eternity to Nicholas. When he opened his eyes he said, "I think we will have much to discuss, Nicholas. But Andre has encouraged me to call you Papa Noel. I like that, and will use that name if you agree?"

"I'm doomed to that name, Father. Feel free."

Father Fritz shook his head with the vigour of a man convinced. "No, you are not doomed to use this name; you are liberated by God with this name, this appearance. Andre has explained to me the confrontation with the demons in Cite Soleil, and the storm when you were baptized. Most of all, he has told me of your miraculous survival when your airplane was destroyed. It is clear to me, Papa, that Satan has taken as deep an interest in you as Jesus has.

"You are one of the elect whom God calls on from time to time throughout history to make a great change in the world. You may not see it, but others see it in you. Andre has called you a brilliant soul. In Haiti that has a special meaning. But it is a concept as old as the Bible. Moses and Abraham were brilliant souls. Saul, whom we know as Paul, was another brilliant soul. And the one you have been named for, Nicholas, was brilliant in a more modern sense. Mother Theresa of Calcutta was one of these and perhaps an easier example for you to understand: she brought change to the world in the acts of sacrifice she performed for the poor, the dying, and the children. You have been given this gift."

Nicholas thought he'd have a chat with the priest about his experience in Cite Soleil, and perhaps his baptism. He didn't expect this, for lack of a better word, anointment, as a Saint.

"Father, I'm not in the league of any of those people. I had a run in with — well, demons — but I'm not here on a mission. I came to Haiti to escape publicity. I just realized that I was selected by God to survive that crash. That has been a dramatic change and darned humbling. What I need is a plan on how to deal with the changes in my appearance and to limit the damage I do by annoying demons. I don't want anyone else to get hurt."

Father Fritz stood up and paced for a minute in the sunshine outside the tent. When he returned to the shade, the man Nicholas mistook for a gardener vanished. A figure of illuminated brilliance shined forth. Not an aura of light, but a powerful presence that spoke of God's wishes channelled through this man. A conduit to Heaven and the dictates of God using this man as a platform, much in the same way a television can bring a public figure into your living room. It was as shattering to Nicholas as anything in his life. This must be how the Israelites felt when Moses came back from the mountain with the tablets.

"Nicholas Bacon, you are one of God's chosen. You are new to your faith, but the seeds have been in you all along. It took the storm of the fight between good and evil in Haiti to germinate and bring the shoots of that faith above the surface. Haiti, for centuries, has been torn between darkness and light. Voodoo and worship of Satan have fought with the Kingdom of Christ since early days. You are here as a pivotal figure in that battle.

"You can flee if you wish. God never forces you to do anything. Free will is one of His gifts. But He has chosen you for a reason: you are a man of pure heart. I feel it; I know Andre feels it. You will lead the forces of good in some way in this nation. If you leave now, you deny God. You deny your own place in His Kingdom. But the choice is yours. Others will be hurt in any event if you let evil run riot over this nation. Since the earthquake it has gotten worse, not better. Our businesses and industries are well on the way to recovery, but our spiritual lives are in precipitous decline. Soon we will descend into madness like Rwanda, or Iraq.

134

Christians will be slaughtered on this island in battles to come. God will triumph in the end, but here and now, we will lose the fights that make up this war."

Nicholas stood and faced the priest, "If I have free will, won't my leaving Haiti stop this war? What if I'm the catalyst that has set it off? I can leave this afternoon and things will go back to normal. I don't want to foment a holy war. I'm not meant to lead anyone into battle. I was never even in the boy scouts, much less the army. What should I do, Father? Help me. I'm begging."

Father Fritz pointed at Nicholas's chair, indicating he should sit down. He walked over to his pile of gear and rummaged for a moment. He returned with a small glass bottle. Unscrewing the cap on a vial of golden liquid he said, "I'm going to bless you, Nicholas of Haiti. You are a part of what happens here no matter where you go. You can choose to be on the side of good or to flee your obligation to the people of this island. You cannot stand in the middle."

The oil was the consistency of warm molasses and the fragrance of spikenard exploded into the air as the bottle was tipped. Father Fritz covered Nicholas's head with a wave of the luxurious substance and began to pray over him in Creole. Andre took up station behind Nicholas and rubbed the anointing oil into his scalp and beard. The tingling sensation that first covered Nicholas's head spread throughout his body. He felt as though he was in the midst of a cold flame. He saw the world around him through a haze of shimmering blue light. His spirit lifted up above the tent, climbing high in the air like an eagle soaring above Port-au-Prince, able to see the entire island of Hispaniola as he climbed ever higher. The words of the priest, the touch of Andre's strong hands, the shade of the tent, faded into nothingness as he rocketed towards the heavens. In moments, he was above the atmosphere, looking down on the island, it being the sole focus of his worldview.

He had no idea how long he spent in that state, but when he returned to the chair, Father Fritz and Andre were toweling him off and speaking to him in voices one used to sooth a small child. The words penetrated the fog that encompassed his brain and emerged from the humming of his stupor: "Be blessed, Nicholas of Haiti. The Lord has summoned you, and you have decided."

Nicholas cleared his throat. "I accept the responsibility. I will obey God's will. What will He have me do, Father?"

"I can't tell you that, Nicholas. But the feeling of destiny is strong in your presence, and Satan's forces are in open defiance of you. It will not be long. When it comes, you will know it without question. Seek guidance from God, Nicholas, and you will be fine."

Andre extended a hand and helped Nicholas stand. "We must go, Papa. You are very tired, and the others will be coming from the airport. Let's go clean you up and pray in the mission house."

Nicholas embraced the priest. "Father, please pray for me. I'm so unprepared."

CHAPTER THIRTY-FOUR
Port-au-Prince, Haiti
March 18

The fingers caressed his eyebrows with a gentle, loving, stroke. Nicholas shifted in his bunk and enjoyed the sensation for a moment before opening his eyes. Eighteen inches away was the young girl who haunted his dreams. Nicholas assumed it was another dream, as he never saw any children around the mission houses. "Hi. What's up? Long time no-see."

She peeked into the corners, and looked at every object in the room, as surprised as Nicholas to be in the same room with Papa Noel. "I am Violene. I have dreamt of you. I am told you will help me escape my owner."

Nicholas's back locked up in tension. Swinging his legs over the edge of the bed, he scrubbed his face to clear the last of the cobwebs. Violene turned away and sat on the bunk opposite him. As she passed through the shimmering shaft of sunshine and hot air slamming into the room from the window, Nicholas was struck by the vivid scars across her back, thighs and shoulders, visible through the sundress she wore. Reaching up to close the window and turn on the air conditioner, Nicholas said, "Why me? How did you get here? How did you know where I was?"

The young girl was speaking in the smallest voice she could muster. It was a voice smothered with pain and foreboding. "I asked God what to do now. He said you would be able to help me. You are the one known as Papa Noel, are you not?"

Nicholas nodded.

"I have been praying for help since I went to the main house. Now — now it is going to get very bad. The woman in town said I must flee. But I have no place to go. I have no money or food. If I leave, they will say I stole from them, and I will be sent back and punished. I prayed to God so hard my head hurt, Papa. He said that you were sent to Haiti to free me. Are you buying me for yourself? Is that what God is wanting?"

Nicholas was appalled at the idea of buying another human being. Until he'd come to Haiti he had no idea that slavery even existed in this

Hemisphere, much less with Restevek children so young. He assumed that his dream girl was the victim of domestic abuse. He never imagined that this girl, Violene, was a slave.

Two of the missionaries that had left that morning were part of a group fighting human trafficking in the United States. They opened his eyes to the extensive trade in children and women throughout the world, even in nice places like Nicholas's hometown. Chalk it up to ignorance, or wilful blindness, but Nicholas never realized how extensive slavery was in this world. That this girl existed, and wasn't just a dream, struck him to his core. She was the one who was with him for months. His purpose was not just revealed, but its genesis was at his elbow.

"No, Violene. I do not know what God told you. I am here to — to avoid some people where I live. God has not told me that I am to do anything for you. You're not in danger here; my friend Larry will arrange for you to have a place in the orphanage where you will be safe. My friends have built a beautiful home for children where you can stay and even go to school. Doesn't that sound good?"

Violene shook her head. "You do not understand, Papa Noel. I am not safe here. I cannot go to a home for children. I must get back to my work or I will be whipped. I must go, Papa Noel. Please do not forget Violene."

He reached for her hand, but the door started to open, and she slipped out before he could catch her.

Andre stepped through the door the instant she left. "Grab her, Andre. She needs our protection."

Andre gave Nicholas a puzzled look. "Grab who, Papa? There is no one in the mission house right now."

"That little girl. She must have bumped into you when you opened the door."

"Papa, you must have been dreaming. There was no little girl in the hallway. I would have seen her in such a small place. Are you okay? Your head feels fine?"

"Andre, she was as real as you. My God, what's happening to me?"

***

138

Across town, at the grand home on the hillside, Violene awoke with a start. She'd crawled into a cupboard to fetch a bowl for Cook and laid down for a moment, falling sound asleep. Her dream seemed so real.

Who was this Papa Noel, and why would he help her? It did feel as though God sent him: her heart told her to trust him. She didn't know where to find him, or how to get a message to him. She now knew that there was an orphanage and a man named Larry where she could find sanctuary. After the morning's events, she burned with the need to flee and soon. She would pray some more after dinner. She must get back to work or be punished. Dreams were wonderful, but reality summoned her in the moment, and it was anything but lovely.

CHAPTER THIRTY-FIVE
Port-au-Prince, Haiti
March 18

"That pretty much covers the current situation. As I said, it's got the potential for being very dangerous, and we didn't want you to undertake this mission trip without full knowledge of what you might face. I'm sorry that we couldn't tell you about it until you got to the mission house, but frankly the airport wasn't a safe location, and there's nowhere else as secure as this compound.

"I spoke to the board late this afternoon, and they agreed that given the situation, it was an individual decision. If any of you want to return to the United States, I understand. We will refund your air fare and mission fees, and you're welcome to come back on a future trip. If you're not comfortable talking in front of the others, let me know in private. I'll be up in my office for the next hour. Again, I am so sorry for the loss of your members at the airport. I'm sure you can see we are fighting a spiritual battle here, and I'm afraid those folks fell prey to the dark side of the battle."

Larry looked out over the stunned group of missionaries in the commons room. These poor people had travelled since three in the morning to get to Haiti, witnessed the violent deaths of three of their friends at the airport, and the first thing they do at the mission house is get a briefing on full-blown spiritual warfare in the offing. He hated to do it, but it wasn't fair to ask them to stay if things got more dangerous and put their well-being at risk.

Nicholas was waiting in Larry's office upstairs. He was looking at a blank page on the word processing program adorning the monitor. His sister asked him to start the book over a week ago and he was getting nothing down on paper. It was hard to write when your head was filled with dreams of cataclysm, and visions of long lines of children waiting to see him. The last one just didn't make sense unless he was destined to be the first shopping mall Santa in Haitian history.

Neither Larry nor Andre blinked when he told them of his vision this afternoon. Andre described their journey downtown, and the meeting with

140

Father Fritz, and while Larry wasn't happy that they'd left the compound without notifying him, he understood that there was a revelation ordained by God during that meeting.

Larry gave Nicholas the boot from the desk and sat down. Andre shifted in the corner and continued to crunch on a package of corn nuts. The silence didn't last long before Nicholas spoke up: "I'm sorry to have brought this all down here with me, Larry. I can't imagine this is helping you with your mission."

Larry gave a dark laugh. "It's not on the brochures we hand out at churches, if that's what you mean. But today has been really rough."

Looking at the list of people scheduled for the group in the room below, he took his pen and underlined three names on the list.

"We lost three of the mission team at the airport. We've never even had a serious injury. Seems they got off the plane and one of them, a woman named Finseth went berserk. She started running across the tamarack, and two others tried to grab her. One woman on the team, Ms. Davis, held onto Finseth's arm as her team leader grabbed her around the waist. Finseth started to break free and dragged both the team leader, Mr. Grove, and Miss Davis into the propeller of a plane taxiing to the runway. Instant death for all three. I don't know how it could get any worse around here."

Larry stared at the list with no expression on his face. Moments passed in silence before he shoved his chair back a few inches, swiped at his eyes, and continued.

"Nicholas, the people who come down here on mission trips are pretty dedicated. They know they risk illness, civil unrest, traffic accidents, all sorts of stuff. But there's a saying that almost all of them embrace, "Lord, break my heart with what breaks Yours." They want to help these people; they know there are going to be challenges. This is just a tad more than most are ready for when they hit the airport tarmac. You don't get a spiritual warfare form with your customs declaration. I just talked to them, and I have to ask you guys to go out on the patio and hang until they have a chance to talk to me. Andre, kindly go down and ask the remaining trip leaders to send people up one at a time, or as families if we have any, so that I can talk to them in private."

Andre nodded and headed out. Nicholas got up and grabbed the MP3 player on the desk. "I'll be outside listening to the Gospel of Luke. He seems to have some connection with me that the others don't. That ever happen to you?"

Larry grimaced. "Right now, I'm feeling a certain kinship with Job."

Nicholas sat in a darkened recess of the balcony listening to Johnny Cash read Luke and prayed while the 20 members of the new teams marched up and down the stairs, in and out of Larry's office. No voices raised loud enough for him to hear them over the recording, so that was a good sign.

Within an hour, they had all spoken to Larry. After the three remaining leaders of the mission trip walked back down the stairs, Larry waved in Nicholas and Andre.

Larry took a minute to write out something on his legal pad before flipping it over and looking at Nicholas. "Want to guess how many are going back on the 1:20 flight tomorrow afternoon?"

"I guess 75 percent of them?"

"You are 100 percent wrong." Larry flipped over the pad, which proclaimed "Praise God, they're all staying!"

Larry flipped the pad around again and started writing. "Let's list all the things we need to do to get this bunch of people, and ourselves, up to speed. First, we need to make sure they take time to drink water. It's pretty hot every afternoon, and I don't want anybody getting dehydrated. Second, let's make sure they take their malaria medicine and use plenty of bug and sun spray. Third, we need to have everyone, including any staff on site, pray together tonight. They know Nicholas is at the center of this, but they haven't met him or spent time with him. If we're asking them to go to war, we need to introduce the general to them."

"Whoa. I'm no general. I'm just…"

"Yeah, you've told us, you're not an escalator, you're just an engineer. I get it, just a guy. Listen, Nicholas, like it or not, all this hinges on you. Signs and wonders have taken place and you're the leading edge of this whole confrontation. You might not know what's going to happen quite yet, but you'll know before we do. The fact you had a vision about a Restevek girl this afternoon tells me God's pointing you toward the enslaved children. Perfectly appropriate given what has happened. I'm not sure how to go about it either, but let's start out at the orphanage and clinic. Lots of kids out there: perhaps there's another sign to this that we have yet to see. Remember, I saw the Holy Spirit manifest over your head while we were eating lunch with the children at Mercy Orphanage.

"There's something important about that place that we can tap into. Tomorrow, early, we are going to head up to the village and turn this Hands-and-Feet ministry on full blast. Half this team is medical, and we were planning on doing surgeries this week. So, let's get them prayed up tonight. We'll take the other team with us, have them visit elders in the village before lunch, and play with the kids after lunch."

"Fine. But what am I going to do? All the equipment that we could install is assembled and tested. I'm a fifth wheel."

Larry drummed his pen on the pad. "You don't get it. You're not the fifth wheel, you're the steering wheel. Let's go down and pray. I want everyone to get some sleep. Tomorrow is going to be the roughest one yet, unless I miss my guess."

CHAPTER THIRTY-SIX
Titanyen, Haiti
March 19

The morning chugged along without incident. No dark clouds on the horizon, no demons storming the gate, not even a lot of sick children. The morning wound clinic saw fewer than half its normal number of patients. Doctor Eric was unhappy about that and expressed his concern to Nicholas: "If they don't come back to get those wounds followed up, they risk losing the limb. Sometimes they do heal up without our help, but it's not very likely. I wonder what's keeping them away."

He got his answer after lunch when the clinic reopened for adults. The line stretched out the door, off the veranda, and partway to the gate of the complex. Patients unseen in the clinic for weeks were all there to be treated. Most couldn't afford to come very often. They left their fields or animals to come on a bus. It wasn't cheap, and very few of them could afford the trip. Eric was shocked at the line. He sent one of the nurses to find a translator so that they could get to the bottom of the mystery. Andre loped across the yard and entered the clinic. "Sorry, Doctor Eric, I was at the fish farm. I did not think you would need me today. Where is the translator assigned to the clinic?"

"Don't know, don't care, Andre. What I do want to know is why all these people chose today to come to the clinic. We were slow this morning, now it's packed."

"Give me a few minutes and I'll find out."

Eric called in the first patient and was examining her while Nicholas held the old woman's hand. Eric finished cleaning the wound and was asking Nicholas for a piece of tape when the woman snatched a hair from his beard, tucking it into her pocket in spite of fingers crippled by arthritis. Eric laughed, but Nicholas didn't enjoy the experience.

"Go ahead, Doc. Next one will want some of that ginger on the top of your head. See how you like it."

"I don't think they will, Papa Noel. I found out where the crowd came from this afternoon. You are the reason."

Nicholas braced against the table and shook his head. Now what?

Andre hugged the old woman and saw her to the door before he spoke. "The children you treated the last time you were in clinic have all been healed. None of them has any wound on their body. All of them, in fact, are quite well. I believe Doctor Eric would call them thriving: they are gaining weight, no coughs, nothing. There is also a lot of talk about our rescuing Madeleine and her baby from the stream. You are credited with raising the dead, Papa.

"Word spread through the local villages as you came in this morning's tap-tap. Each village brought their sick to be healed by you, Papa. The little boys who ate with you and took the hairs? They are claiming to have seen miracles since then. They are gaining weight, and infirmities are gone. Smooth skin, no scars. It is miraculous. I am sure many more are coming. There is traffic up and down the coast. Come to the roof and see for yourself."

The three of them slipped down the hallway and climbed the ladders up to the rooftop. Looking down the mountainside they could see the coastal highway and the ocean beyond. Andre was understating the situation: there was a traffic jam in this remote part of Haiti, and every vehicle appeared to be heading toward the orphanage and the clinic at the top of the hill.

"There is another thing, Papa. Some of the children said they saw you in a vision. They cannot say what you are supposed to do for them, but you are very important to the small ones. I am told many more will be coming."

Eric looked down at the crowded roads and turned toward the stairs. "We better get Larry. This could become dangerous if we get overwhelmed."

The clang of the gate closing a hundred yards away caused every head to turn and look. Larry was putting a bar through the fitting on the wall and the security staff was assembled near him. He scanned the compound and caught sight of the three men on the roof. Indicating that they should stay put, he jogged up the hillside.

A minute later he joined them on the roof. "Thanks for the warning, Andre. We got it closed just in time."

Seeing the puzzled looks on their faces, Andre explained to Nicholas and Doctor Eric that he ran across Larry on the way to the clinic and let him know what was happening.

"Hope you guys got your toothbrushes with you, because we aren't going to be able to get out of here tonight. I need some time to figure out a plan, but it will be okay. We can stay in the old dorms. The kids are all in the new family-style homes we just finished. Tomorrow I'll get the President to send some people up here to calm things and we can get back to normal. I think."

The crowd below at last noticed them standing on the rooftop and began to chant, "Papa Noel, Papa Noel, Papa Noel." The cries grew louder and louder until Nicholas waved at the crowd. It broke into a wild cheer and shuffled in place.

"What are they doing?"

"I think they're waiting for you to say something, Papa."

"I don't speak Creole, what should I say?"

"That is simple, my brother: Jezi renmen ou."

"Jezi renmen ou – I'm pretty sure I know that one, but I want to be sure what it means. Andre?"

"It is the truth. Jesus loves you."

Nicholas turned toward the crowd from the edge of the roof. Leaning on his walking stick to balance himself, he looked out over at least a hundred people inside the compound. He felt like a fraud intellectually: he was, as he told others, just a guy. But a voice prompted him inside: "It is the truth, Nicholas. Speak My truth to them and then heal their wounds."

Raising his staff, Nicholas held his arms over his head as the crowd grew even more quiet. When he spoke, it was not a fat engineer from Minnesota with a long beard, a white t-shirt and a pair of shorts. No, it was Nicholas of Haiti. "Jezi renmen ou!"

His voice thundered across the valley and down to the ocean front below. A chorus of honking horns and cheering people pelted back up the hillside toward him from over a mile away. Nicholas looked toward Heaven and in that instant, knew what his mission in Haiti was: heal the sick that come to you. But first, free the Resteveks. And then, put an end to human trafficking on this island.

146

CHAPTER THIRTY-SEVEN
Titanyen, Haiti
March 19

It was clear that the people inside the compound must be treated or they would have a riot on their hands. They had made long journeys in most cases, and many were desperately ill. Most would have died in painful isolation in some remote village under normal circumstances. Today, for the first time in their lives, they hoped that a miracle might cure them. Nicholas argued for a short time with Larry about his course of action. Larry wanted to protect the missionaries and staff, but most of all he wanted to guard the safety of the children in Mercy Orphanage. Nicholas laid out a simple plan: they would see each patient as long as he could hold out.

He shared what God told him on the rooftop, and said, "Larry, He's got His hands cupped around us. I feel very strong and His power is inside of me. We can see them all. If I do have the power to heal, I should be using it for these people. If we get all the missionaries and staff to organize the people down there, outside the gates, we can take care of them without risk to the rest. Some will leave when darkness falls, and all will be hungry. Is there some way we can get food brought in for them?"

"We've got food here, Nicholas. Enough to feed all these people but then we'll be short for other things in the coming weeks. My next container of food doesn't come for a couple of days. We have to collect it in Port-au-Prince and then truck it up here. That's assuming Louis releases it without a bribe that's worth more than the contents. I have serious doubts that he'll do anything to help right now. He's holding out for a huge bribe on the medical equipment, and he absolutely will use food for orphans as a lever."

"Much as I want to fix that for you, Larry, God didn't mention containers in His message. I'm pretty sure that water and food are part of the healing process, so we need to risk it."

"Nicholas, you don't understand: we're out of supplies if Louis won't release that container. Seriously, no matter how much money I have, without the container we have no food."

147

"An hour ago, I would have agreed with you. But now — Larry, He'll provide. We need to do this, and He will take care of the details. Besides, if we need the food, I'll charter an airplane myself and fly in all we need. If we get the press involved, petty tyrants like Louis can't stand in our way.

"My sister tells me I'm worth five million dollars when that book is finished. I bet I can get an advance, and I can get her to con some network into providing the food and the airplane. God is doing miracles today, Larry. Right here, right now. Aren't you the guy who challenged me to step out on faith this week? Let's do it, brother."

A quick meeting was held, water distribution organized, and volunteer cooks sent to help with meals in the dining hall. The plan was to bring each of the patients in for an examination with a doctor. The wounds would be treated medically, and Nicholas would lay hands on the patient and pray for healing. Belt-and-suspenders healing is what they were calling it at the clinic. Each patient was cleaned up for treatment, photos taken of the injury, vital statistics gathered, and then they were ushered in to a room with the doctor and Nicholas. After treatment, and prayer, the patient was taken out and fed before leaving the compound. No base was left uncovered if Nicholas's miraculous cures were not miracles but statistical anomalies during the last clinic.

This went on for two hours before they started to hear of miracles taking place. Doctor Eric and one of the paramedics with the team went to the dining hall to talk to the patients who claimed to be healed. Comparing the wounds with the pictures taken just an hour before, it was clear that miracles were afoot. They would stick with the protocol, but it was obvious that something special was taking place on this dusty hillside.

Working through the afternoon, and into the evening, the tide of people never wavered for a moment. Once the initial people inside were treated, the gates were opened a crack so that they could leave, and new patients could come in. It was announced to people outside that everyone would be taken care of and a flutter settled over the hillside, broken by prayer and an ongoing hymn sung by everyone present. It rumbled the ground beneath their feet and carried for miles on the evening air. The words spread across the land like a flow of molten lava from a volcano, igniting fires and embedding the song in hearts as far away as Port-au-Prince.

The cooks and children from the orphanage began taking food and water down the hill to the people, reaching halfway to the coastal road before turning back. People in the line were sharing what they brought, and a brisk business was done as temporary markets were set up along the road and up the hill. Someone called the brewery in Port-au-Prince and trucks full of sodas, water, and beer arrived just after eight in the evening, further reducing the demand on the mission. Larry walked down and talked with the truck drivers. After a series of phonecalls back to the bottling plant manager, Larry promised to purchase all their stock as long as they stayed to distribute it to the people waiting. Larry, well known in the business community of Haiti, was a good customer and his trade was welcome. The thing that mattered most? His credit was massive.

Just after nine that evening, the clinic ran out of sterile dressings and most medications, yet the line still extended for half a mile. The doctors were short on gloves as well. A council of war decided to clean wounds and pray over the patients, as this wasn't about traditional medical treatment any longer.

Into the night, and until the next morning, the patients came through the gate. The nearby church was packed for hours. Those whose wounds were healed gave thanks and praise for the miracles of the evening. Larry was sitting in a chair, on the roof, praying for the people of his mission and all of Haiti. This much goodness could not go unchecked by the forces of darkness.

At 3:45 in the morning the last patient came through the door of the examination room. It was a fourteen-year-old girl with deep wounds on her back and legs. Nicholas flashed back to a memory from the day before: Violene had the same marks on her.

"What are those marks, Eric? What makes that happen?"

"It is the wound from a rigwaz, Nicholas. It's a Haitian whip, and it's used on children rather often. Restevek kids are often marked up like this. These are pretty bad, and they're dirty. It's not like whips get sanitized between uses. Andre, ask her what happened."

Andre sat on the exam table and took the girl's hand. She would not make eye contact with him but answered his questions. Andre talked to her for a few moments and comforted her before explaining what she said.

"She is a Restevek. She broke a window two days ago while cleaning it. Her chair tumbled, and she cracked the glass when she fell against it.

149

The woman who owns her used the rigwaz on her until she passed out. She said there are more scars on her bottom, but she doesn't want to show them to a man. I guess she has been…"

"Raped. That's the word she used, Andre. You don't need to shield us from what happened. Nicholas, it sickens me what people do with these children. They are supposed to take care of them and give them a better life. That's why the parents turn them over to the slave holders. But instead they are starved, and beaten, and raped. Andre, ask her if we can have a female doctor help her. Explain that we will treat her other wounds, but it is important to clean all of them."

Andre spoke in hushed tones to the girl for another moment. She began to cry and shudder. Nicholas reached out to put an arm around her, and she buried her head in his chest. He stood there, sobbing along with her, while the female doctor treated her wounds and examined her for sexual trauma. Nicholas's usual shyness was nowhere to be found when this little girl wouldn't let go; he remained at her side throughout the examination. Once the wounds were cleaned and ointment applied, the girl put on new clothes the orphanage director brought her. Andre explained to her that she did not have to leave; she was welcome to stay with the other children in the orphanage. She wiped her tears on a tissue and blew her nose. A torrent of Creole flew toward Nicholas, confounding him.

A plea-filled look toward Andre brought the translation. "She said, Papa, that God told her to run away and to come to the orphanage. She was told in a vision that you would be here and take her with you to safety. She is afraid to leave you and go to the orphanage."

Nicholas bowed his head, looking deep into the child's eyes. "I will not abandon you. You are safe here. I have prayed over your wounds, and the doctors have treated you. You will have a new home with us, here at Mercy Orphanage. You will never be mistreated again. We will find your family and get you back to them if that's what you wish. Now go with my friend and she will find you a bed with a family."

The girl, smiling for the first time since she was taken from her family's home two years before, gave Nicholas a hug that almost crushed the wind from him and said, "Mesi, Papa Noel. Bondye te vre. Se mwen menm ki lakay yo. Ou e sove mwen."

Looking again to Andre for a translation, he had already heard the answer in in his heart: "Thank you. God has been true. I am home. You have saved me."

It was over an hour before Nicholas was able to quit weeping.

The blinding glow on the wall announced the passing of noon at the orphanage. Nicholas rolled over on his cot and tried to go back to sleep, but the support post in the middle dug into his hips.

He almost gagged when he got a whiff of himself. It seemed that handling dirty, dusty people, and sweating like a firehose for seventeen hours straight wasn't conducive to good personal hygiene. Across the room, Andre shifted in his chair and set a cup of coffee on the counter.

"Bonjou, Papa Noel. It is nice to see you awake. Would you like some coffee?"

"Uh, eventually, Andre. Right now, I want to clean up and put on some fresh clothes. But none of those is very likely, now is it?"

"You would be wrong, Papa. Once the roads cleared, one of our staff brought out clothes and toothbrushes for everyone. I even have that red shirt you like so much! It is not your toothbrush, but it is brand new. The water here is potable; we filter it all from the well before we pipe it to the buildings. So, drink your fill, and rinse your brush with tap water. Once you do that, I will take you to the dormitory where you can shower and change. If you hurry, you can still have lunch. I have asked the cooks to save some eggs and avocados for you. You must eat many calories today, Papa Noel, for you worked very hard last night."

Andre handed him a cup of hot coffee. "How is it you always have hot drinks hot and cold drinks cold, Andre?"

"I am very attentive to my friends, Papa. Now, finish your coffee and we will do the rest."

Nicholas stood up and walked to the window. There was already a line down the hillside. More desperate people in need of healing and food. The two were interchangeable in a nation where so many died of malnutrition.

"Are we seeing patients today, Andre?"

"Larry and Doctor Eric are waiting to talk to you about that, Papa. Some other things have happened that must be addressed, but it is for them to talk about it with you. They will be waiting when you have showered."

Nicholas threw some water in his face at the sink and brushed his teeth. When he looked into the mirror to inspect his work he was shocked at the reflection he saw. It wasn't Nicholas Bacon in the mirror, but an old man with a very long beard. The features were similar, but he looked to have aged twenty years in just a day.

"Oui, I see it as well, my friend. You are changing. The work is taking a toll on you. But, Papa, you were involved in many miracles last night. We have proof. Hundreds of people were treated and healed. Word of the miracles has spread to Port-au-Prince this morning."

Half an hour later Nicholas felt like a new man. A very old looking new man. He no longer looked like a forty-something engineer. He took on the appearance of a saint in some church triptych you'd find in a village outside of Moscow. The reflection in the mirror was unsettling on one level, yet he found it comforting to assume that mantle. The miracles of the day before weren't quite real to Nicholas, but as the minutes ticked by, he was getting a powerful sense that this was just the beginning.

The children finished eating and the people seeking treatment weren't admitted to the compound yet. The air was dusty and silent, like the streets of a Wild West town before a gunfight. He felt forces much larger than himself swirling around the compound as he headed toward the dining hall. When he entered the room, the cooks rushed into action, and Larry and Eric both jumped up from the table in shock. Nicholas guessed that he changed even more overnight than he observed in the mirror. Andre seemed unperturbed by the changes; a calm smile covered his beautiful face.

The men sat down at the table as juices and coffee were brought out, and a few minutes later, a calorie-laden spread was placed before them. A brief blessing was said before the wholesale destruction of the food began. Within fifteen minutes all that was left on the table was one pathetic slice of toast. Andre snapped that up and munched on it while the others talked.

Appetites satisfied, Nicholas took the lead for the first time. "I'm thankful for all that you've done for me, guys, but I sense that gathering of evil that we talked about the other morning. I feel like I should be apart from all of you before anyone innocent gets hurt. These kids and the missionaries don't deserve to get in the middle of this battle."

Larry started to respond but Doctor Eric interrupted him. "Are you going to abandon the people who've come for healing? If you do that, where would you go?"

Nicholas hadn't thought of it in those terms. "I'm not abandoning them, I'll be back. But there's something coming that will bring death if I'm around all of you. That's clanging in my soul like a burglar alarm. I have a good idea what I'm supposed to do, and I'm sure I should be doing it alone. You'll have to trust me on this."

Larry held up his hand like a schoolboy. Nicholas smiled and pointed at him to speak. "We need to talk about that "something wicked this way comes" feeling, Nicholas. I know what a part of it is. A couple of things happened this morning. The first was a call to our house-mother. It came in on her personal cell phone from your sister."

"How could Jean get that number? Why didn't she call you?"

"Your sister is a very capable person. She had a private detective look up my social media friends, find anyone who lived in Haiti, and then get their phone numbers. Once the detective called the mission house and verified the right people, your sister called her and filled her in on what was happening. It appears that the Department of Justice has issued a warrant for you as a material witness in the bombing of your plane. They found out you were in Haiti and have a team of agents arriving here this afternoon to take you into custody and bring you back to Salt Lake City."

"Why? I don't know anything."

"That's the point. This is all part of the evil working against you. Nothing good ever comes from any government that needs a scapegoat, and it appears that ours is being used to obstruct your work here in Haiti. I don't think the Haitian government will stand in their way, either. Seems that rumors are exploding all over the country about your being here to rescue Restevek children. A dozen calls from local businesses said that they're under pressure to cut us off if we participate in your work."

Nicholas didn't have anything to say. Any effort to destroy him was going to hurt these people. It was just as he felt this morning when he woke up. But instead of physical force and danger, it was the slow starvation of supplies, support for the orphans, and the rest of the mission here.

While Nicholas was contemplating the problems he'd caused, Larry delivered another arrow to his heart. "Do you remember Louis at the

154

airport? The customs guy? Well, he called me. He thought I should know that until this "nonsense" about freeing child slaves passed, he would not be able to release any more of the equipment I brought down, the food container due for release this week, or allow any more missionaries into the country for visits without work visas. Nobody gets a work visa in Haiti, so that pretty much ends our operation here. He also suggested that my airplane leave within seven days or be impounded. But that would be fine, because all Americans here on visitor visas with the organization have to leave within 96 hours."

"Super. I've single handedly brought this mission to an end."

"Depends on how you look at it. I prefer to think that you've completed the first phase of the mission work, and now we're getting to God's work on a massive scale. Nicholas, the miracles yesterday were a blessing to everyone involved. If I died today, I'd be so blissed out that I'd go with no regrets. Last night you said that your true goal was to end human trafficking in Haiti. We will help you in any way. That's such a wonderful goal that all the rest will take care of itself. The Haitian staff can keep this place running if they get food and supplies. They don't need us here; we've always worked toward them doing it themselves. Maybe it's time.

"But freeing all those kids in slavery? I would never be able to do that in a thousand years on my own. You, with your spiritual connection to God, and the miracles you've performed? You, my brother, can make it happen. That's why God sent you here. That's why He spared you on that airplane. Don't waste that gift. What we need, and I'm relying on you to provide the plan, is to tell us what to do and when. Are you up to leading this new way of life through to its birth?"

"I am. I need your guidance, Larry. I don't know Haiti well enough to make all this work smoothly. What would you do if God gave you this gift?"

Larry sat back in his chair and sipped at his coffee. Closing his eyes, he took a deep breath and was very still. "I had a dream last night, Nicholas. In that dream, we drew all the clergy of Haiti into our battle. Without them, you're just a rumor that can be dismissed by the press. They'll turn you into a sideshow freak and a fraud. Once that happens, you'll have a hard time making anything take place without twice the work. In my dream you met with church leaders at the Hospital for Terminally Ill Children. The nuns know everyone on the island. You go there, meet with

155

the Bishop and the top church leaders, and let them see that you're for real. They will back you and put pressure on the government to end child slavery. The benefit of meeting there is that it's very private and we can get you in and out without being seen.

"It's not going to be easy. There is a huge stake in the Restevek business for a lot of wealthy people. People who control the way things happen in this country. You'll be upsetting every family that has a slave. That's about 10 percent of the populace — the top 10 percent for the most part. I don't think that it can be avoided after the rumors started spreading yesterday that you were sent by God to free them, but the slave holders will fight you tooth and nail. That's why we're being pressured about our mission. Satan also has a role in this: he thrives on human misery. What could be more miserable than selling human beings into bondage?"

"What about the people down the hill? Won't they riot if I leave without seeing them?"

"No. We've got food and water to keep them in good shape for a day or two. You go into Port-au-Prince, meet with the clergy, and avoid the federal agents that are on their way here. Just keep it low profile until the church speaks out. That's the key: backing from the church. They're expecting you this afternoon, Nicholas. Andre knows how to get there, and I've got it all set up. Before you go, I want to pray for your success."

The men pushed back their chairs and cleared a spot next to the table. Dropping to their knees, they formed a small circle and joined hands to pray.

For the second time in as many weeks, small tongues of fire appeared over some of the heads bent in prayer in a simple dining hall at an orphanage.

CHAPTER THIRTY-NINE
Titanyen/Port-au-Prince, Haiti
March 20

Twenty minutes later Nicholas and Andre left from a remote gate, far from the crowds out front. They had backpacks full of water and energy bars, and Nicholas' walking stick was strapped across his back. The two rode dirt bikes across the ridge until they met up with boys from the orphanage who were waiting with a tap-tap. The boys rode the bikes back while Andre watched the scenery and Nicholas sat on the floor, out of sight below the windows on the trip to Port-au-Prince.

Once in town, the tap-tap ground deeper into the city until it reached a street crammed with whitewashed buildings. The street itself was paved, free of ruts and potholes, and clean. Trim, small homes with colorful window frames fronted one side of the road, while on the other there was a long, high wall topped with razor ribbon and security lights. The tap-tap pulled up to a gate like the one at the mission houses and honked. A security officer carrying an ancient, but well-maintained, MP5 machine pistol stepped through a small door in the gate and spoke to the driver. He walked around to the back of the vehicle and looked in to inspect the contents, finding Nicholas and Andre curled up under the bench seats, doing their best to hide from view. Neither one fit into the space well. A grin split his face.

"Papa Noel. You are expected. Be blessed, my brother. Rescue them all."

Nicholas turned to Andre, "Super security. Did they put out a broadcast on television, or just radio?"

Andre laughed until tears ran down his dusty face. "You may not realize it, but the vision of you has spread across the island. I heard the children who were Resteveks talking about it at the orphanage. On the roads from the city, we passed thousands of children walking toward Titanyen. Papa, there is no way to hide this sort of thing. Do you sense evil when he spoke to you?"

Nicholas relaxed. "No, he was genuine. I enjoy this, Andre. I don't know if I'll want to give up this work when we finish."

"All you can do is your best, Papa. That is what the children expect. It is what I know you will do for them. And, who said this is a single mission that you will finish. God may have many other things for you to do beyond the coasts and borders of Haiti."

Turning to the gate, the guard signaled an unseen sentinel above him to roll it open and admit them. Once through the gate, the tap-tap turned in a wide circle and headed back toward the gate, stopping in the center of a large courtyard filled with dozens of newer vehicles and a few relics.

Andre surveyed the vehicles. "These are the big ones, Papa. You will find the leaders of many churches here, but most of all, the Catholic royalty. Be yourself. They will know you are real."

Leaving the back of the vehicle they were greeted by a woman in the dull khaki habit of the order that ran the hospital. No taller than five feet, she had a weathered face that told a story of sunshine, wind, and heartbreak.

"I am Sister Genevieve. Welcome to our hospital. We have our people waiting for you in the chapel, and I know they have set forth an agenda. But that can wait until we get to know each other a little bit. Do either of you want a drink? I have both water and juice."

"I'd love some water, Sister. But aren't they waiting for us and anxious to start?"

Her smile was chipped but radiant. "Oui. They wait and while they do they are taking care of other business. Before you meet them, Papa Noel, I have been asked to sit with you a bit. Do you mind?"

Nicholas liked her smile. It burst forth from skin the color of ripe peaches with a leathery but unblemished surface. She could have been forty or seventy, but it didn't matter. Nicholas sensed a kindred soul with a love for children.

"It would be an honor to sit and talk with you, Sister."

"Let us then go to the courtyard. You can see a bit of our operation there and perhaps meet some of the children."

Entering a sun-blasted courtyard filled with white rock and surrounded by white-washed walls, Nicholas was glad he was wearing sunglasses. He felt uncomfortable wearing sandals, shorts and a red shirt. He knew little of Haitian culture, but the reserved formality he encountered with others told him that he was improperly dressed for such an occasion.

158

The three of them took a seat on benches facing out into the courtyard, protected from the sun by a canvas awning. "Sister, I apologize for my attire. I didn't have anything else when this was arranged."

"Papa Noel — or should I call you Nicholas?"

"I'm getting used to Papa Noel if that's okay with you. My mother is the one who called me Nicholas, usually when I'd done something she considered terrible. It's Nick to my friends."

Her brown eyes twinkled as she examined his beard and face. Her eyes lingered on his walking stick for a moment. "I think Nicholas is more appropriate. He was a wonderful saint, and a protector of children. He, too, rescued children from a life of slavery and abuse. Nicholas, do not be ashamed of your simple clothing. We know that you fled the orphanage to come here. We understand how times are in Haiti. We are glad you were able to come."

While they were talking, one of the nurses brought out a small child and handed him to Sister Genevieve. The nurse set a small bowl with chopped up hard-boiled egg and some gruel on the bench next to Sister Genevieve and went back inside the nursery building. The baby was emaciated, close to death from starvation.

"He has refused to grow. We cannot persuade him to eat. All he does is struggle and cry. I am afraid he's not long for this sad and fallen world. I am blessed to be the one who can calm his cries, but even I cannot get him to take nourishment."

The baby was calming a bit in her arms, but still kicking and making noises. "His mother was a drug addict and died a month after his birth. He was brought to us two days ago."

The tiny skeleton of a boy locked his eyes with Nicholas and reached out with stick arms towards him.

"Nicholas, it seems he likes you. Would you like to hold him?"

He had never held a baby this small. Yet there wasn't anything he wanted more to do in that moment.

"Yes. I'd be glad to hold him."

Accepting the bundle from Sister Genevieve, Nicholas shifted him until he was resting in the crook of his arm and settled. Nicholas could feel the child's bones through the blanket: the boy could not have weighed more than six pounds. As he shifted him to make him fit better in his arms, the small boy began to smile and relax. Within a minute he started to gurgle in glee and reach toward Nicholas' beard.

"Is every child in Haiti going to trim my beard, Sister?"

The little child entangled Nicholas' beard in his tiny fingers. With a strength borne of desperation, the child pulled himself closer to Nicholas; he seemed to be trying to look deep into Nicholas' eyes. There was a moment of recognition on the boy's face, and then he settled in to the space he created in the shade of Nicholas's beard, cuddled in close to the big man's chest.

"You have a friend. He likes you and trusts you. Would you like to try and feed him?"

"Uh, sure. I'll try."

Genevieve handed him the bowl, which Nicholas held in his left hand near the boy's head. "What is his name?"

"Espere. It means to hope."

"Good name. Bonjou, Espere. Non mwen se Nicholas."

"You speak Creole? I was not aware of this."

He blushed, his face turning even more red than his shirt. "Andre is a good teacher. I don't even realize that I'm learning when I'm around him. He takes good care of me, Sister."

Nicholas stirred the contents of the bowl, not wanting to know what all it contained. It didn't smell bad, but it evoked images of an old movie he had watched at the rehab center, and the gruel the orphans were fed. Taking a large spoonful he was about to feed it to Espere when Sister Genevieve intercepted his hand with a soft touch.

"He is very weak, Nicholas. Maybe a fifth of that to try. I don't think he could swallow much more than that, even if he wants it."

He knocked the gruel back into the bowl, taking a much smaller amount on the spoon and steering it toward Espere's mouth.

Like a baby bird taking worms from its mother, Espere opened his mouth and accepted the food. Nicholas smiled and continued to feed larger dollops to the boy until a quarter of the bowl was gone. He took a towel from the sister and put it over his shoulder.

"This is how you burp them, isn't it?"

Sister Genevieve said nothing but nodded, a tear running down her face. A couple of gentle pats on his back and Espere let loose with a belch that would do a sailor proud.

"Whoo, you got the mojo, kid. They heard that one in Miami."

Nicholas cradled Espere in the crook of his arm again and continued to feed him until almost half the bowl was gone. He would have gone further, but Espere was sound asleep. "Guess we could call this 'Feed my sleeping children.' He's all yours, Sister."

Genevieve took the child, and in response to some signal he had missed, the nurse who'd brought Espere came and took him back inside.

"Nicholas, come with me for a minute? I want you to meet the rest of the infants."

"Sure. Aren't the Bishop and the others wondering where we are?"

Genevieve laughed. It was a clear, wonderful sound that raised the hair on the back of Nicholas' neck. There was something special in that laugh that spoke of God's direct hand in her creation.

"My friends, they will wait until we are ready. I promise. They spend most of their time with others waiting on them. A bit of humility is a blessing that God does not bestow often enough in my opinion. Nicholas, we are all servants to Jezi, and it is important that we humble ourselves before Him from time to time."

Sister Genevieve stopped at the door of the nursery and asked them to wait outside for a moment, saying that she would return quickly. While they were waiting, Nicholas asked Andre if he knew Sister Genevieve.

"Yes, Papa. She is the Mother Superior of the order. A very holy and powerful woman. Many say she can heal the sick as you do, but perhaps not so much as you."

Genevieve returned to the door, "Come in, my friends. Please meet the children."

Turning inside the doorway, they went through a small hallway and entered a nursery that was straight out a movie about the horrors of orphanages in 1920's America. Inside a fifty-foot by thirty-foot space were rows and rows of iron cribs painted with infinite layers of white paint. Each one had a number on its side, and a child's name and age written in marker on a plastic tag next to the number, when the name was known. Only two cribs were empty, leaving over forty children crammed in that small space. The noise level was unbelievable as they entered the room: crying and wailing screams of despair permeating the stagnant air. Nicholas came through the door behind the other two.

As he entered the room, a hush settled on the space. The nursing staff gave each other puzzled looks; the only sound in the room was the two small bells at the top of Nicholas's walking staff. One by one, older children stood and reached out with arms barely larger than the spindles on the sides of their cribs. Not sure what to do, he walked down the rows, placing his hand on the head of each child and saying a small blessing. All anyone heard was the shuffling noise of his sandals on the linoleum and the gentle "ting" of the two bells each time he set his stick down. When he finished making rounds of the room, all the children were sitting up in their cribs, even the children too weak to roll over on their own just minutes before.

Gentle spasms of fresh air flowed in through the shuttered windows; cool as a night's breeze. Smiles graced the faces of starving children. For the first time since the building was occupied many decades before, joy had a place in this room where children were sent to die. With confusion visible on the staffs' faces, Nicholas turned to look at the bowls of gruel placed on carts, waiting for the meal to be served.

Taking a bowl from the tray, Nicholas closed his eyes and said a blessing over the carts of food.

"Father, these children need you more than I ever have. Please bless them all, let them thrive, and have good lives. I ask that you grant me the strength that you deem fit to carry out your work."

In a silence underlaid with the beautiful soft cooing of happy children, Nicholas fed each child a few morsels of food before handing the bowl off to one of the nurses. Over the next few minutes, word spread throughout the wing, bringing nuns and nurses to help with the feeding. Nicholas stood at the doorway, tears of joy running down his dirty face, leaving little drops of love mud on his red shirt. He was whole for the first time in his life.

"I think, Nicholas of Haiti that we should meet with the Bishop now."

CHAPTER FORTY
Port-au-Prince, Haiti
March 20

Violene was lucky: the man who saw her jump into the bushes was a farmer headed home from a market in Petionville, not her owner. Pulling off the road, he grabbed couple of cookies from a bag on the seat next to him and shut off the engine. Getting out of the truck, he shuffled to where she was hiding.

"I won't hurt you. But you look like you've run away from your owners. You need food. I am sorry I am out of water, but I do have these sweets to share. I will set them on this rock. If you want a ride, come to my truck and I will give you one. If you do not, you can stay where you are, and the cookies are yours. I will wait two minutes for you before I drive home."

Violene thought he was ancient. He looked like her grandmother's age: at least fifty if not older. He was wrinkled like a fig from years in the field with a hoe welded to his calloused palms. His hands looked like spiders, a central body and bony fingers splayed in a crooked array with arthritis and abuse. Those spider legs scratched at his whitened eyebrow before they moved to his lips. The tremble was slight but very common in old men and women who suffered malnutrition as children.

What to do? If she stayed in the bush, he might leave and then she could continue to walk toward Papa Noel. If he did not leave, someone would find her before she reached her destination. She didn't know if she could trust him. Her options, however, were limited. She stole some cash from her owner's dresser the night before when he brought her to his bed. He was drunk, and cruel, but he passed out before he could finish what he'd brought her to the room to experience.

She shuddered, crossed herself and thanked Jezi that her owner had a drinking problem. If not for that small mercy, the slaps in the face would have been followed by something much worse. She touched the corner of her mouth without conscious thought. It was still sticky with crusted blood.

Violene stepped out of the bushes, knowing that her owner would notice the money was gone and begin looking for her in earnest. It was just a small amount but nonetheless could earn her an hour with the rigwaz. Her back hadn't healed from the last time.

"Where are you going? "

His voice was kind. Soft. He didn't move well due to his age; she could outrun him if she had to do so.

"I am heading toward…" She didn't know the name of the place, so she pointed where she thought she was supposed to be heading. It felt right, her hand swung to that point like a compass needle to magnetic north.

Following her arm with his eyes, he smiled. Three cracked and weathered teeth on the bottom, four on the top. None of them had seen a dentist since God formed them in his skull, but they gave a wonderful smile despite the surface that looked like a tea-stained buffing rag, complete with fuzz.

"You are joining the children's crusade toward Titanyen. I should have known. I wonder why God has chosen Titanyen?"

Violene didn't know where she was heading; just that Papa Noel was at the end of her journey. She had no more control over her motion along the roadway than a salmon heading up the Columbia River. Nature, God, magnetic fields, providence, random choice — all were explanations, all were irrelevant. She just knew this is where she was to be, and whatever was supposed to happen, would happen soon.

"I had a dream. Jezi told me to go there to see Papa Noel. You would not understand."

The old man levered himself up into the truck with a grunt. It wasn't very high off the ground. Violene felt better about getting in now; he wouldn't have the strength to hold her if she needed to get out. He was very old indeed.

Lighting the stump of a cigarette sitting on the dashboard; the old man drew the smoke deep in his lungs.

"You are a Restevek. I was too as a child. I also dreamt of Papa Noel last night. I think all of us who have suffered dream of him."

Jamming the gear shift into low, the old man let out the loose clutch as though it were going to bite him, until the truck jolted from its lethargy and started to rock along. Shifting into high gear, it was still a plodding farm truck with manure on the undercarriage.

164

"I can take you much of the way, but I go East at the junction and you want to go West. Will that help?"

Violene met his gaze. "Yes, Granpapa. That would be wonderful. Thank you for taking me."

"Have another sweet, young lady. You have a long walk ahead. We will stop for water. I wish this happened when I was a boy. You are safe with me. If we are stopped, you are my granddaughter. What is your name?"

"Violene, Granpapa."

"Indeed. So that is the name of the granddaughter I should have had in my life. Enchante, my granddaughter. Now, shall we talk of God? For it is He who brings Papa Noel."

Violene adjusted her back so that her stripes would not rub against the rough material and springs behind the truck's thin padding.

"I do not know enough about God, Granpapa. But I want to know more. Can you tell me?"

Flicking the small nub of the cigarette out the window, he began to speak of his youth as a Restevek, and how he came to know God. It was a long drive, the traffic thickening with every meter as they came down the mountainside.

The reason became clear when they came out of a tunnel of trees on a winding stretch of road and hit a straightaway where the scene ahead was fully visible. The road entered the outskirts of Port-au-Prince's most populated areas, and now it was a tidal surge of children as far as the eye could see. Everyone was headed toward Titanyen.

It was a sea of human misery fleeing bondage and seeking a new life.

The tiny chapel at the hospital was packed. A table was set in the middle of the room with six chairs. Nicholas came in with Sister Genevieve holding his arm and pulled up short when he saw so many people standing in a semi-circle waiting to greet him.

"Please wait just a moment here by the door, Nicholas of Haiti. I must speak with the Bishop in private."

The small woman approached the Bishop and bowed, taking his hand to her lips, kissing his ring. He pulled her up straight and embraced her like a long-lost sister. The two walked to the far side of the room and put their heads close together in conference. The other attendees stared politely at Nicholas and Andre as they waited. There were smiles, but each face was laden with questions and curiosity.

Satisfied with Sister Genevieve's words, the Bishop gave her another hug and walked back to the front of the group. He crumpled in slow motion, as dignified as his frame and age allowed, falling first to his knees, then prostrating himself on the floor in front of Nicholas, the others falling to their faces as well. Sister Genevieve remained standing.

"I, too, would do the same, Nicholas of Haiti, but at my age I am afraid I would never get up again. The Bishop has asked me to present his compliments and ask for your blessing on this group before we begin."

Nicholas stuttered, "Sister Genevieve, it is my honor. Please, all of you, be blessed and get up. I want to see your faces. I came here for your help, not your obeisance."

One by one, the men on the floor got up and approached Nicholas, introducing themselves and explaining where their churches were, or what office they held in the Catholic Church. The smiles on their faces were immense. Joy was palpable in the room. Each took a turn. When Nicholas was finished with the handshaking, the Bishop pointed to the table and asked Nicholas to join him for something to drink. There was an assortment of bottles and a carafe of coffee on the table. Nicholas stood next to the table until it became clear that he was to take his seat first.

Once they were seated, the others grabbed folding chairs from along the walls and formed a ring of concentric circles around the five senior figures at the table. Nicholas had brought Sister Genevieve with him to the table and she sat at his right hand.

The Bishop spoke first, in a voice that all could hear in the room. "Nicholas of Haiti, we are honored to have you join us today. God has blessed this nation with your arrival. We know very little about you, but word of your miracles, and the visions of your work, have spread across the country in the last twenty-four hours. Normally, we would spend a great deal of time vetting your claims, but the Holy Father in Rome has asked us to meet with you. It seems that visions of you, and your promise to free the slaves of Haiti, have spread to all nations. There is great chaos churning in much of the world as a result. We are but the tip of an iceberg here in Haiti, if such a thing could occur in this climate. The Holy Father wants to find out more."

Nicholas still thought of himself as a baby Christian without the sense to come in out of the rain. These men, and the Pope as well, were interested in him? He'd never led anything in his life, much less a worldwide campaign against human trafficking.

"I am honoured. I'll follow your advice and see what I can do to help. But I'm not somebody you need to bow to, or honor for that matter. I am at your service, not the other way around."

The Bishop lost his smile. The mood changed in the room.

"Like many before, you have been called to service. We heard of the miracles from many sources, but now the beloved Mother Superior has validated your gift. I felt His presence when you walked into this room. Nicholas, all of us, have been powerless without you. God has spoken to you and given you visions. He has inspired thousands of slave children to assemble in Titanyen; they are waiting for you outside the walls already, with many more clogging the roads to greet you. Follow those visions, act as you see fit, and keep in prayer. That is all any man can do for God."

"Bishop, I'm afraid that people will worship me. I don't want to become God; I worry about what I'm doing, afraid that I will bring great harm to innocents through my ignorance. I feel a strong calling to do this but have no clear path. I just don't know where to go next."

The Bishop relaxed in his chair. "Have no worries, we do not think you are God. There is but one God and we all serve Him. What we see is a

167

man who has been unexpectedly and abundantly blessed. You are a man whose presence strikes fear in the heart of demons and casts them out. You are a man who holds the destiny of innocents in his hands. Nicholas, we will pray for you and keep you grounded. Like Moses, we will lift your arms above your head when you tire. Just like Moses, however, we need you at the vanguard of this task."

The Bishop bowed his head and prayed with the others for what seemed a long time. Nicholas' eyes drifted away from the table and saw a familiar sight: Cite Soleil. In his vision, he was leading the clerics through the streets, marching toward the oceanfront. When the prayer ended, he knew what to do, and when he was supposed to do it.

"Bishop, I know what we're supposed to do next. Here's my plan..."

CHAPTER FORTY-TWO
Port-au-Prince, Haiti
March 20

A dozen tap-taps pulled into Cite Soleil at sunset. Each one held a mixed batch of clergy from the churches of Haiti. If Nicholas took time to look, he would have seen many shadows in the crowd. Some of this group was loyal to the other side.

Like the last time he visited Cite Soleil, Nicholas saw boiling thunderstorms roll over the area. This time, he wasn't alone in being able to see them; most of the people with him pointed at the sky and shouted. The clouds shared explosive lightening, and if you turned your head just right, you could make out angels and demons hurling those bolts at each other, with the bigger flashes coming as they grappled hand to hand. Battle was taking place in the skies above as Nicholas and his crew prepared to exit the tap-taps.

Sister Genevieve took his hand in hers, "Nicholas, be very strong. God is your strength, but Satan is strong in this place. People will find their destiny this night among us, and some will not leave with us. Pray, my friend. Pray as you never have before."

Nicholas bowed his head in prayer and reached out to God. He felt that strength flow through him, and it made his skin taut with spiritual muscle. When the tap-tap came to a stop, deep in the slum, Nicholas was the first one on his feet.

"God is with us tonight. The New Testament said that Jesus gave all of us the power to heal and to cast out demons. Follow in the footsteps of Christ this night and let's free the people of this city."

The vehicles parked, facing deeper in toward the neighborhood. Tonight, they were not preparing for a retreat to safety. This was an assault on the fortress of darkness that held the people of Cite Soleil in bondage. There would be no warning horns, no running from trouble. Tonight, might not have been the end of evil in Cite Soleil, but it was the beginning of the end or certainly the end of the beginning of wiping out human slavery in that benighted area.

Linking arms in a wedge, Nicholas at the tip of the formation, the group marched through the streets and headed toward the oceanfront. Along the way, thousands of children joined to march along behind them, as well as some adults. Every block or two, a group of demons appeared in windows or on rooftops, throwing garbage and rocks toward the group. Each time the demons retreated as a wall of shouted prayer and Nicholas' eerie booming voice shattered their resolve. This continued until they were just a hundred yards from the ocean, in the poorest part of the slum. Ahead, a barricade of trash and broken furniture was constructed. Behind the barricade demons the size of NFL linemen stood like statues on Easter Island. They were waiting for the approach of the clerics. A pack of snarling dogs ringed the intersection, protecting the demons with their snapping jaws and aggressive lunges.

To an outside observer, all of this looked like a group of priests and nuns walking down the darkening streets, shouting at the gangs that were defending their turf. Not many locals looked upon the scene and saw its spiritual component. A select few blessed with second sight were privy to the enormity of the conflict taking place on those trash-strewn streets between the open sewers.

Nicholas sensed a change in the demons facing his group.

"Bishop, what's going on with that bunch at the end of the block? They're different."

"I've never dealt face to face with demons before, Nicholas. I'm guessing that what we're seeing is related to the rankings of angels and demons. You are young in the church, so you do not know. There are warrior angels that God has given strong powers, and so there must also be demons that match them in strength. I suspect these are the demonic equivalents of Gabriel, Michael, and the like. They will not retreat as quickly as the others you met in Cite Soleil have done. They have come to test our mettle. Watch out, for they will focus on you, probing for weak points and attacking you with lies that hurt the most. Listen for God; He will be speaking as well, deep in your heart. His is the voice you must give credence to at all times."

Nicholas pulled apart from the others and advanced alone toward the demons behind their barricade. He maintained eye contact and ignored their jeers and the occasional piece of rotten food or excrement hurled his way from the back of their pack. The dogs spread wide to avoid Nicholas and then scurried to join the demons behind the barricade.

Standing in front of them, an arm's length away from the one who appeared to be in charge, Nicholas thumped his staff on the ground. In a flash of brilliant light, the staff once again took on the form of a serpent with a copper head, just as on his first visit to Cite Soleil.

"I'm here to evict you from this city. It no longer belongs to you, it belongs to God Almighty. Leave now and go back to Hell where you belong."

The lead demon chortled.

"Nicholas, you are an imbecile. Don't you know that Hell is not the home of our kind? We come from Heaven as well, and one day we will be taking it back. For now, we are comfortable in this city. We like the weather and the food. You do not belong here, you miserable cur. Why don't you go back to your sad, pathetic, and loveless life in your empty house? Oh, that's right — you have nothing since that shack burned down. I'm told the fire was bright with all of your things burning at the same time. You don't even have that to retreat to in your misery. So sad."

The choir of demons behind the leader laughed and made sad faces while pointing at Nicholas.

"I can get another house. I can buy more clothing. But you will not be able to do the same, because I'm casting you out in the name of the Nazarene. Be gone!"

The lead demon howled in agony and began to shrivel as though melting. In an instant he doubled in size and his fury was exquisite.

"You know nothing of God, nor of us. Do you really think that mentioning a name would make us flee? All you know is what you learned watching movies. Try again. Every time you fail, we grow stronger. Every time we grow stronger, your retinue shrinks. Look behind you if you don't believe me."

Nicholas looked over his shoulder. The ranks had thinned quite a bit in just the last few minutes. The Bishop and Sister Genevieve were still in the front row along with Andre and several others. But some faces were missing.

The demon grabbed his attention with a snapping of his fingers. "How's your sister? I heard she had a bad accident this evening. You probably will get a call from the hospital in a few hours when they're done amputating her legs. Crushed, you know? That's a tough break. Maybe you should go and take care of her instead of wasting your time here, in a place where you can never win, no matter what simple parlor tricks you bring to amaze us."

Nicholas was heartsick at the thought of Jean being injured. But he'd been warned that the demons lie about that which he most loved. It was now time to break out the heavy artillery and put an end to this confrontation.

"What is your name?"

"You don't need my name. That's another of your movie myths. Call me Dennis if you like."

The demon was ducking Nicholas' question. He must be on the right track.

"I'll call you out is what I'll do. I believe that God will channel His power through me and deal with you. We're all ambassadors of Christ according to the Bible. I'm presenting my diplomatic carnet right now. I command you, in the name of Jesus Christ, our Saviour, to take your abominations with you and leave this place. Leave Haiti and release these children and this neighborhood from your bondage. You cannot argue, you cannot win, God will triumph. Again, be gone minion of Satan."

The mystical voice that accompanied the empowered Nicholas was once again in full throat. Buildings near Nicholas shook, and tin walls bent. The demons recoiled at the force of his prayer. The lead demon diminished to his original size, just a bit larger than Nicholas.

"You will never win this battle. We are strong across the world. The trade in humans has been going on since time immemorial. You may gain ground here, but you will find it grows stronger in some place like Arabia. We are not leaving. Not now, not ever.

"You are alone, Nicholas. Your sister is dying; you have no wife, no parents, no offspring. No human loves you and even your God sends you out as a sacrifice to be given so that He can gain a few more followers. We will gain even more when our might is revealed."

Nicholas began to respond when he felt a gentle hand on his back.

"Papa Noel, he is wrong, you are much beloved. Hundreds of thousands in Haiti are calling on you to help them. They believe in your gift. I believe in you. Do not listen to this demon, he is cruel and weak. You will triumph over his kind if you stay strong."

The demon was eyeing Andre as though taking his measure. "You are not human. Are you Nephilim?"

Andre grew three feet in an instant, and huge wings sprouted from his back as Papa Noel looked on in wonder. Brandishing a flaming sword and a shield that sparked in brilliant tones of orange, Andre cut down the demon with a single stroke.

"Now, Nicholas of Haiti. Cast them out!"

Nicholas turned his face toward Heaven. "Father God, I beseech You to cast these demons into the ocean and drown them like the herd of swine in whom Jesus allowed demons to lodge. Hurl them far out to sea, where none may survive."

In an instant, every single demon fled the body of the man they possessed and transformed into a new pack of dogs. Snarling and rending each other's flesh, they ran into a crashing surf and vanished under the waves.

Silence settled upon the square. The waves vanished and the quiet harbor returned. Nothing in sight moved for almost twenty seconds.

A ragged cheer went up from the crowd behind him.

Nicholas turned to Andre and said, "I'm exhausted, Andre. Help me back home."

Andre put his arm under Nicholas' knees and hoisted the exhausted man in his arms as though he were a toddler. The bishop grabbed his staff from the ground and followed as they moved back to the tap-taps.

"It is not over, Andre. We're not safe anywhere. I've seen it in a vision."

"Non, Papa Noel. You are safe for now. God protects us all in this moment."

Like one of the small children he was sent to protect, Nicholas fell asleep in the arms of his guardian angel as he was carried out of Cite Soleil, and on to his destiny.

173

CHAPTER FORTY-THREE
Near Titanyen, Haiti
March 20

Violene started walking toward Titanyen after the truck driver dropped her off at the crossroads and vanished toward the East. He had stopped along the way to buy her a large bottle of water, and when she got out, he gave her the rest of the cookies.

Still, it was a long day of intense fear, anxiety, and uncertainty after escaping from her owner. She was nearing the end of her rope.

She had walked less than five-hundred meters when she saw a group of children huddled under a shelter, they had made by stringing a bed sheet between some gnarled cacti on a hillside. Wanting nothing more than to get out of the sun and sleep, Violene climbed the loose dirt and took a closer look. The girls ranged in age from eight to fifteen, all were in the same state of dishevelment and despair that she was on this hot afternoon. Given their shabby clothing, all of them were Resteveks like Violene.

"Bonjou. May I sit with you?"

"Do you have anything to eat?"

"Oui. I have cookies. And water. I will share if you are hungry."

"No, we have plenty; we were concerned that you had nothing. Come and share with us."

Moving under the shade, Violene got a good look at their faces. They looked like typical Haitian Resteveks. Tattered clothing, weary eyes, and an aura of fear about them. Like most children in her situation, Violene was wary, and thought she had a good eye for who might want to hurt her or steal from her. This group seemed okay. On the plus side, they did have food. More substantial food than a few cookies. And, they shared. After a bowl of corn mush and rice, Violene filled her stomach for the first time in a day. She finished her bottle of water and put her head down on the empty container after wrapping it round with a plastic bag that had snagged in the cactus. Her light snores amused the other girls.

She slept in peace as the sun worked its way across the sky, and toward the ocean in the west.

***

The sun was low in the sky when the six of them set out for the orphanage. Violene was refreshed from the food and her nap. The others seemed in good spirits as well. They walked close together, one always in physical contact with her as they traveled down the road. For whatever reason, the older girls took her under their wings, and made sure that she was safe. None of them could ever explain it, but it was a feeling they all shared. What was not visible to anyone was that angels formed a screen around Violene to shield her from any demons that were sent to take her from her appointed destiny. They herded the girls in close to provide a travelling screen around Violene.

Turning a bend in the road, it became obvious that traffic wasn't going any further: thousands of people blocked the road ahead.

The lead angel hovered in front of Violene and whispered requests to the men and women in front of her to move from her path. Unaware of what was happening, they shifted 18 inches to the left or right, opening a small gap where the group of girls could press through. The children seemed to move of their own accord, as though they were sensitive to the presence of angels and knew that they must be allowed to pass.

Four hours of foot-sore trudging brought them to the dirt road that led up to Mercy Orphanage a kilometre distant. There were still tens of thousands of people between the girls and the gates. Violene was glad when the other girls said that they were going to stop and eat something and lay down for a while. The moon overhead provided a beacon to travel by not that different from a star two thousand years ago. This time, instead of beckoning wise men to the presence of their Saviour, it brought tormented children to the temporary residence of their greatest champion on the planet.

Violene heard people saying that Papa Noel was ahead in the compound, and that when the sun came up, she might even see him in person. She was exhausted but wanted to move closer. She was debating getting up and moving toward the front of the queue when sleep grabbed her in its narcotic embrace, pulling her down to dream. The leader of the angels hovering over the crowd relayed a message to the others:

"She will sleep the night. Cover her; there is a great threat here tonight. Once daylight comes it will be safer, but for now, we must make sure that she rests and moves closer to the gate as the day goes by. She must be ready to move through the gate at nightfall tomorrow. Until then, she must remain hidden in our midst."

The angels unfurled their wings and covered Violene with a blanket of protection and concealment as demons moved within the crowd, seeking victims. Most of all, they sought Violene whom they'd been told to kill. Her death would stop this movement in its tracks, according to the one who commanded the legion of Satan's followers in Haiti.

They intended to carry out their orders. Both sides.

CHAPTER FORTY-FOUR
Port-au-Prince, Haiti
March 21

It was after midnight when they finished tending to the cuts and bruises from the battle with the demons in Cite Soleil. The chapel in the hospital was used as a makeshift emergency ward so that they would not disturb the sleeping children in the hospital proper.

The Bishop sat in silence at the table, drafting a message to the Vatican while the others drank water and got stitches. Nicholas slept with his head in Andre's lap in a quiet alcove of the church. After an hour, Nicholas awoke with a jerk and looked around in panic.

"Andre, where are we?"

"We are at the hospital for dying children, Papa Noel. It is safe. You cast the demons out of Cite Soleil, and we are safe for the moment."

"I did, didn't I? I couldn't have done it without you, Andre. You are an angel, aren't you? Can I know your name?"

"My name is indeed Andre. Not all of us have fancy names like Gabriel and Michael. I am one of many who are soldiers in the army of angels. I have been your guardian all of your life, Papa Noel. I have taken on many physical aspects over the years, but it was always me to protect you in vulnerable moments. Tonight, I revealed myself to you, because the demon was about to disfigure you. I could not allow that to happen. I did not allow the others to see what happened, and I revealed it to you because you have special reasons for knowing who I am. I do not believe the Bishop or Sister Genevieve know, and they are alone in being as vibrant as your soul."

"You've been guiding me all this time, haven't you, Andre? Is there a reason you didn't tell me who you were when all the trouble started happening? Hey, were you there to pull me out of the airplane? I mean, you've been in Haiti for years now…"

The bright teeth glowed for an instant in the dark corner of the church. "Oui. I was told to guide you to your destiny. I never changed anything; I merely provided the opportunities you needed to recognize your place in the Kingdom of Heaven. It is not many who become Saints in their own age, Papa. Just a handful throughout history. You are doing better than most I have seen. And I have seen a few in my existence.

"The airplane? God Himself set that up. You were not flown to the earth or any such thing. It was all physics and powdered snow. He is very clever like that: many miracles have been dismissed as random. I think it is His sense of humor. He makes us laugh quite often. I am always with you, just like Jezi. I can be in Haiti and at your side – the laws of physics do not apply to angels as they do to humans. I have several I look over all the time. You see my body around, but my spirit can be many places."

"Why me, Andre? Why as Papa Noel?"

"That, Papa Noel, is known to you and God. I am sure if you think about it for a time you will realize the reason. I do not know with certainty, but I have my suspicions. He gives me direction, but rarely explains things in the way you understand it. But it seems to me that Papa Noel fits for a very human reason, one that I picked up on the day you stepped off Larry's plane."

"Okay, don't keep me hanging in suspense. I've thought about this for days and have no answer except that it's an extended fat joke at my expense."

Andre started out chuckling, and then burst into full-throated laughter. His nose ran and tears formed in his eyes as he laughed ever harder. Even in the darkness, those tears glistened like mercury caught in a laser beam.

"Papa, who is the most trusted man on the planet? Is it not Papa Noel? People tell their children not to fear him; they pose for pictures with him, leave food for him in their locked houses, and sing songs about him. He is always kind and generous, and Nicholas of Myra rescued little girls from enslavement. Does not every child in this nation at least know of Papa Noel? They may not know Jezi, but they know Papa Noel. In Haiti, he holds a special place. Christopher Columbus landed in Haiti on Saint Nicholas day. The place Columbus landed on December sixth is named Mole Saint-Nicolas, and it was the beginning of the European presence in this land. In spite of the history of white men and this land, Saint Nicholas is revered. Every single child trusts you to do the right thing for him or her. They don't even have to write letters: they just know in their hearts that you will save them from a life of misery."

"What do we do next, Andre? I know we cast the demons from Cite Soleil and freed the slaves there, but there are slaves all over this country. All over the world when you think about it."

Andre pointed toward the interior of the chapel.

"I suggest you coordinate with the others in there, Papa. I am done guiding you; my mission is strictly to protect you for now. The demons know me after tonight, so I will be less effective than before. You have good people to count on in what remains of this group, and they will help you find the path you seek. I am sure of that much."

Andre helped him to his feet and handed him his staff.

"This thing rocks, Andre. Did it have these powers when my sister gave it to me?"

"The walking staff has no power by itself, Papa. You command it on behalf of the Living God. By itself, it is just a piece of wood with a bear and bells on top."

The Bishop looked up as he heard the tinkle of bells heralding Nicholas of Haiti's approach. Jumping to his feet he said, "Are you well, my brother? You were quite exhausted after fighting with those demons. I read that passage many times in the Gospel of Mark, and never expected that I would see it re-enacted in my life. That is one of many miracles today. Please sit and join me."

Nicholas lowered himself into one of the chairs. This was a soft leather cushioned chair with ornate wood, not a folding chair. Nicholas gave a quizzical look and the Bishop explained:

"I brought some things from my office. I thought we might be here quite some time."

A phone trilled nearby. A moment later a man said, "It's for you, your Excellency."

Taking the phone, the Bishop spoke to someone in English and looked at Andre and Nicholas every few minutes. Ending the call with profuse thanks, he hit the power button and handed the phone back to his assistant.

"That was your house-mother at the mission. You cannot go to the mission house tonight as you planned. There is an American federal agent named Gabler along with the Haitian police in the courtyard. My people also tell me that the Tonton Macoute are offering a large reward for your capture. You have brought out the worst of our people, Nicholas. Satan has many allies in his pursuit of you."

"Great. Schimmler is the one I expected all along, but my sister killed him. Gabler was his partner and he's been after me for months. If he gets me, Bishop, I'll vanish from sight and pop up again after I'm past retirement age. Who are the Tonton Macoute?"

"They are the henchmen of Papa Doc Duvalier, a former dictator. They must be old, or they have recruited new members. They are the ones who tortured and murdered his opponents. Very bad people.

"The media has descended as well. How could they get a television crew here so quickly is beyond me; they even brought a truck on a cargo jet. I am told that your biggest news network has pictures of a burning Cite Soleil running nonstop, and they are blaming you, and me, for leading a group of vigilantes through the slum to exterminate drug dealers. It seems that Breitbart was right: Satan controls the American media."

The Bishop waited a double beat before laughing at his own joke. "I went to Loyola. Never cared much for the type that took up a microphone in your country."

Nicholas applied all his mental assets in his exhausted state to get the humor in the Bishop's words.

"Cite Soleil is burning?"

"Yes. It was the final wound inflicted by some of the demons. It is coming under control, but we are all being sought for questioning. We are not safe here, and I do not wish to endanger the children if the government sends soldiers to arrest us. Or, even worse, the United Nations troops. They don't care what happens to any of us in Haiti. History bears witness to that fact."

Nicholas looked at Andre and said, "We can't use our tap-tap, it's too well known. Can we borrow someone's car to leave? It's me that they want: I'm the one upsetting the apple cart for the slave holders. If we have something inconspicuous, we can get out of town and hide at the orphanage. That's a secure place. They'd have a hard time taking us from that hilltop without a full assault. I don't think they'll want to do that with the press around. I'm guessing that at daybreak there'll be reporters staking it out just like the mission house."

"They are already there, live reports and all. How will you get past them? Not to mention the roadblocks throughout the city?"

180

Nicholas pointed at one of the monks standing along the wall. "He's my size. If you will allow it, Bishop, I will wear his cloak. I can shave my beard as well."

"Do not shave, Nicholas. I think there is something of Samson in the Old Testament with your beard, or God would not have grown it so luxuriously. Wear the robe; beware to tuck your beard inside of it. That will get you past the roadblocks. But it is a long drive and the roads will be blocked near the orphanage."

Andre leaned in and spoke in a low pitch so that nobody beyond the table could hear him. "I know a road through the hills. It will take half of the night, and we will be far from help, but it is beyond the orphanage and unwatched as it is so remote. We will park below the hill and walk the last miles. It will be a simple monk and a man walking along a dusty road. God will protect us until we can make it to safety."

The Bishop stood up and beckoned a monk to the table. "I hope, Papa Noel, that you don't mind giving up your shorts to Brother Ignatius. I'm guessing that he's blessed with nothing but underwear under his robe. It is far too hot to wear pants. Modesty must be preserved."

Nicholas headed for the alcove with the monk. He stopped halfway and said, "If that's our biggest problem tonight, Bishop, we are in the clear."

CHAPTER FORTY-FIVE
North of Titanyen, Haiti
March 21

"Next time you borrow a car, Papa Noel, could we ask to inspect it first?"

The darkened road rang out with Nicholas' laughter. He was so exhausted that he had passed giddy and moved on to punch drunk.

"Sure, Andre. I'll make sure we get at least a Monsignor's car the next time, they get paid better. Bound to have better wheels. You're the warrior Angel; can't you just pop those wings out and carry me to the orphanage?"

"Union rules, Papa Noel. It is not permitted. Before, when I protected you it was required because the demon was liable to hurt you with his surprise attack. I would be interfering with your hero's journey if I flew us to our destination. God has reasons for the hardships we face on our trip."

"Hero's journey? Andre, you sound like my college English professor. I'm an engineer. I look for logical, easy solutions — never mind. I've got the powers of Moses, the face of Nicholas of Myra, and the blistered feet of a Bataan Death March survivor. There's not much logic involved in any of this, is there?"

"It is logical for God to select one such as you, Papa. You are far from perfect in your faith, yet you are risking your life to save others. You are tired, hungry, thirsty, and dirty yet you continue to walk toward your destiny. You do not know what that destiny is, yet you willingly move toward what is likely to be your personal cross. That, Nicholas of Haiti, is why God selected you. You are everyman, yet you are in His image. It has been a great joy for me to see you transform here in Haiti. You have gone from a man who denied his own gifts to one who is open to God's power and mystery. You are obedient even at the expense of your own well-being"

"Andre, I'm humbled by your praise. I'm also astonished by your smart guy comments. I didn't know angels went in for snappy repartee."

"We do many things, Papa Noel. Including a bit of burglary."

Nicholas stopped in his tracks. "You're a burglar?"

Andre's smile shone in the darkness. "Not yet. It won't be a true burglary. I have money, but at this hour, I do not wish to awaken the storeowner and draw attention to us on this remote road. We do, however, need something for you to eat and drink. I will arrange for the door of this shop to open and we will leave a generous amount for what we take. Not quite burglary, but I ask that you remain quiet while I get us lunch."

Andre walked up to the small structure next to the roadway and turned the knob as though it would be unlocked even at night. It opened with a well-oiled swishing noise, and Andre went inside. Nicholas stood in the undergrowth across the roadway, the full moon throwing shadows as long as the night itself across the dirt road. Andre came out with a pair of plastic bags, two children's string backpacks and a handful of licorice whips.

Moving a hundred yards down the road, he plopped down under a tree and bade Nicholas to do the same. Handing him a backpack, Andre divided the food and soda equally between the bags at first, and then took back most of the bottles of orange soda for his own pack.

"Uh, Andre, I really am thirsty and I prefer the orange stuff over the colas if you don't mind sharing."

"I merely thought I should carry the bulk of the weight, Papa. You are welcome to carry more if you wish…"

He smiled back, caught out at being suspicious when dealing with an angel. "Sorry, Andre. That was stupid of me. By the way, how much did you leave for all of this stuff?"

"Three hundred dollars. It was all I had."

Nicholas gagged on the cookie he was cramming into his mouth. He took a sip of soda and washed it down before he spoke: "That's about twenty times what this is worth, Andre. You didn't have to do that. I'll reimburse you when we get back to the mission house."

"You do not understand, my brother. I do not need money beyond this adventure. You will not need me much longer; and the demons will have already spread the news of my presence here in Haiti, making it unlikely that they will attack you directly. We did not drive all of them out of the city and into the sea, and others saw me while watching from the shadows. All did not reveal themselves. A few of them were in our midst, behind us in the parade through Cite Soleil. My effectiveness as your guardian angel is at an end. I will soon be with someone else for my next duties."

Nicholas struggled to his feet and slung the backpack across his shoulders. Hoisting his soda for a long drink, he drained the bottle and started to throw it to the side of the road. Just what Haiti needed — more trash. Instead, he slipped the empty bottle into Andre's pack after crushing the air out of it.

"How am I going to get along without my guardian angel?"

"You will be fine if you trust in God. You are no longer naïve about what you face in this battle. Your staff is formidable, and you will find others who will take care of you. I have been with you for this season, until this time, because you were not ready to take care of your own soul. Since you flew out of that plane, you have changed."

Nicholas thumped down the road, and the gentle tinkling of the bells on his staff warned off night animals. It also, however, alerted more malicious beings of his presence. Stopping for a moment, he started to place one of the empty grocery bags over the bells.

"Do not do that, Papa. Jezi said do not hide your light under a basket. This is your light. We do not need to shout, but we do need to boldly walk in opposition."

"You've got a nice turn of phrase, Andre. I've got another question: you said you'd be done as my guardian very soon. What is going to happen?"

Andre walked for a full mile before he spoke. "We will face a great test, Nicholas of Haiti. You must pray tonight, while we walk. With the light of day, you will be facing the opposition I spoke of, and it will require your heart and your mind to be fully engaged. Do you remember your Bible from our studies?"

"Most of it. Themes and intent. Why?"

Andre smiled in the growing light. "There are some things that should stick. One is Ephesians, 6:11. Do you remember that one?"

"Nope. Not by number. But since I'm about all-in, how about you tell me? I'm guessing you met the guy who wrote it along the way."

Andre chuckled. "Oui, Papa, I have met him. The passage tells us to put on the full armour of God to deal with the demons around us. But in addition to the armour, you must trust in God's strength and turn the burden over to Him. Papa Noel, you must be as brave as the three boys when they were thrown into the ovens in Babylon when your time comes."

Nicholas kept putting one foot in front of the other, unsure of his bravery but willing to put his faith in God. Not knowing what armour was at hand, he resolved to buckle on any that he could find. Andre sure picked some strange metaphors to instil courage, but Nicholas knew that he'd make it with God on his side.

CHAPTER FORTY-SIX
Titanyen, Haiti
March 21

Nicholas was exhausted when the sun edged over the mountains and started to put a glow in the morning sky. He and Andre had walked for hours, and the sandals that were so comfortable when he was sitting on the couch in the mission house left raw meat on his blistered feet.

"Is it cheating, Andre, for me to heal my own wounds? My feet are in grim shape."

"You notice them because you can see them. Until the sun came up, they didn't matter to you. The same sun is showing you something better: our destination.

On the horizon sat the ridgeline above the clinic and the orphanage. On the other side of that ridge, they would find rest, food, water, and a chance for his feet to heal.

"How far do you think it is? I'd guess about two kilometres."

"You are close: it is 1.7 kilometres from here."

The fact that angels came with a built in GPS didn't surprise Nicholas. Nothing was all that surprising to him anymore.

"We must leave the roads very soon, Papa. The local people are moving about as they begin their day, and we may be recognized. Just ahead, we can take a small road that cuts across the hillside above the village. Most of the path is within the tree line. It is rocky, but it is not far: just over a kilometre. Can you make it?"

"I don't think there's an option for us, Andre. Since the sun came up, I've felt more and more of a tug toward the horizon. I also saw some visions while we were walking. Either that or I'm so tired I was walking and sleeping at the same time."

"They were visions, Papa. God takes those moments when we are at a physical and spiritual low to provide us with guidance. What were the visions you had?"

Nicholas saw the first full light of day on the hillside ahead. A moment before it had been just a glow in the air. Now the sun was visible above the horizon behind them. With the increasing light of day, the visions became more dreamlike and distant.

"I'm not sure, Andre. It seems like God put it there for me but tucked it away for future use. I know it was important, but other than providing answers for a question I never even asked, I don't understand what He was showing me. Part of the time, I was sitting in a classroom back in graduate school. Part of the time, He was showing me something here in Haiti. I assume when the time comes it will all gel and make sense."

Andre pushed Nicholas into the bushes on the left side of the road and dove in after him. A moment later an armored car roared around the bend in the road behind them and a cascade of dust and diesel fumes were pulled behind as it charged toward the same ridgeline that they sought.

Both were deep in the shadows of the bush and maintained their quiet until they were sure the vehicle wasn't stopping. Its roar declined to a hum, and then vanished as it took another switchback in the road.

"What was that thing, Andre? I didn't know the Haitian government drove anything that big."

"It is from the so-called peace keepers, Papa. The United Nations has many vehicles like that here. The white paint with blue highlights is the key. We were lucky they didn't see us. Again, Jezi provides. The question is, how many more are coming this way. I think they are surrounding Mercy Orphanage in hopes of catching you. At least one of the men with the Bishop must have been a demon. They know your time is very close and want to stop you at any cost."

"Why am I such a threat to the United Nations? I'm not declaring war on anyone."

"You are wrong. If you free the oppressed, and comfort the sick, you are declaring war on Satan. Many in power on this earth have given their souls to him, and when you diminish his power, you take away theirs at the same time. If this crusade to free children works, the structure of power in Haiti will change in a most dramatic manner. It will change with much violence in other places as well, and powerful men are opposed to what you do here. No matter where this goes, the threat to them is very real. They will stop at nothing to put an end to your quest."

Nicholas didn't think about the upheaval in global terms. Andre was right: slavery was all over the world. If he helped put an end to it here in Haiti, the movement had to spread to other places. Not because he was so powerful, but because once God's people began to understand what was happening, they would awaken from their complacency with prayer and righteous anger. Not even Satan could stand against that kind of power."

Another set of engine noises caught their attention, forcing them deeper into the bushes. This time it was Haitian police in a large truck, officers armed to the teeth hanging off the back of the vehicle. The men were scanning all around them as the truck zoomed by in its own cloud of dust and debris.

A second vehicle sped by, an American sedan with four men inside.

"Nuts. I didn't expect that jerk to show up here."

Andre bobbed his head. "The one you called Goebbels was with the Tonton Macoute in the car. Very dark presence, Papa. They will not take you into custody: they will kill you if they can."

Nicholas knew that Andre was correct. Gabler had hunted him for months along with Schimmler. There were no rules here, no sign of his sister to help bail him out of trouble. But he did have Andre.

"We are very close to the orphanage, Papa. But now we must go off the road and run. I will take your pack if you wish. We cannot stay here, and we cannot let them get into position and cut us off. Follow me: we must get on the road for a hundred meters or so before we can move up the trail I told you about. Pray as we go, we will need His help to defeat the forces arrayed against us."

Andre moved out on the road and reached back for Nicholas. Nicholas stumbled out and adjusted his robe as the two began jogging toward the ridgeline and praying that they could outpace the armed men who were hunting them.

CHAPTER FORTY-SEVEN
Port-au-Prince, Haiti
March 21

"Welcome to Haiti. I am Michael. Larry sent me to bring you to Mercy Orphanage. Do you have bags?"

"Nope. Just my carry-on. Where's our car?"

"I have bad news: there is no car. I have a motorcycle in the lot. You will ride on the back. Is that acceptable?"

Jean Silver had spent the last 24 hours following the events in Haiti via cell phone and news reports. It seemed that her brother was wanted by the Department of Justice in the United States, and now he was on the run for fomenting a riot and burning down some slum in Haiti. He'd always been such a goody-two-shoes that she almost laughed as she read the news reports about what a terrorist he'd become. Nicholas wasn't going to get out of this unscathed without her to blunt the impact of the world press. No matter what he did, he was still her brother and she would do anything for him. She flew all night, and solely by virtue of the fact that she collected more VIP miles than the president of the airline every year, she got a seat on the first flight of the day to Haiti. The rest of the plane was crammed full of bureaucrats in suits and the type of skuzzy reporters who drank their breakfast.

"Yeah, I can handle the back of a bike. Please tell me you have a helmet for me?"

"Oui. It is my wife's. It should fit you as well."

The two slipped past the hundreds of people inside the terminal and even more just outside the doors. Offers of cabs, hotel rooms, resort accommodations, and other assorted items of a less-than-legal nature assaulted them in a barrage of English, Creole, and French. The heat was another story: it was like a fist to the side of the head. Pushing her sunglasses back until they were smashed against her face, Jean followed Michael toward the parking lot.

It wasn't so much a motorcycle as it was a glorified dirt bike with a luggage rack and a giant toolbox bolted on the back. Michael handed her a helmet while he donned his own.

"No way, pal. You wear this one, I'll wear yours."

Jean held out the canary yellow helmet as though it was an oozing block of toxic waste with a chin strap. She couldn't be faulted, as it had antennae sticking out of the top and a pair of wings festooning the sides – right next to the lightning bolts. There was no way she was wearing this thing and risking a picture of her along the way.

"I would, but it is too small. It is my wife's. She is very artistic. I am sorry if you do not like it, but you do not have to wear it if you do not wish."

Watching the traffic as it honked, revved, and roared out of the parking lot, Jean made an existential decision: wear the helmet and risk the picture, or not wear the helmet and risk her life with these crazy drivers.

Shrugging the helmet on, she attempted to maintain her hair in some fashion of order. After the fourth try, she just crammed the thing on, buckled the strap and got on the back of the bike so that Michael could bungee cord her roller bag on the back along with his grimy looking tool box.

"Do you need all of what is in here? I am afraid the rack won't handle the weight."

Jean bit her lip before replying, "Yes. Every bit of it. How about you throw out some tools instead?"

Michael hefted the bag again, weighed it in his mind, and bungee corded it down with the heaviest cords left on the rack.

"I think it might be okay. Let me know if you hear any noises from the brackets."

Threading his leg between Jean and the handle bars, he heaved himself into position. With a vicious kick to the starter, and a yank on the throttle, Michael revved the engine to life. It was a bike without benefit of a muffler, just straight pipes burned blue with heat. Lowering himself into the saddle, he slammed the gear shift without apparent use of a clutch and careened toward the exit with all the other maniacs in Haiti.

"Hear the brackets break. My God, I'll be lucky to hear my own screams. Welcome to Haiti: see the island and die." Jean's shouted complaint was lost on the wind as they headed toward the remote orphanage and her brother.

190

CHAPTER FORTY-EIGHT
Titanyen, Haiti
March 21

Weaving in and out along the tree line, Nicholas and Andre were concealed from view for the first portion of their climb along the path. The trees ran out twenty yards past the edge of the village, and all that was left was exposed ground between them and the walls of the orphanage, hidden by the ridge in front of them.

"Now, Papa, we must run as fast as you can until we get to the gate. If you look straight ahead and visualize, it is near that group of rocks. Once we go over the top, it will be on the left side of the wall near three smaller structures. Do you remember the purple paint when we left? Well, it only appears on the gate, and the road we departed is on our left side. So, go straight ahead, over the ridge, 100 yards or so, and then to the purple gate near the three small buildings."

The morning sun brought the temperature up to over ninety degrees, and it was not yet eight in the morning. Nicholas could see the rocks, but they blurred in and out with the beads of sweat in his eyes.

"I'm ready, Andre. Say the word."

"One thing remains. You must leave your robe here. They are looking for a monk and an Haitian. The island is full of people that look as I do, but you are the only monk for many miles. Many of the people from the mission school go out and jog in the morning. If we are lucky, they will think you are one of them. Leave your robe here under the bushes and make the final run without it. You will trip if you wear it."

Nicholas started to laugh. He was so tired, and so beat up from the long walk that he was on the edge of collapse. It would feel good to get rid of the robe. The thing wasn't that heavy, but it was warmer than he wanted.

"Andre, there aren't too many white guys with long beards in this neighborhood, so I think I'll keep the robe. All I've got on underneath is my superhero underwear. My sister thought they were funny when she packed them, and I sure didn't plan on ditching my shorts last night in trade for this robe. I'll be darned if I run across that ridge wearing underwear that identifies me as a guy who flies and shoots power rays from his hands and chest."

"You have a point. My apologies for suggesting it. I sometimes forget you look so different than the rest of us."

Nicholas took that as a compliment. Over the past few weeks he'd grown to love the big Haitian as a brother. It turned out that his brother was an angel, but that didn't change the fact that the two of them were friends. He was gratified by the love he felt from Andre.

"Andre, if you weren't my guardian angel, would we still be friends?"

"Without a doubt, Papa Noel. We are all part of His Kingdom and His children. We will still be friends after this as well, no matter where we go. Now, enough talk. Leave your pack here and gird your loins. We must run for the gate before the police get off the lower road and go up the hillside. They appear to be ready to move out."

Nicholas looked down the road and saw that the troops were indeed dismounted and formed up in ranks. They were being briefed by Goebbels before they moved up the hill. Nodding his assent, Nicholas set the backpack under the bush and got set to run. Andre counted down from five and the two of them sprinted toward Mercy Orphanage, just over a quarter-mile up the hill.

The first two hundred yards were the smoothest, some grass clung to the hillside here, and the path wasn't eroded by the occasional coastal rains. The rest of the run was exposed along the entire route, and a sea of apple-sized rocks, designed to twist an injudicious ankle, were the basis of the path. Nicholas was dodging one rock and missed another which sent him sprawling in a cloud of dust. That drew the attention of the armed men on the road and their shouts reached up to Nicholas as he struggled to his feet. Andre was already turning back when Nicholas got to his feet and made it a full ten steps before tripping over his monk's robe. Slamming to the ground even harder this time, he rolled to his back trying to orient himself and get his wind. He felt a violent tug as things went dark for a moment before the sun blasted his face once again. Andre was pulling him up by the hand and hurling his robe in the other direction. "Come, Papa, they see us."

Glancing down the hillside, he realized that he and Andre were equidistant from the safety of the orphanage and the men storming up the hillside toward them.

Running as hard as he could, Nicholas struggled to keep up with Andre as they approached the ridgeline and dropped over the other side. Once clear of the ridge, they immediately saw the structures outside the wall, and the gate beyond them. From this angle, the gate was not visible, but he knew it was getting closer every second. Andre was shouting for them to open the gate and let them in, but his cries were met with silence. There was a guard on the gate under the circumstances but, where was he?

Bullets ricocheted off the side of one of the small outbuildings and whined off into the distance. Some of the soldiers flanked them to the right and were firing from almost a half-mile away. Andre hit the gate first, pounding his fist on the metal. He could hear the soldiers getting closer, and from the far side of the gate he heard someone shouting to bring the key. The gate would never open in time; the soldiers would be there in fifteen seconds at most.

Pivoting to his right, Andre threw open a panel in the middle structure outside the walls and climbed inside, pulling Nicholas in backwards. Clamping his hand over Nicholas's mouth, he whispered in his ear, "Be quiet Papa. They could not see where we went; they will think we made it."

The two men huddled on a slab of hot stone and waited. The stench of wood smoke and burned bread was overwhelming. Somebody burned breakfast and not very long ago. In seconds, they heard the tromp of heavy boots running past the structure, and a thunderous hammering on the gate. Demands to open the gate echoed between the structures and the wall of the orphanage. Nicholas prayed harder than ever that the troops wouldn't kill him when they opened the panel and found them hiding. He pledged himself to do anything God asked, but to be spared until he could rescue the children of Haiti.

The noise made when the first panel was opened next to theirs was unmistakable. Vicious swearing accompanied the clang of the panel hitting its stops, followed by mocking laughter. The door to their hiding place opened a crack, and jeers erupted just before it clanged shut.

Orders were shouted to the troops to move around the corner and search for another door in the fence. Silence reigned after the shuffle of boots moved away.

Andre reached around Nicholas and opened the panel with his left hand, allowing both to peek out. They confirmed the space between them and the gate was empty before moving. Both saw the gate open a few inches and a set of eyes poke out for a look.

Lowering the panel, Andre pushed Nicholas out and toward the gate. The two ran for the safety of the compound, the gate opening just wide enough for them to pass. It shuddered closed as Nicholas cleared the rail in the ground that guided the heavy gate in its path.

Nicholas stood, hands on his knees, naked except for his sandals and his superhero underwear. His favorite red shirt had come off when Andre yanked the monk's robe over his head during their run up the hillside and was laying where he'd fallen. Andre stood grinning, while the gate attendant stared in shock at the two men.

"Come on, I don't look that crazy, do I?"

The old man who'd opened the gate dropped to his knees and pointed at them, babbling in Creole.

"I give. What's he saying, Andre?"

"He is saying it is a miracle, he is thanking God for our survival."

Nicholas shook his head. Big deal: he ran up a hillside and got lucky when the troops picked the wrong panel to open. "Okay. Fine. Can I get some clothes? It's kind of naked out here if you know what I mean. I don't want everyone to see me like this."

The old man continued to make the sign of the cross on his chest and babble. This wasn't just about a run up a hillside, but Nicholas had no idea why he was so upset.

"Andre, what is he saying? Please don't condense it. He seems super upset."

"It is because of where we hid, Papa. He is the bakery assistant. We hid in his ovens. Remember when I told you to be as brave as the boys?"

"Yeah. So?"

"The ovens are named Meshach, Shadrach, and Abednego. We were hiding in Shadrach. He brought them up to full temperature this morning; they are to be baking bread and making pizza in them in a few minutes."

For the first time, Nicholas noticed smoke curling from his beard and Andre's clothing. Close to igniting, but not quite there yet.

"You could have warned me, Andre."

"We had no choice, Papa Noel. Besides, your faith was strong, and you made it."

"True. But I may never eat another wood fired pizza. Who knows what naked guy was hiding in the oven that morning?"

CHAPTER FORTY-NINE
Titanyen, Haiti
March 21

Larry quit laughing long enough to find some pants and a clean shirt for Nicholas. His bloody sandals were taken away for cleaning while Doctor Eric tended to his wounds.

"I don't know why I'm wasting my time on this; he's healing faster than I can treat his wounds. Just sit there and eat your breakfast, Nicholas. Let God do the healing. I'll save the supplies for emergencies."

The leaders of the orphanage and the mission teams gathered in the dining hall, all of them spellbound while Nicholas told his tale of the confrontation in Cite Soleil and their escape from Port-au-Prince. Silence hung over the room when Nicholas told the story of Andre stuffing them into the oven while they hid from the pursuing troops.

"That was close, Nicholas. I got up on the roof a few minutes ago, and when your feet are healed, I think you need to look as well. There are tens of thousands of children outside the gate, and another hundred thousand people on the hillsides toward the ocean. In the last few minutes, they've started coming from the countryside along the road you guys took. It's amazing. The thrum of their singing is eerie. They all know something huge is coming, but the praise and worship aspect is overwhelming. The sounds of people worshipping God are the only noises coming from the crowds."

Nicholas lifted his head up to listen. He walked outside the hall with bare feet. It felt good after the grinding of the sandals the night before. He knew it would be a long time before he volunteered for any nature hikes.

Standing in the bright sunshine, the noise was louder. He listened and hummed along for a moment before breaking out in a huge grin and walking back inside the dining hall.

"I don't know what you folks heard earlier, but that's not a worship song. Matter of fact, it's not even vaguely religious. But I like it. Of all the things I've seen and heard in Haiti, "Santa Claus Is Coming to Town" sung in Creole by twenty thousand children is the best."

Sitting down at the table, Nicholas said, "I'm so glad to be here today. I know this is where I belong; God's been bringing me here with increasing frequency over the last two weeks. I don't wish to put anybody in danger. If you want me to leave, I'll walk down the hill right now. I'm sure Goebbels would be glad to take me into custody if we do it in front of the cameras out there. I'll be okay. I never expected this many people to be outside, waiting for whatever happens. I won't be upset; I understand the children must be protected first and foremost."

Larry spoke for the group, "Nicholas, we know your heart. We know it's about the children. Most of our children were Resteveks before we were able to rescue them. You have done more for the child slavery issue in two days than we have in ten years. God is moving you on this chessboard. I don't want to be a pawn, but I don't want off the board. The others feel the same way."

"If those soldiers want to drag me out, things will get bloody, Larry. Can we all agree that we can put an end to this if they break in here and start shooting?"

A new voice chimed in from behind him. "Not on a bet, Nicholas Bacon. We're going to kick their butts."

Nicholas jumped up at the sound of a familiar voice and spun toward the door. He rushed forward and grabbed his sister in a bear hug. "I didn't know you were here. When?"

"Holy smokes, I recognized your voice from behind, but I wouldn't have picked you out of a line-up. Nicholas Bacon, you've been transformed."

Jean stood and stared at her brother. The combination of amazement and upset on her face roiled her features. She clearly hadn't expected him to be so physically different. It literally took her breath away for a few moments.

Once she'd regained her composure she spoke: "Uh, I just got here. On a dirt bike. I bet I look great. Where's Larry?"

Larry stood up and offered his hand.

"Larry, you're a trip. Thanks for the ride, but next time could you arrange for a car service? Michael's a good guy, but his driving is marginal."

197

Nicholas thought about the mob on the road up to Mercy Orphanage. "How did you get past those people on the road? It's jammed for miles in both directions."

"It's amazing where you can go if you don't mind cutting a few fences. Michael carried a wire cutter in the toolbox on that thing he rides. He was kind of excited to have a rider that knew how to use the things. We went cross country the last couple of miles."

Nicholas hugged her again. Pulling out a chair for her, he waited until she got something to drink. "You don't think that the troops on the road and the international press are a problem. Why?"

"Everything, my dear brother, is spin. They aren't going to attack you here in an orphanage with children surrounding you. There's got to be twenty-five thousand kids outside that gate. They're expecting something to happen, but they're looking this way, not towards the troops down the hill. Nothing bullies hate more than being ignored. I take it you have a plan of some sort?"

He lowered his head and thought about his words for a very long time before speaking.

"I have seen things in visions that may be the most amazing... I have a plan, but they have to talk to us to make it work."

Nicholas stood up to pace around the table. "I know what God's laid out for us to do here today. But if we negotiate this with the people outside the walls and nobody knows what we discussed, they'll bury the whole thing. We need to be live to the world when we do this, but I feel that the news outlets are here to vilify me for some reason rather than tell the real story."

Jean's face twisted into a smirk before she spoke, "Darned right. Back in the States they're making you out to be somewhere between Rasputin of Moscow and the Charlie Manson of Haiti. I'm sure the Haitian press is even worse, but back home your name is Mudd. You're taking the blame for the plane blowing up, riots in Haiti, and a threat to kidnap children from their foster families. Sound about right?"

"Yeah. But how do we get around that?"

"Larry and I talked about it before I got on the plane down here, and we can get the word out without the press. Remember all that stuff you installed at the clinic?"

"Of course."

"Wasn't one of the items a video-conference center with a satellite link?"

Nicholas pumped a fist in the air, "Yes! I wired it myself. That thing has great bandwidth. But who will put our stuff on the internet?"

Jean pointed a thumb at her chest. "I've got more geeks building websites for my narcissistic clients than you can shake a stick at, brother dear. I just have to get some dope from you now that I'm here and we can livestream this on a dozen celebrities' websites at the same time. I'll pay for doing it in the long run, but they'll calm down once they realize the benefit to their shallow little lives. All we have to do is get the heavies to come in here and talk to us without their bodyguards."

"They'll never come in here without firepower. What if we could get them to video link to us, and we just mix the signals?"

"If you can do that, it would be perfect. But isn't this a medical conference thing? I can't imagine it being able to do the mixing."

"That thing can conference on up to six feeds at once. Right now, we've got both landline and satellite links to the equipment. The landline is Ethernet over copper. It's the first in Haiti and has got enough bandwidth to do video with the local people. If you can get them to come in on the landline, they won't know we can put it out on our satellite. They won't even know we're live on the internet until we've been up for a while. Can your geeks promise that we're going out to the world?"

Jean dug in her luggage and pulled out a sleek laptop. "Larry, if you've got internet, we can test it before we try it. Where's the camera gear we're using?"

Larry led the group to the clinic. Ten minutes, and three short, cryptic phone calls later, the link was tested. If Nicholas could mix the signals, the geeks could put them out live around the world on some of the most heavily trafficked internet sites around.

Larry's cell phone rang as they headed back to the dining hall. Stopping in the courtyard to talk, he turned a bit pasty. Motioning for Nicholas to take the phone, Larry led the rest of the people into the hall.

"He needs a minute to take the call in private."

Half an hour went by before Nicholas returned. He glowed like a man who knows where he wants to be in history.

"Ladies and gentlemen let me tell you about what we're going to do today. Our plan is ready to execute."

199

CHAPTER FIFTY
Titanyen, Haiti
March 21

"Mr. President, thank you for joining the conference. I apologize for beginning without you, but time seems to be of the essence for some of the others. Let me just recap, we have the President of Haiti, the Attorney General of the United States of America, the Port Captain for Port-au-Prince, and the commander of the United Nations peace-keeping force on the conference along with the members of my mission whom you see with me, including Doctor Eric Swendsen and Mister Larry Timmons. I thank you all for joining the conference this afternoon."

The Attorney General was the first to speak.

"Mr. Bacon, you realize that the United States government considers you a fugitive from justice. We're asking that you turn yourself over to our agents in Port-au-Prince and return to the United States. I have reached an agreement with the Haitian authorities that if you willingly return to our shores, they will not pursue charges regarding the riots and arson in Cite Soleil. If you fail to do so, the United Nations contingent is prepared to assist the Haitian government in arresting you and bringing you to trial for acts of terrorism in that nation."

Nicholas nodded and turned to face the Port Captain who began to speak on the next screen.

"...without reservation. That would be a tragedy. But if you do not surrender, we cannot guarantee the expeditious delivery of supplies to Mr. Timmon's organization in the future. It is suspected that he is involved with you in your activities against the people of Haiti, and that you have abetted his smuggling to pursue your own interests. His bringing you to custody could go a long way toward allaying those suspicions."

The President of Haiti sat looking sad and tormented during both of the other men's little speeches.

"Mr. President, what do you have to say about this? I am a guest in your nation. I have heard that you are a fair and decent man."

"Mister Bacon, I regret that I have to ask for your surrender as well. I promise that you will be treated well and allowed to return to the United

States to face your own government. I do not believe that you present a threat to my country, but you are a distraction from our dealing with the problems of Haiti."

'Gentlemen, I've heard you out. Now it's my turn. You've seen the people on the hills surrounding my location. They came here in a peaceful manner, so I hope you have no plans to storm this orphanage. Any bloodshed would be on your hands, and I'm sure the press around the world will turn on you if that were to happen.

"You know that I've committed no crime against anyone, either in Haiti or the United States. This is all a dark strategy to suborn God's plan for the children of Haiti. I am here because God is using me to gain worldwide attention for the problem of human trafficking. I suppose you might try me for practicing medicine without a license when I was involved in miraculous healings, but that's about it…"

"You might think you're a comedian, but the government of the United States has some serious questions that you need to answer, Mr. Bacon. I suggest we get on with it and arrange your surrender before this charade goes any further."

"You know, Mr. Attorney General, I listened quietly while you spoke. Now please shut up until I'm done."

The sharp intake of breath from all the participants told the tale. Nicholas skated to the edge of the precipice.

"Let me set out for you exactly what I require, and then you can continue to threaten me. I'll make it simple: I'm demanding the release of all Resteveks in Haiti. I want the United Nations to provide the material support needed to take care of these children on behalf of the Haitian government. The Government of Haiti will need international assistance in housing, educating, and providing for these children. I am sure that they cannot be ready to do this on their own fast enough. This is non-negotiable. Moreover, it must be immediate. Not one more day of these children being abused and enslaved."

"You're probably wondering how I can make these demands and who is going to pay for all of this? Gentlemen, let me introduce a friend of mine, His Holiness the Pope."

On the video feed, yet another frame exploded to life. There, in his apartment overlooking Saint Peter's Square was the Pope.

201

"Gentlemen, I bring you the good tidings of Jesus Christ. I have been in conference with the Bishop of Haiti for the last twelve hours. A little while ago, I contacted Nicholas and asked what I could do to assist him in his work in Haiti.

"He has suggested that we use the church's resources to take care of the enslaved children of Haiti, and to help free this entire nation from human trafficking. I have agreed to provide the funds, and the logistics experts, to ensure this goal is met. In return, he will join me in an effort to eliminate human trafficking in every nation. We have allowed the abomination of human enslavement to go on for too long. I am pledging the resources of my church to the elimination of this scourge, this black stain on the soul of mankind, in the next five years."

Around the world, news outlets were picking up the feed from the conference. At first, it was just entertainment networks and other websites that saw the feed coming from celebrity websites and wondered what was going on. When the Pontiff joined the conference, he utilized his resources to broadcast the conference live on Italian television as well as the church's websites around the world. Within moments, microphones were muted in all the offices participating except the ones in Rome and the orphanage. Hurried conferences were held off camera, and one by one, the participants returned to the table.

"I trust you've discovered our conference is available to the entire world. Good. I just wanted everyone to realize that we've got nothing to hide here, this is all above board. Now, Mr. Attorney General, I'm letting you know that I have no intention of leaving Haiti in the near future. I have a lot of work left to do here. You see, I'm planning to supervise the Restevek relocation program. The Pontiff and I talked about it earlier this afternoon. I'll be working with the good people of the mission here, and several other groups the Pontiff put us in touch with today."

"Mister Bacon, I am not going to allow you to stay in Haiti. You have disrupted my entire nation with your behavior."

"Mr. President, I'm sorry to hear you say that. What if I could bring something to the table that will enrich the people of Haiti and ease the poverty of this nation forever?"

"I cannot imagine what would be within your power to change my nation forever."

"I am offering to the people of Haiti a solution to your eternal lack of fresh water, and the rampant deforestation. If you agree to free the Resteveks, end human trafficking, and provide for those children as they grow up, I will show you an economically-viable process for obtaining limitless fresh water. I will work with your agricultural officials and teach them a new planting method, which will reforest Haiti and allow you to grow sustainable crops for substantially less than it costs to import food. I will do these things by providing the knowledge, and the Vatican has offered to provide funding to build the pilot plants, so that you will understand we are sincere and able to fulfill our promises."

Skeptical laughter came from most of the screens. The Pontiff and Nicholas maintained their composure while the President of Haiti appeared intrigued by the offer.

"Look, Bacon, you're nothing but a scam artist. There's no way you can do that short of magic. I'm not impressed with your promise. I'll be waiting for you to get serious while I'm building my perpetual motion machine."

Nicholas smiled back at the Attorney General of the United States. "You can laugh all you want. Mr. President, what would it take to convince you?"

"I want to see proof of the things I've heard about. Are you able to do some miracle or other…?"

He trailed off and turned off camera for a moment before resuming. "I understand you can heal the sick. What if you show us your sincerity by doing that again?"

Nicholas shook his head.

"It doesn't work like that, sir. I'm not a circus monkey to perform tricks to amuse you. I believe that God has revealed this to me so that I can share it with the world. Your Holiness, please tell them the rest?"

"Once Nicholas brings this to Haiti, we will ask the governments of the world to free all the slaves on every continent. Each country that does so will receive the support of the church, and Nicholas' technology to bring fresh water and agricultural plenty to their people. We will accomplish this within five years. We believe that it is the will of God to end all forms of human trafficking on this planet."

"One thing I need to clear up. It is not my technology, it is God's. He revealed it to me in a series of visions, and I am merely the messenger.

Gentlemen, I will give you until ten this evening to talk amongst yourselves and get back to us with your answer. Your Holiness, my thanks for your help today."

"Nicholas, be cautious. I know this goes to the whole world, so I am going on record: you are in great danger. Be careful, my son."

The videocast ended and a screen saver went up stating that it would resume at three in the morning, Universal Coordinated Time.

Nicholas relaxed and fell sound asleep in his chair.

CHAPTER FIFTY-ONE
Titanyen, Haiti
March 21

Nicholas awakened on a cot in one of the examination rooms. He'd been asleep for over two hours. His body ached, and his legs were twitching. He knew from experience in hot climes that he was short on electrolytes to the point of danger.

Rolling over and sitting up the first thing he saw was Andre sitting across the room.

"I don't know how I'm going to get anything done if you're not sitting right there when I wake up. You make a habit of anything for too long and it becomes a requirement."

"Papa, you need to drink this. It will help with your muscles. You are close to exhaustion and dehydration. Please, drink it all and I will get you more when you are done."

Nicholas took the large bottle and drank it as fast as his stomach would tolerate. It was energy drink, and he experienced a sense of physical inflation as the fluid seemingly pounded through his stomach lining directly into his veins. When he finished the first one, Andre handed him a second one. Flavored with Papaya, the second one was carbonated and helped clear the last of the road dust from his throat. That walk to the orphanage in the night was still clinging to his beard.

"Where are the others, Andre?"

"They decided to feed the children outside the gate. Larry took everyone to the container farm to collect food just a few minutes ago. Without the container at the port that they are holding ransom, we will be out of food after tonight."

Nicholas looked at the clock on the wall. There were two hours until the conference resumed. "Let's go and give them a hand. I want to meet some of those kids in person. I feel drawn to them just as they are drawn to me."

Walking across the compound, Andre and Nicholas could hear voices singing hymns outside the walls. He began to lift his feet higher, and his stick thumped with a tingle of bells in ever larger arcs of stride. Crossing

205

between the containers and the buildings, Nicholas saw the missionaries lined up to take packages from the last container in the row.

"Hey, Larry. Need a hand?"

Larry thrust his arms out and hugged Nicholas.

"Nicholas! Are you okay? Last time I saw you you'd passed out in your chair. That was one tough negotiation with those vipers. I kept wondering when you were going to reach for the Pope in your pocket."

Larry started to snicker and then bang the side of the container with the flat of his hand. He stopped laughing and began to weep. He looked like a man who was losing it.

"Whoa, Larry. What's wrong? I didn't mean to freak you out."

"It's not you, Nicholas. I just realized that the Pope in Rome can't do anything for all those children outside the gate. There's under half a container of meals left here, and that won't feed more than a thousand or so children. We can't take care of them all. That will give the government the leverage they need to break up the crowd and win the battle. If he were closer, maybe. But Rome is a long way from Haiti."

Nicholas knew what he had to do. He dropped to his knees and then prostrated himself on the dusty floor of the shipping container. After five minutes, he got up and asked all the missionaries to join hands and stand in the opening of the container.

"Father, we're on a hillside near the ocean, just like Your Son was so many years ago. We need to feed a multitude as well. We ask that You help us to find the food in this container that we need to nourish these children who have nothing except faith in Your miracles. It's not fish and bread, but we call upon You to spread them in the same manner. Please, Lord, help us feed these starving children."

The missionaries shouted an "amen" and formed a line replete with wheelbarrows to carry their loads. Nicholas asked Andre to help him empty the container and then motioned to Larry.

"You need to make sure that adults don't take the food from the kids out there tonight. If you handle that end of the line, and keep sending your people back here, I'm sure God's going to provide what we need."

Larry embraced Nicholas and said, "How is it that just a few weeks ago I was the teacher and now I'm the pupil?"

Turning on his heel, Larry grabbed the first wheelbarrow in line and waited as Nicholas and Andre carried out boxes of meals. Loading two in

206

each of the wheelbarrows, they filled the available carts as fast as they could. Some of the older children from the orphanage took the large boxes and broke up the contents so that the smaller children could carry out individual meals. After some time passed, a trickle of wheelbarrows came back, pursued by smiling orphans who grabbed meals and ran ahead.

For the next three hours this continued unabated, Nicholas and Andre drenched the floor of the steel cargo container in sweat. The children brought them a series of soft drinks and water, but they never were able to keep up with their fluids. Neither man took a break, just paced back and forth to the wall of boxes and prayed as they worked that the supply would be enough.

At nine that evening the wheelbarrows quit coming back to the container. The children came to say goodnight, and Larry stood in the door of the container with a flashlight summoning Andre and Nicholas from the interior. As they walked out, Larry took a look at what was left. Stopping 10 feet inside the container, he said, "Nicholas: we have one more for your list."

"List of what, Larry?"

"Miracles. See the marks on the inside top of the container? Those are so the people who load these know what percent of capacity they are at. It's important to load balance the container so the weight is spread out equally."

"Yeah, that makes sense. Don't want to flip a truck over or capsize a barge. I get it."

"See the mark above the row of boxes you were emptying?" Larry pointed his flashlight at the top box. "That's three feet closer to the front of the container than when we started. I track these extremely carefully, so that I know how much pressure to put on the Port Captain to get our supplies released. Nicholas, there's more food in here than when we began. We just fed over fifteen thousand people and we have more food."

Nicholas felt that wash of power again that he'd felt at the lunch table when the Holy Spirit consumed and filled him. The choice of the scripture he cited wasn't random; he heard the words about loaves and fishes in his head when he got ready to speak. God worked another miracle this night.

Larry shined his flashlight on the containers up and down the row. Perplexed, he walked up to the first and examined a customs seal on the door. Grabbing a softball sized rock; he pounded on the seal until it split.

Cranking open the door, he sank to his knees and started to laugh again. This time it was laughter rich with joy.

Nicholas and Andre walked over to the container and saw that boxes of food packed it to the top, right up to the door.

"I thought you were out of food, Larry. I'm not complaining, but we could have fed some adults if I knew we had this much."

"They were all empty except your container, Nicholas. I rechecked them all myself about ten minutes before we began."

Larry took his rock and smashed the seals on three more containers, finding each of them packed with food as well. There was even a container full of baby formula and electrolyte packs to deal with dysentery. By the end of the row, Larry was bouncing up and down like a little boy.

"They can't make us leave, Nicholas. We've got enough supplies to last for months in these containers. One of the containers even has a tank full of diesel fuel for the generator. I've never ordered fuel that way; it always comes in a tanker truck. If the President of Haiti still wants a sign, bring him up here and let him look for himself."

CHAPTER FIFTY-TWO
Titanyen, Haiti
March 21

Violene ate her fill with the other children on the hillside, and with hours of effort, and squeezing between thousands of expectant youth, she moved her way up close to the gate. The staff of the orphanage was keeping the children out, and the little refugees seemed to know that they shouldn't enter the grounds without an invitation. Walking up to one of the security staff, Violene asked, "Is Papa Noel here? I have not seen him coming out to bring the food."

The security guard nodded, "He is here. I am told he is helping load the wheelbarrows."

"Please tell him that I am here to see him? He told me that he had a bed for me at the orphanage when I talked to him the other day."

The guard heard a lot of stories over the years, but this one was the most original. He turned to look for one of the leaders when he felt a hand on his shoulder. Looking up, it was Larry.

"Open the gates and let the children in, but not the adults. Nicholas wants to meet his friends."

Pointing at the narrow opening in the gate, the guard said, "Larry, this one says she knows Papa Noel personally. He told her to come and he had a room for her."

Larry walked to the gate and knelt. Speaking to the girl in Creole, he asked her name.

"Violene. I talked to Papa Noel the other afternoon. He said his friend Larry would have a place for me at an orphanage. I am sure this is where I am supposed to be."

Larry tenderly grasped her hand. "You are in the right place, Violene. Come with me and meet Nicholas of Haiti. He is the one you call Papa Noel."

Looking out over the hillside, Larry took in thousands of lights, small campfires burning across the barren landscape. They stretched as far as the eye could see in every direction. Where on earth had the fuel come from, the area was a desert. Turning back inside the compound, he told the guard to let children in and have them go to the school playground.

The gate rolled back to its stops, hitting them with a musical clang. Twenty thousand or more children got up from where they were seated and followed Larry and Violene to the large playground where Nicholas and Andre were having something to eat and drink in the cooling air.

Nicholas got up and walked toward them, but Violene broke into a run and finished the final ten meters in a full sprint. Throwing herself around Nicholas in a grip that could never be broken, she was enveloped in his arms as his long beard touched her face. Both pulled back and were smiling as widely as was possible with the human anatomy.

"Welcome to your home, Violene. I am so glad you made it after our talk the other day. You can stay if you want, but I think we'll be able to reunite you with your family very soon. Would you like that?"

Stunned, the little girl sat transfixed and nodded once Andre translated Nicholas's words. Nicholas looked deep into her eyes and said, "Andre, ask her if she's okay. I'm concerned she may have been raped. She was afraid of that when I talked to her the other day."

Andre spoke to the child and she shook her head.

"Good. Now, ask her if I can see the scars on her legs and back."

Once again, Andre translated the words. In the dim light of the compound, Violene revealed a series of ugly scars. Nicholas traced his finger across each mark, overcome with anguish and love. As though his finger were an eraser, the marks faded and vanished with his touch.

"Larry, can you make sure that someone is in the conference room to start the meeting? I'm going to be here a while. If anyone is impatient, please ask the Pontiff to take over for me. That guy gave me the negotiating strategy; he's more than capable of handling things for me."

One by one, for over four hours, Nicholas went to work healing the children of Haiti. Each child was presented to him singly. He ran his hands from their head to their feet; some of the scars began to heal before the child was released. When he was finished, the external marks were gone. But what scars would remain inside of them for the rest of their lives?

CHAPTER FIFTY-THREE
Titanyen, Haiti
March 22

Nicholas was empty from seeing so many abused children. His favorite aunt had been a social worker, and she painted a bit of the picture for him one night many years before. Even her tales failed to prepare him for the pain he had witnessed tonight.

Stepping into the conference room, the Pontiff was praying and the Attorney General braying. Taking his seat, he tapped the microphone in front of him and apologized for being late to the conference.

"I've just spent the last few hours with the Restevek children of Haiti. Earlier we talked about our requests for their release. Your Holiness, what have they said in response to our conditions?"

Several voices started to chime in from the attendees. Nicholas held up a hand and said, "Please. I need to hear just one man: The Pope. Sir?"

The Pope put his chin in his hand. "They are obstinate. They will not force the issue until we provide the technology and the horticultural secrets to prove we aren't bluffing."

Nicholas shook his head.

"You are not getting it, boys. This isn't me talking; God has ordained this whole enterprise. He's the One who provided the knowledge to me, and He's the One who will make it all work. I think there have been a reasonable number of signs provided. Now it's time for God to bring you to heel…"

Nicholas was interrupted by the sound of helicopters coming in for a landing in the plaza outside the clinic. The plaza was filled with children with no place to go. Nicholas bolted out of his chair and ran outside.

There were at least eight helicopters with spot lights blazing down in the courtyard. Shock troops were starting to rope down toward the compound so that they could deposit their forces without having to land the helicopters.

Nicholas raised his staff to the sky, and in the same eerie voice that had boomed through the streets of Cite Soleil, he thundered, "No. Never. Be gone."

211

In an instant, a strong wind raced across the courtyard like a battering ram. Starting 30 feet above the ground, the hurricane force wind swept upward and out toward the sea. The helicopters were flung 10,000 feet away from the compound, gaining at least 5,000 feet of altitude. None of the troops lost their grip, and the helicopters were able to form up over the ocean and fly off to the capital of Port-au-Prince.

Nicholas stumped up the stairs into the clinic and took his place at the table. The attendees were getting a play-by-play from their forces via radio. The Pontiff greeted him when he sat down, the others shunned him.

Nicholas let them carry on for a few moments more and then he interrupted them.

"You know by now that your forces were unable to land and capture me. You don't understand, do you? This was never about me. It is about the children. And if you think that's another fluke of nature, I'll go and stand on a hilltop in some remote area. God, gentlemen, has His hand cupped over me. I cannot fail with His love and protection while I'm doing what He tells me."

Silence penetrated the room. After a very long pause, the President of Haiti spoke.

"Nicholas, my apologies for that stupid stunt. I have surrendered too much sovereignty to the United Nations over the last few years in hopes that they could provide aid to heal my country. I am done bowing to anyone but God. How do we arrange for the children to be taken care of properly? I'm sure the United Nations will not be all that helpful after you scattered their forces."

"If I may, Nicholas," the Pope said, "the members of my staff have drawn up a plan to take care of the Resteveks. While we were waiting for the meeting tonight, they have purchased several tons of clothing, shoes, personal care products, and begun loading them into shipping containers in Miami. We have chartered a fast cargo ship to bring them to Haiti within the next three days. All we are waiting on are for several dozen other ships to load with portable housing units."

"In the interim, we have sent emergency supplies to dozens of regional airports and purchased thousands of tents across the southern United States. These will be loaded into chartered aircraft and flown to Haiti and the Dominican Republic beginning at dawn. The Dominican Republic has graciously granted us emergency landing permission, and I'm presuming that the Haitian government will do the same. Is that correct, Mr. President?"

The President of Haiti nodded as someone off screen was showing him something that was distracting him.

"One moment, please, Your Holiness." He muted his microphone and shielded his mouth from the camera.

"I am told we will need some special air traffic control help to coordinate the aircraft that will come to Haiti. Is it possible for the United States Marines to come and help our controllers?"

Nicholas smiled.

"I'm sure that the President of the United States will be glad to send Marines, Mr. President. I think that the Pontiff and the Attorney General can get that done without any trouble. Is that correct, Mr. Attorney General?"

The man was fuming, but he realized that he'd been outfoxed. Anything he said, or didn't say, was being broadcast live around the world. If he denied a request for humanitarian assistance under these circumstances, the administration was done for what was left of the President of the United States' term.

"Of course, Mr. President. I will call the White House and make the arrangements. I'm sure we can have controllers there within the next twelve hours. If the Pontiff would be so kind as to hold off until then, I will make the arrangements."

The Pope nodded on camera, making no attempt to hide his joy.

"Gentlemen, it has been a very long two days. I want to put our meeting on hold until the relief effort is well underway. You have my word, and that of the Pontiff, that we will do as we have promised. Goodnight, everyone. We'll talk again in three days."

CHAPTER FIFTY-FOUR
Port-au-Prince, Haiti
March 29

The meeting that Nicholas and the Pontiff scheduled kept getting delayed because Nicholas wanted to make sure the release of the Resteveks was happening at an acceptable rate, and partly because it was taking longer than anticipated to arrange shipping of the relief supplies that the church had obtained.

Over the intervening days, normal travel to Haiti and the Dominican Republic became impossible, as the island of Hispaniola was flooded with medical teams and organizational specialists from dozens of countries. Instead of launching into the venture with little or no planning, the efforts were being coordinated and ramped up as new people were assimilated. Much of the equipment came from the United States Navy and Marine Corps, who sent their air traffic control teams, as well as the single group of specialists who could build whole villages in the matter of a week. The storied SEABEES were the leaders in setting up temporary housing and feeding installations across the northern rim of Port-au-Prince. Without them, chaos could have ensued.

The main reason for the delay was the world-wide rumbling over the end of human trafficking. In an unexpected twist of events, people all over the world demanded immediate change, not a gradual five-year period proposed in the original meetings. This meant that governments were scrambling to avoid revolution within their borders, and the violence that would take place if slaves overthrew their masters. The history of Haiti spoke volumes to this problem, and the Haitian President offered to host an international summit at one of the new resorts. This resort was built in the years following the earthquake that almost destroyed his country and was the future of the nation. It would be more than a showcase for economic recovery; it would be a showcase for the basic decency of humans across the globe in putting an end to this form of misery.

In a private teleconference between the Vatican and Nicholas' team in Haiti, it was agreed that they had to make their good faith technology transfer available to the whole world. For the first time in many decades,

214

the world seemed to be on the same page, and delaying the release of this information might cause skepticism to overrule the good will generated.

An international broadcast was scheduled for the next evening. Nicholas planned to reveal his vision for solving the fresh water shortages around the world. The agricultural piece of the puzzle would wait until inspection teams verified that human trafficking was eliminated in any given country before the transfer took place. Nicholas was to be joined by the Pope at the orphanage, the two of them to broadcast together.

The following afternoon the airspace over Port-au-Prince was quiet for the first time in days as the Pontiff flew in a small jet from Miami. Rather than take ramp space with his usual aircraft, the Pope elected to make the final leg of the flight in a small business jet.

Nicholas and Andre were at the airport to meet the Holy Father, along with a host of dignitaries from every nation in the Western world. Clad in a pair of slacks and a button-down shirt that were a perfect fit, he was no longer the grimy vision of Saint Nicholas who had walked through the night to Mercy Orphanage. His beard and long hair were a magnificent white, and he took on a subtle aura that those attuned to God could sense.

Andre, contrary to his announced plans to leave Haiti the day following the miracles at the orphanage, stayed on for the duration. When Nicholas asked him about this, Andre replied that "My superiors thought you might need further help for some time to come."

The Pope's aircraft taxied to the terminal, and the same band which met Nicholas and Larry when they landed just a few weeks before greeted him as he approached the terminal. The band played with unbridled fervor in front of the whole world, as the terminal was swamped with camera crews.

The two men, Nicholas of Haiti, and the leader of 1.2 billion Catholics, met in person in the poorest nation in the Western hemisphere. Not sure of protocol, Nicholas greeted the Pope with a firm handshake and a clasp of his shoulder. The Pope replied with an offer to exchange his shepherds crook for Nicholas' walking staff.

"I have wanted to see that stick since I first heard of your miracles in Cite Soleil. Truly, it does have a teddy bear on the top. God has a joyous sense of humor, doesn't He?"

"I know He does: He picked me to lead this emancipation. I couldn't have asked for a better partner than you, sir. You are the sharpest negotiator I have ever met. Remind me not to play poker with you."

The Pope laughed from deep down in his being.

"I can already imagine the pictures of that game being splashed on television screens around the world. I'm sure that my staff would drop of apoplexy if we did such a thing. In public, anyway. Are you ready to go to the resort and start our conference?"

Nicholas shook his head. "Holy Father, I want for you to come with us to meet the Resteveks of Haiti. There are thousands of children gathered around the orphanage that have heard you are coming. Many have expressed an interest in meeting you. I would like you to meet them as well. I have taken the liberty of asking the leaders meet us at the orphanage, and we can hold the first meetings in the church on site. We have moved a television camera into the sanctuary to cover the events. After we meet, we can go to the resort tomorrow."

"I am at your service, Nicholas. Please lead the way."

Nicholas, the Pope, and Andre all walked through the terminal to the surprise and deflation of the dignitaries who were standing in a line to get their pictures taken with them. Instead, they walked out the other side and stopped under the awning.

"We'll take my car, if that's all right with you?"

The Pope looked for his body guards and realized that God was all the protection he needed for this journey.

"Certainly. Where is it?"

Nicholas pointed at the garish tap-tap parked next to them. "It even has padded benches. Andre made sure we have water and snacks for the trip. I promise you, it is the best way to see Haiti: it is how the missionaries travel from place to place."

Caressing the side of the vehicle as though it were a beloved horse, the Pope said, "I was once a missionary as a young man, Nicholas. It would be an honor to ride in this vehicle with you. Can you provide me with some informal clothing for when we meet the children? I want to play some soccer with them. I may be old, but I can still kick."

Andre reached under the bench seat of the tap-tap.

"I brought a change of clothes for both of you on the chance you agreed. These should fit."

With a radiant smile, the Pope walked to the back door and pointed at the steps.

"I will need a lift; I haven't climbed one of these in decades.

Andre climbed the rungs and reached down to grab the hand of the leader of Peter's church. When their hands touched, the Pope looked into his eyes and knew in an instant who Andre was in his eternal form.

Not a word was spoken as the angel pulled the old man in front of him up to the passenger compartment. Nicholas clambered in behind the Pontiff. Leaving them in the back, Andre jumped down, closed the door, and got behind the wheel.

The motorcade, almost a mile long, was led by a team of motorcycle officers, followed by a tap-tap that resembled the Partridge Family's bus, and several dozen armored cars and police vehicles. In the back, the two men chatted as though they'd been friends for decades while the Pope changed into a pair of khakis and a shirt like Nicholas's.

CHAPTER FIFTY-FIVE
Titanyen, Haiti
March 30

After a long ride across the coastal plain, and almost an hour of meeting children and playing soccer on the dusty field outside the orphanage, Nicholas had arranged a meal for them. Several of the children, including Violene, joined them for the simple meal. The Pontiff dazzled the children with his attempt at Creole.

After they ate with the children, the two talked about the broadcast for a few minutes while the Pontiff changed back into his robes. The two of them walked toward the church with the rest of the mission team, the bells of Nicholas' staff announcing their arrival to the assembled leaders inside from across the courtyard.

Violene spurted between Larry and Jean Silver, and grabbed Nicholas by his hand, tugging him down to her level. He looked her in the eye as he crouched to face her. Andre translated her words:

"Papa, why are you leaving?"

Nicholas looked at Andre in confusion, assuming that he'd misunderstood the translation. Placing his hands on her shoulders, he said, "I'm not going to leave you. I'll be here with you for a long time. I'm not..."

His words were cut off by the roar of an automatic weapon. A fusillade of bullets chattered across his back as a uniformed security officer stood over him and shot down at the helpless, kneeling man. The shots ended when Andre swung a mighty fist and knocked the rogue security agent unconscious.

Nicholas, life draining from him, smiled at Violene. His body had shielded her from certain death. Andre, his sister Jean and Larry all knelt next to him in the pool of blood seeping from his wounds. Andre reached over to touch Nicholas on the face, and gently stroked Nicholas' forehead while Jean cradled his head in her lap.

"You're fired, Andre. You were asleep on the job."

A tremendous puddle of blood was forming under Nicholas as Andre whispered in his ear, "No, Papa. Jezi is waiting for you. You completed your mission and your soul is safe. I have a new charge, and you have helped me start on those duties."

Nicholas gave Andre a quizzical look. Andre nodded his head to where Violene sat on the hard-packed earth, covered in her rescuer's blood, and sobbing.

"The girl, Papa. She is very important. I am to take care of her from now on. You have done well, Nicholas. You will be remembered always in this land."

Doctor Eric ran over and knelt with the others in the red mud surrounding Nicholas. He squeezed the hand of his friend and shook his head in response to Jean's questioning look. "He's got a strong healing power, but I don't see how he can survive this much damage. He just doesn't have the time to heal."

With a final wet cough, Nicholas Bacon – Nicholas of Haiti – departed this earth and went to be with his Father.

The Pontiff, shaken by the horrendous attack, ministered to Nicholas for a time. His robes soaked in the blood of the newest Saint: Nicholas of Haiti. Composing himself, he got to his feet and walked toward the waiting conference. Taking his seat in front of the dignitaries and assembled cameras, the Pope quietly prayed for success and the freedom of all people from bondage.

Turning to face the bank of cameras in the back of the church, the Pontiff began speaking to the world:

"Good evening. I have very sad news this evening. My friend, Nicholas of Haiti, was murdered a few minutes ago. I am sure he wants me to go on with this mission, as we agreed that it was the most important thing either of us had ever done.

"As he promised you a few days ago, we are releasing the process to provide sufficient fresh water to meet the needs of every human on this planet. You might say that it is the product of what we know as "living water" in my faith. You do not have to be a Christian to receive this technology for fresh water, but if you want to know more about living water, I have provided a simple website that will explain many of your questions at www.thenewlivingwater.com.

"Now, the moment you have all been waiting for: the technology. All this information will be available on the website as well, so there is no need to take detailed notes. I am not a technical man, and Nicholas, God rest his soul, assured me that it would explain itself when the time came."

Pausing to wipe away the tears flowing for his friend, the Pontiff nodded to a staff member, stiffened in his chair, and took on a look of steely resolve that shook some of the assembled dignitaries. As the schematics and papers that Nicholas drafted were released on the websites, the world began to change. Once all the uploads were complete, the Pontiff spoke in a clear, strong voice.

"You know the part in the Bible where Jesus is at the wedding feast and turns water into wine? Well, it's almost that simple…"

THE END

DISCUSSION QUESTIONS

1. Was Nicholas Bacon a man without religion, a man without faith, or a man in need of guidance?
2. There are two major turning points in this novel for Nicholas Bacon. Name them.
3. Was Andre a success, or a failure, as a guardian angel?
4. Nick Bacon listened to the Bible on stereo headphones instead of reading the book. Is that an acceptable way to study the Word?
5. There are number of missionaries mentioned in this book, including Larry Timmons. Did they play a role in Nick's destiny? If so, how did they impact him through their examples and testimony?
6. Are miracles a matter of physics that we don't understand, or God's unseen hand?
7. Why do some places suffer under the hand of the devil (Haiti) and yet others are blessed by God?
8. In real life, are miracles like those Nicholas Bacon performs real, or has that time passed with the coming of Christ?
9. Describe how the abuse of the Restevek children impacted you as a believer, and what you might be able to do to help.
10. Is the influence of Satan as visible in our daily world as it was in this book?
11. What is slavery? Is it the same as human trafficking?
12. Have you ever been on a mission trip? Where and will you do it again.
13. Are there really people who live their lives as Larry Timmons' missionaries live? Are they just in third-world countries?
14. Who turned Nicholas Bacon's life around toward Christ?
15. Do you believe in guardian angels? If so, do you have one? What has yours helped you with?

16. Are there frequent battles between good and evil? How can one protect oneself from evil and do good?
17. In what ways was Violene blessed even though she was a Restevek?
18. Where are the slaves in your city?
19. Can people foment miracles with their own actions? How?
20. What should you do if you find someone in a slavery situation?

AFTERWORD

Nicholas of Haiti deals with the problem of human trafficking in ways that most of us never see give little thought to over the course of our lives. The simple fact is that there are slaves all around us, not just "somewhere back in time." Slavery did not end with the American civil war. Right now, in the United States, there are people held in slavery. Today we call it abuse, or human trafficking. In some parts of the world such as Haiti, it is an active part of the culture. In many Islamic areas, especially those engaged in warfare with non-believers, slavery is often justified on a religious basis because non-believers deserve to be enslaved.

But it is slavery. Whether it's the fourteen-year-old girl being turned-out by her pimp, or the cook at the ethnic restaurant who speaks no English and is being forced to work off the smuggler's fees in the back room. Neither of these people are free, and both are worked as slaves have been since time immemorial.

There are other subtler forms of slavery as well. Did you ever wonder about the mentally challenged woman who's always at work in the local establishment you frequent? The mentally ill, and the mentally challenged are often forced to work for little or nothing, being told that they are there as a duty of some sort, or that they have committed a crime and need to work it off or face incarceration or institutionalization.

The point of the story, literally and figuratively, is to be aware of the existence of human trafficking/slavery. Look for the signs, do some research, seek out church groups working to combat this scourge. And pray.

FINAL NOTE

While Nicholas of Haiti is a fictional character, the very real Nicholas of Myra is the most popular saint in western culture outside of the Virgin Mary, and the apostles. He was a man of great courage, kindness, and many miracles.

I used to consider myself a bit of a scholar regarding Nicholas. You see, I am a professional Santa on top of the other pursuits that I have. Nicholas is the basis for the modern Santa Claus, and as one of his helpers I thought I should know more about him. Little did I know that Nicholas of Myra was credited with almost all the miracles in this book until after it was completed. Some were transposed in the modern era, like his surviving a plane crash versus a shipwreck. But he is credited with all these miracles by different sources I've read along the way. Except for his staff: I stole that one from Moses.

I have a special place in my heart for the character and legend of Nicholas. Being mistaken for this saint is a blessing in my opinion.

If you would like to read a beautiful book about Saint Nicholas, I recommend: St. Nicholas: A Closer Look at Christmas. Written by Joe Wheeler and Jim Rosenthal, it contains beautiful illustrations, and a lot of the contextual history that will bring this saint to life for modern audiences.

I'd also like to encourage you to be a little more like Saint Nicholas today. The world would benefit greatly from that kindness.

Made in the
USA
Monee, IL

13781791R00136